Quiet, W
Sings

By

Diane Calton Smith

New Generation Publishing

Also by Diane Calton Smith:

A Georgian House on the Brink

For Janet,
with best wishes,

Diane

12.2.18 .

Afterthought

I can write now, now that there is time and space. I can write it all down from the perspective of someone who has learned to see all sides of events as they unfold, seeing everything as does a fly on the wall. Not quite impassive, certainly not without self interest, but as a narrator does, telling it all from a clear and lofty vantage point.

Perhaps it all began with the party, maybe earlier than that, with a holiday in the sun. Who knows when these things truly begin, when the first tiny tiles in the mosaic start to be laid in place? But it has to be told from some starting point, so I'll begin where it feels best; at the party.

Chapter One

The first person I should introduce is Henry, dearest Henry. He used to have lots of parties, but I'm not sure how much he enjoyed them himself. I was never invited to any of them, of course, but from my vantage point of fly on the wall I can see everything. All parts of the story.

Henry Blanchard on the day of his forty-fifth birthday was wearing his habitual puzzled look, the one he wore when anyone mentioned smart phones, tablets, satellite navigation or any other item of pointless gadgetry. He'd been born at the wrong time, really, into a world where technology would soon be sprouting up all around him, yet he never seemed ready for it.

'What about CDs, then?' Bruce Ryan was asking in exasperation, 'Surely there are some o' them hanging around the place?'

'Well, no. Never bothered with them. Nothing wrong with my record collection. It was Dad's and I've carried on collecting. There's more than enough music for tonight.'

'Some people would say that vinyl was rather cool, actually,' ventured Pamela Ayling, though what she said sounded a bit silly, even to her.

'Not when the vinyl collection ends at 1969,' Bruce muttered as he watched his host squat down before the old turntable. Little bobbles of dust clung to the arm and to the edges of the casing and Henry had to blow a grey fluffy ball off the needle before he could place it, crackling and hissing, onto the outer rim of the record.

Pamela paced over to the window and rubbed a clear patch on the misted pane, ignoring Antonia's silent and simmering disapproval.

'All right then, who's coming tonight?' she asked, 'not just us, surely.'

She tried to sneak a glance at her watch as she pulled her hanky out of her sleeve, but without her glasses it told her nothing whatsoever. A medley from "The Merry Widow" was scratching its way into life from the turntable, filling the room with about as much fizz as the warm prosecco in her hand.

'Of course not,' Antonia replied lazily, 'my darling other half, Henry, has invited all his old friends, so there should be at least five of you, ha ha ha…'

'Hilarious,' commented Henry as he stood and brushed dust from his trousers, 'Look, just stop fretting. Everything will be fine when they all get here. Have another glass and cut out the whining, the lot of you.'

'Ah yes, everything will be just tickety-boo,' grated Pamela's sarcasm from the window, 'Eugenie the Party Animal has arrived!'

'No need to be bitchy,' murmured Henry drily, coming to join her. His secretary, Julia, who could never bear to have Henry out of her sight for long, trotted up behind them. The three of them watched Eugenie's slow passage up the drive, her silhouette caught in the moving headlights of a passing car. Her head was bowed before the blast of the January wind, her arms stretched long by the weight of the carrier bags she clutched in each hand. She was out of breath already and in no state for a knees-up. Which was just as well, really.

'You shouldn't be so unkind about her,' complained Julia between sips of gin and tonic, 'You know she means well.'

'So did Laurel and Hardy, but I wouldn't want them at my party,' said Henry, 'Where's Ted? Don't say he's making some pathetic excuse again. Anyone would think my parties weren't up to much.'

'Could be you put him off that time you let it slip about only inviting them to make up the numbers,' remarked Antonia. As far as she was concerned, though, the whole crowd of them was only there to make up the numbers. The doorbell sounded with smart electrical efficiency and,

4

wearing her most dignified lady-of-the-house sneer, Antonia strolled into the hall to answer it.

'But Eugenie, darling, where's Ted?' came her brittle, false and dutifully sociable voice from the hallway.

'That's my Antonia,' muttered Henry, 'all heart and warmth.'

'Put another record on,' requested Bruce.

'Oh, come on, you know what she's like.'

'No, put another record on. "The Merry Widow" has finished and your needle's hopping about like it was made in the 1970s or something.'

Henry gave him a look. Eugenie appeared, complete with carrier bags, in the living room.

'Hello everyone! Sorry Ted can't make it, but he couldn't be bothered. Too engrossed in that film on Channel 838 or whatever.'

'Thanks a million,' growled Henry.

'But darling, *I'm* here! Surely that's all that matters!' wheedled Eugenie, dropping the carrier bags and grabbing the birthday boy in a tight embrace, engulfing him in her large brown cardigan. He suffered it with his usual dignity, aware that his guests needed a laugh.

'Well,' she stated, addressing the immaculately attired Antonia, 'I've iced the cake but left the crispy wontons at home because I know you're eating less fat these days. Have you made cheese and pickle?' Her voice trailed off as she plodded behind her hostess towards the kitchen. Henry could picture his partner's reaction to Eugenie's idea of a buffet. Antonia couldn't have been any less cheese and pickle if she'd tried.

He leafed through his glorious collection of old vinyl, some so treasured, such a part of his life and his dad's before him, that the sleeves were reduced to paper tatters with bits of ancient sticky tape hanging off in yellow flakes; remnants of past attempts to mend them. With a smile he selected Bing Crosby. You could trust old Bing to get things going. The doorbell rang, then again and again. More shrieks from the hall, more air-kisses, and before

5

Bing had crooned his way through his second number the room was full of people.

'You know, mate,' commented Bruce, as he caught his friend in the kitchen later, 'I could get all your music on to your phone for you, save you all this mess and then you could chuck this rubbish away...' He was holding one of Henry's cherished records, rubbing carelessly at its dog-eared sleeve. Henry snatched it out of his hand.

'And there was I, thinking you were my friend!' he grinned, 'and as far as I'm concerned, phones are for ringing people with. Nothing else.'

Bruce gave up. Against all odds, the party gradually staggered into life. Henry, determined to be jovial, found himself facing Eugenie over another glass of prosecco.

'So,' he beamed, definitely more relaxed now, 'which film is Ted watching?'

'Oh, Heaven knows! Something in grainy black and white where all they say is 'Achtung!' all the time. Something he's seen five times before, I should think.'

'I can see the attraction,' replied Henry drily.

'I hear Antonia's made blinis,' continued Eugenie, changing the subject without a pause, 'I do like blinis. It's just that all those little bits of caviar get stuck to your top lip.'

Henry escaped from Eugenie, only to dance with Antonia, as he supposed he ought to. She was looking good tonight, he had to acknowledge. She'd had her hair coloured and cut again and the blonde highlights suited her brown eyed, rather heavy, yet handsome face. Had it been her looks that had attracted him to her in the first place? He couldn't remember. They'd been living together forever, or at least it felt that way. He just couldn't recall when it had stopped being pleasant.

Next, and almost as dutifully, he danced with Pamela, listening to her verbal destruction of just about everyone in the room. Then he escaped to the more peaceful company of Julia. She was an utter treasure as a secretary and rather pretty in a petite, blue eyed and fair haired way, but he had to admit that she really wasn't his type. He even felt that dancing this closely to her was somehow wrong, though she seemed perfectly at ease with it. He was relieved to move on again, dancing with Sylvia Farrah, who made him smile with her clever jokes. She was looking as beautiful as ever and he danced with her for as long as he could get away with, before being grabbed for a peculiar sort of lunging two-step with Eugenie. As she barged her way around the room, loosely attached to Henry, her elbows frequently came within millimetres of Antonia's Chelsea and Meissen figurines that decorated every horizontal surface.

Dancing duties out of the way, Henry had a quick drink with Ronnie and Malcolm, the Barnstone twins, who were usually all right until they'd had too many whiskies. Then their bragging started, which was enough to send Henry out to walk the dog. They told everyone they were farmers, but in fact they'd inherited a large house and medium sized farm and employed other people to run it for them. They had probably never done a single day's work on the farm, but liked to act the part, wearing expensive tweeds and country clothes from the covers of magazines you usually found at the dentist's. Tonight they had brought with them a couple of youngish, expensively groomed dark haired beauties, who were doing a lot of low-pitched, upper-class sounding guffawing. Pamela remarked, as soon as they were out of earshot, that their Lycra tops were far too low cut for January, but then Pamela would.

Frank Sinatra was singing about his kind of town as the party goers attacked the buffet table in the dining room. Left alone for a brief moment, Henry leaned one elbow on the marble mantelshelf in his sitting room and looked into the embers of the fire. Out of nowhere, he felt a wave of pride. He was hugely proud of their lovely late eighteenth century house in the small village of Bridgewell. Once a farm house, it was solid and handsome, its old red bricks softened at the edges now. It looked out over the Well Creek at the front, with the broad Fenland stretching away in all directions at the back. He was not the greatest fan of

7

the Fens, being an in-comer, but the house itself gave him a feeling of comfort when all else failed.

He was not a shallow man by any means but could justly be described as vain. Though he wasn't all that keen on entertaining, he had to admit that he gave these parties occasionally to show off his house and to reinforce the status he felt he deserved. The trouble with being in the financial services industry was that other professionals seldom acknowledged him as an equal. However well qualified and experienced, however good he was at his job and however successful as a business man, the title of Financial Advisor did not earn him the cachet of an accountant or lawyer.

'Blimey!' Jeanette Radley's high pitched exclamation from the dining room pierced his thoughts like a cocktail stick through a sausage. 'You don't 'arf need double glazing…there's a hell of a draft coming through them windows!'

Henry heard Antonia's tinkly laugh in reply.

'What? Double glazing in Henry's Georgian windows? He would have a seizure!'

He found himself wincing in agreement as he bent down to fish more coal from the scuttle at his feet, watching as the fire briefly dimmed, then glowed back into life. He was still standing there when his guests began to wander back from the dining room with plates of food. Jeanette was soon smooching with Bruce, her empty plate abandoned on the carpet by the sofa. Jeanette Radley, landlady of the Dog and Duck, attended without fail every party in the district, invited or not. She could smell a free drink from miles away and somehow managed to get cover for the pub every time. Once the pub gossip grapevine had brought tidings of a party to her eager ears, she simply turned up. These days, everyone in the area seemed to accept this, but why, Henry demanded of himself as he fed the fire again, why did everyone just put up with her? She was well-oiled already and was staggering around the place. Fortunately, Bruce had a pretty firm hold on her, though at any minute something was bound to be knocked off a shelf and broken. He caught the look on Antonia's face as she entered the room just in time to see Jeanette picking up one of the Meissen figures to gawp at before replacing it unsteadily on the shelf.

Eugenie went past with her plate piled high with blinis and stuffed olives. Already, there was a little pattern of caviar around her mouth. The trouble was, he thought crossly, these parties were always dominated by the same boring old cronies, repeating the same lame stories and exhausted jokes. And always, there were the same hangers-on at the end.

Food eaten, dancing done, same old jokes repeated and cackled at, by midnight the party had lost all its vitality and most of the guests had left. The night had never reached the sort of fever pitch that legends were made of and now it was done. Yet still it dragged on to the death.

And by two o'clock they were still there, as predicted; the usual nucleus of old cronies, trying the last shreds of Antonia's patience and the last dregs of Henry's booze. Pamela, Julia and Bruce were slumped on the sofa. At any moment Bruce would fall asleep, though it was cold in the room now. As a subtle hint, Henry had long since stopped feeding the fire.

Uninvited, Julia helped herself to yet another gin from the cocktail cabinet. Henry wondered why she couldn't give his bottles a rest for once and start on the hip flask in her pocket, though as usual he said nothing. He was tired. He'd had enough. Why couldn't they just go?

Eugenie was sprawled in the chintz covered armchair closest to the dying fire, her head thrown back and her mouth open. When she began to snore, Henry pulled himself out of his chair and caught Antonia's eye. But she just stared back at him. His party. His job to throw them out. They'd discussed it earlier.

'Come on, party's over!' he yelled at last. Eugenie gave a huge, raucous snore.

'Come on, Sylvia, help me out here!'

Sylvia, walking gracefully into the room from the kitchen, looked at him out of tired eyes and smiled. In all honesty, she was the only one he didn't mind being there. She was one of his clients who made a living out of doing historical research for all sorts of people. She was never the life and soul of a party but usually had something interesting to say and he liked talking to her.

'Yes, Henry, we really should all be leaving.' She balanced herself on the edge of a chair, holding her refilled wine glass, as if to make the point that she was only finishing her drink and didn't intend to get settled again.

'Well, Sylvia,' Antonia joined in, 'At least someone realises that there's life after this darned party! How many people are there in the kitchen now? I shall want it soon to eat my muesli in.'

'Oh, the usual lot. The twins look like they've moved in permanently, and their ladies of course…' Henry let the sound of her voice wash over him. He loved its calm, the music of it. He even loved the fact that in describing the hangers-on she didn't seem to include herself. She was tall and slim, her silver hair cut in a very feminine way. She was in her late fifties, but it was hard to tell her age. It was as if age was totally irrelevant to her and she was undoubtedly one of the most attractive women he knew.

Hastily gathering his thoughts, he realised that Antonia was staring at him again.

'Yes, all right!' he snapped, 'I'll chuck them out in a minute.'

'There aren't that many,' Sylvia repeated, 'just the Barnstones, their girlfriends and the young lady. Don't know her name.'

'Young?' queried Henry with an extra long sigh, 'None of us here tonight could still be described as young. Apart from the Barnstones' bits of stuff.'

'Steady on!' barked Antonia, leaving the room with a thud of the door behind her.

'Don't be mean, Henry dear,' soothed Sylvia in her calming, velvety voice. 'The lady *was* young. You must know who I mean. And attractive. Not like you to miss her! I just passed her in the hall. Go and look for yourself!'

But no one bothered to go. And there was something very decisive about the way Antonia strode back into the room and yanked out the plug of the record player, so that Nat King Cole slowed and droned to a most undignified finale. The lady of the house then spoke.

'It would appear that my other half is either incapable or unwilling to bring this social event to a close. I am therefore doing it for him and have just thrown everyone out of the kitchen. This party is at an end.'

Pamela grunted and Julia giggled, sensing that this meant her too. Henry was smiling at her with a satirical look, the one he was especially good at.

'And did you, Julia, my dear faithful secretary, happen to see a fictional, attractive woman in the hallway, said to be enjoying our hospitality?'

'Certainly not, Henry.'

'Nor me,' added Antonia as she left the room again, 'I'd have chucked her out if she'd been there. Sylvia was dreaming.'

'You see, Sylvia, darling?' whispered Henry, 'Inebriated again and seeing things, aren't you?'

'Certainly not. I am never *that* inebriated.'

On the sofa, Bruce, who had finally dropped off, stirred in his sleep as the young golden retriever came in and brushed its wet fur against his leg. The animal brought with it the scent of earth and damp air from the garden and Antonia's voice could be heard outside now, calling to the cat.

It was the final warning. The party really was over.

'All the same,' Henry smiled into Sylvia's eyes, 'I still say you are five sheets to the wind, darling.'

'All the same,' she whispered back, 'happy birthday, Henry.'

Chapter Two

Henry. Tuesday 20th January

No need to look. Henry knew exactly who it was at the door.

Only Bruce Ryan could make so much racket, pressing the bell so hard and repetitively that it sounded like a major emergency. Only Bruce could forget his coat on a day as raw as this, so that he had to jump up and down on the doorstep while punishing the doorbell. Only Bruce could fail so miserably to understand that when Henry said he was working from home, he really *was* working from home. To Bruce, anyone who didn't turn up daily to his desk or workshop, wasn't really working at all.

He had worked once, very hard too, running his own lawn mower repair business. He had a real understanding of old motors, with the ability to coax even the most hopeless cases back to useful life. The business had done well, enjoying a good local reputation, and he'd employed a small team of people. He was considered a decent bloke who'd do anything for anyone, but he had an absolute loathing of paperwork, something that would be his eventual undoing. Meeting Henry Blanchard of Mason and Blanchard one day in the Dog and Duck, while swallowing a quick pint between jobs, had turned out to be one of his luckier days. For years after that, Henry had helped him with tax and pensions advice and was more than happy to add Bruce's name to his long list of lucrative business accounts. The relationship had been mutually beneficial. Up to a point.

Despite Bruce's reluctance to keep his paperwork up to date, he'd stubbornly refused to hire an accountant. Henry had regularly reminded him to sort something out, but in Bruce's opinion it was perfectly all right to catch up with things every few months. He'd been getting the hang of the tax forms, he reckoned, knew roughly what to do with them. This situation had worked, after a fashion, while legislation remained unchanged. Bruce simply hadn't had time to read all the updates from the Revenue, screwing them into engine grease smeared balls and tossing them into the corner. Despite this, it hadn't been so much the income tax as the VAT that had got him in the end. He must have missed the bulletins that mattered, probably used them to scribble his shopping list on or something, because somehow the VAT had been underpaid. Before long, the arrears had built up and the debt had become so heavy that Bruce's once successful business had collapsed under the weight of it all.

All that had been years ago, but it had taken Bruce a very long time to get over the guilt and shame about his employees losing their jobs. He'd become ill, making it difficult to find work, and times had been very tough. Divorced several years before this crisis, he was also bringing up his teenage son Jimmy, alone. This responsibility, despite all the inevitable challenges, had been the main thing to keep him going, making him determined that he would win in the end.

Lately, Henry had noticed, Bruce had seemed a lot more optimistic and was always on the hunt for a job. Things were bound to work out for him now. And Bruce was not unaware of how much Henry had helped him through the toughest times. He had stayed around through thick and thin, trying to lend a hand whenever he could. Bruce and Henry were an odd pair, viewed locally as a rough diamond and a posh, sad bloke.

The posh, sad bloke at the time of Bruce's demented ringing of the doorbell, was half way through writing a particularly complicated report for a client. He had papers and documents spread over the desk in his study and screwed up balls of scrap paper covering the floor where they'd missed the bin. The last thing he needed right then was to be disturbed. He had specifically avoided the office that morning to ensure that he was not disturbed. And so it came to pass that he was very disturbed indeed.

He carried on writing down the sentence that was in his head, desperately trying to ignore the bell. When it rang yet again he cursed loudly. He thought about pretending he was out, but it was no good. His Jaguar was in the drive. Bruce was never so easily fooled.

Still swearing, he padded into the hall, where Bruce's agitated shadow was dancing like a frenzied elf on the frosted glass of the side window. The door stuck a bit at that time of year, the frame swelling with the damp, and it screeched as Henry yanked it open. Bruce's tall, under-dressed form was still hopping up and down, arms wrapped around his body in the misty cold.

'What kept you, mate? Bloody brass monkeys out 'ere.'

'Heaven's sake, Bruce, why don't you put a coat on?'

'Any chance of a coffee?' Despite his moaning and the cold, Bruce's big grin under the mop of greying dark hair had not faded and he bounced past Henry into the hall, rubbing his hands together with energetic cheerfulness.

Henry gave in, plodding despairingly into the kitchen to fill the kettle, his lips pursed somewhere between irritation and the need to laugh at his own daftness. After all these years, he chided himself, despite his professional appearance, he had never mastered the art of saying 'no'. Already, Bruce was huddled in the big Windsor chair by the kitchen radiator, sharing the warmth with Arnold, the golden retriever and Polly, the long haired black cat, who occupied small beds on the floor. Right next to Bruce's tapping foot, by the wall, was Polly's uneaten breakfast. Henry knew it was only a matter of time before the heel of Bruce's yellow suede trainer landed in the chunky chicken in jelly, coating it in chunky chicken, ready to be walked on to the hall rug.

'So, old mate,' said Bruce as he slurped his coffee, 'What's new? Got any new ghosts? Any biscuits to go with this?'

'No and no. Why is everyone so obsessed with this ghost thing? We had Pamela going on about it again yesterday. For Heaven's sake, Sylvia had had far too many. We all know that. This house is not haunted.'

'If you say so,' Bruce shrugged, 'Not exactly the hysterical sort, though, is she? Sylvia, I mean. She didn't look drunk to me. She saw the woman three times.'

'So she says.'

'Yep, twice in the hall, once in here. Who knows for sure?'

'Look, don't let Antonia hear you mention it. I thought she'd rip Pamela's head off yesterday when she wouldn't let the subject drop. And for once,' he added a little priggishly, 'I agree with Antonia.'

'It'll be for the first time then. Anyway, why aren't you at work today?'

'I *am* at work!' he almost shouted, 'I have a report to write, which has to be done by tomorrow morning. I thought, obviously wrongly, that I might get more peace here! With Antonia playing golf, I thought I might have my lovely, quiet and peaceful home to myself...'

'Just think, though,' interrupted Bruce, totally oblivious of any criticism, 'the lovely Julia will be quite alone in your office today. Do you think I should call in and cheer her up?'

'No, you damn well shouldn't!' Henry objected with a burst of a laugh, 'Just leave her in peace to get on. Like me, she has plenty to do!'

'But, what a waste! Gorgeous woman like that and you don't even look at her. She has it real bad for you and you don't even notice.'

'Rubbish! It's no more than the usual secretary and boss thing. She just looks after me, that's all. But she does like a drink. Bottles everywhere. Can't help but notice. Doesn't seem to affect her work so far, though...'

'That's only because, you blind old idiot, you are the centre of her world. Working for you is the last thing she will let anything spoil. I'm surprised the lovely Antonia hasn't noticed!'

'Why should she care? Just so long as nothing rocks her perfect, idle little world, just so long as I go on providing, the way her Daddy did before me. She never tires of reminding me how much Daddy contributed to the deposit on this house and how much income I need to keep providing.'

'Huh, talk about love's young dream! Good thing she's not saddled with me, then. Since the wife walked out on me and Jimmy, no one wants to know, especially not now the money's gone. No one wants a loser. I wonder if the beautiful Julia…'

'Oh, give it a rest, Bruce! You'll have a lucky break at some point. You did it once and you'll be all right again. You're on the way up again now. And at least you have your freedom!'

'That bad, eh?'

'That bad. Anyway, this will not get that report done and you need to look for a job.'

Bruce grunted and made hard work of getting to his feet, though his amiable grin hardly faltered as he plodded through the hall.

'See you then, mate!' he called, as the clammy mist of January closed around him. Henry watched him jog manfully down the drive to the old white Vauxhall. For a moment Henry paused on the front door step, looking at his winter weary mess of a front garden. Long dead stems of golden rod and collapsed spikes of allium were lying in the drifts of last autumn's beech leaves at the side of the drive. The garden filled him with no enthusiasm whatsoever. He only wanted to shut it out and put off the problem of getting it dealt with for a bit longer. The gloom of it on this cheerless morning, together with what he'd admitted to Bruce about his life with Antonia, had moulded his mouth into a grim line. He rammed the stubborn old door shut, no longer wanting very much to get on with the report, and headed for the kitchen to make another coffee.

Across the parquet flooring of the hall and over the pale oriental rug in its centre, was a faint but unmistakable trail of chunky chicken jelly footprints.

Chapter Three

Rosie. Saturday 17th January

The next person I should introduce is Rosalyn, or Rosie as she prefers to be called. That is to say, me.

It seems strange to talk about myself in the third person, but it is fairer that way. Every story needs to be told equally, from everyone's individual point of view, and that's impossible if the teller of the tale is trapped inside the perspective of just one character.

Rosie was going through a kind of limbo at that time, a lull between two phases of her life. The past, with its loss, divorce and anger, was gone, leaving her in what felt like a grey waiting room. She had been there for a very long time, as if waiting for a delayed appointment, longing for the door to open and let in the light.

There had been some brighter patches, even in that waiting time, but they too were past and brought sadness with the memories. The only way to survive this patch, she'd decided, was the way she'd survived all other past difficulties. She had to keep the past locked firmly away, refusing to dwell on it, even to spare it a thought. Memories brought too much pain.

She was determined to move forward, to get through her time in the grey waiting room without being tempted to look at the glossy magazines that were left there. They only made you feel worse.

But in the end it was the scarf that spoiled things.

Falling like a beam of turquoise light through the darkness, it gathered in a pool of silk on the wardrobe floor. Reaching out too late to catch it, Rosie stooped to pick it up from the rough wooden surface, feeling the silk snag on hidden splinters.

The room was almost dark now, though in all honesty it had hardly reached full light in the whole of that short midwinter's day. The old house was completely silent, stifled by the frost that clung to its window panes and newly painted woodwork.

Normally she managed her solitude better than this. Usually she enjoyed her own company, focusing on the present; her job, her friends and her interesting old house, but today wasn't normal. Today the cold and dark were getting to her. She could feel the chill creeping up between the floorboards and through gaps in the window frames, laughing at the old house's puny attempts to keep it out. And today the scarf had stolen her peace.

The weekends were usually the hardest times, with her neighbour and friends out of town or with their families, but until recently she'd had the renovation of the house to keep her busy. Now the house was finished, or at least as well as it could be on such a modest budget, and she was truly proud of it. She came home from work each evening with a sense of satisfaction. She could hardly believe that she'd renovated the place alone, that she'd put in so much energy and love and had succeeded.

For once, her efforts had not been wasted.

From the roadside, the little Georgian cottage and its adjoining neighbour looked welcoming and cosy, rather than handsome. Once a substantial single farmhouse, it had later been divided into two cottages, then badly neglected for years. Rosie had bought her semi-detached portion cheaply, which had left her with a small amount for its renovation, and over the months she'd grown increasingly contented in her small home in the Cambridgeshire Fens. She loved the quietness, especially at night, when the hunting owls and weather were the only sounds. She loved it even when the weather was bad, when the wind came howling and galloping across the open acres to hurl itself against the back of the house, flinging its cold, wild rain at the windows.

With work on the cottage completed, Rosie was free to enjoy some leisure time. In her newly renovated home that overlooked the River Nene at the front and the open Fen and orchards behind the garden at the back, Rosie was almost happy. She had been born and raised in Fenland, and though her small family was no longer more than a set of special memories in a single photo album, she still had the legacy of this landscape for comfort. Everything was all right. Everything was absolutely fine, just so long as she never allowed herself to dwell on the past.

This self discipline was imposed for good reason. She knew from bitter experience how much damage too much wallowing in difficult memories could do. Her grandmother, a kindly but strict woman, had brought her up from the age of ten, after she had lost both parents one terrible day.

Her mother and father had gone off for a weekend's sailing the south coast, happy and waving and promising to be home by Sunday evening, but she'd never seen them again. Her poor grandmother had had to explain to a sensitive and terrified child what had happened, how somehow both parents had gone overboard from the sailing boat they'd hired.

For weeks, Rosie had suffered appalling nightmares, waking up and crying in the dark. In the dreams she was always drowning, being dragged down in the water, long tentacles of seaweed clutching at her legs as she tried to reach the surface. Her grandmother had tried so hard in those first few weeks, had always been there at her bedside, always there to comfort her when she must have been grieving herself. It must also have been a great shock to her that the child she had offered to baby-sit for a weekend had suddenly become her dependant. But her grandmother's belief in not nurturing grief, in straightening her shoulders and getting on with things, had soon come to the fore. After a while, her sympathy had become edged with common sense, her words sharper, less indulgent, and Rosie had learned to get through it, to return to school, concentrate on her lessons and move forward.

It had been like that ever since really. Whenever something bad happened, she would do everything in her power to avoid the fall-out of grief that might come afterwards. She'd dealt with her divorce in the same way. She'd done her weeping, then picked herself up, looked at her options and moved on. She'd known better by then. The drowning nightmares with their seaweed and terror were never far away; she did not dare to allow them back.

So, when that ridiculous business happened in the summer, all that miserable pointlessness, she'd been adamant that she would not dwell on it. She had to keep to that. She could not allow herself to think of it, especially not on a monochrome day like this when she was so utterly alone. The past had to stay where it was. The present and future were where her focus must be. She had to keep looking forward.

Life was there, waiting, so long as she never looked back.

But the scarf was still in her hand. She was sitting on the edge of her bed, the turquoise silk wrapped around one wrist. Despite the dull light, the silk was bright, luminescent, almost as if it held its own inner light, as if it had absorbed some of that old, glorious sunlight. As if it were waiting for the right time to release it, tantalising her like some forbidden sweetie.

No. Abruptly she put the scarf down and left the bedroom, moving fast along the narrow landing, her hand leading her along the neatly painted rail, then down the stairs.

She cooked moussaka. All that chopping and cooking the ingredients in batches, letting the suspicious looking brown juices leak out of the aubergine as it rested, was a deliberate ploy to occupy her mind. While the moussaka was bubbling away in the oven, she opened a small bottle of red wine and sat in the window seat of her dining room, watching the last of the light fade from the frosted lawn in the back garden.

Later, she put on some music while she ate, but the shuffled selection on her phone blended meaninglessly, one set of chords into another. She couldn't face the thought of television. She washed up, then somehow she was back upstairs, reclaiming the scarf from where it had fallen on the carpet. She held it against her face, as if it might dull some of the pain, and already she was making a pact with herself. If she allowed one more trip into the past, one more luxurious wallow, that would be it. After that, never again. She promised.

Just one more time.

She was back. Back to the place which was almost perfect.

But it hadn't been anything like perfect to begin with. They were just too old for that sort of thing. Rosie and Monica felt, and probably looked, very middle aged, even a little disapproving as they wandered amongst the throng of happy holiday makers. They had booked the May break as a last minute bargain and instead of the nice, quiet little paradise they had imagined, they had come to this; a place of ear-battering din.

The only good thing about it, as they saw things at the beginning, was its location. The Melek Hotel was nestled between two protective arms of mountain that seemed to stretch from the perfect blue of the sky to the unbelievably pure turquoise of the sea. From behind the hotel at regular intervals came the plaintive call of the Imam. The tiny white mosque was almost hidden from the road, snuggled between the small houses and parcels of tirelessly cultivated strips of land. The girls had never been to Turkey before and their first impressions were very mixed. The mosques with their haunting cries had a mysterious beauty about them. The coast with its steep rocks towering above the sea and the deep, dark pine forests that filled the gulfs between the winding mountain roads were exquisite. The hotel, however, seemed like bad news.

It wasn't as if the Melek wasn't beautiful, because it was. The architecture had been sensitively thought out, spacing the little pastel stuccoed bungalows daintily amongst the bougainvillea and fish ponds of a scented garden. When it was quiet, which must have been for all of five minutes between three and four in the morning, the place was an oasis of perfumed perfection. But the noise, the blaring, screaming noise, from kids, loud speakers and animators, seemed determined to turn the place into a mild form of hell. In Turkish, Melek meant 'Angel', but in those early days the place felt anything but angelic.

Now sedately past the age of thirty, both girls considered the world of night clubs well and truly behind them, so the hotel's nightly transformation into a strobe-lit catwalk didn't exactly go down well, especially with Monica.

Even in the daytime, the music went on around the pool and became the background for the animators, that highly strung team of irritatingly cheerful people. They seemed to be under the impression that everyone's idea of heaven was to play every daft pool game known to man. Saying 'no' was no defence. The animators just kept advancing, smiling and cajoling like Godzilla in a swimming costume. This same frantic energy seemed to drive the bar staff and restaurant waiters too. They were forever toiling, forever smiling, forever desperate to please.

Monica decided after twenty long minutes by the pool on their first morning that life was too short to waste it in this way, and moved to the beach. Rosie joined her, sunbathing on one of the beds in a long row that faced the waves. Music and laughter from the hotel could still be heard, but it was muted here and blended with the sounds of the sea.

From time to time the graceful shapes of paragliders appeared overhead, like big yellow birds descending from Mount Babadağ. The wide canopies arched and wheeled in the sky before hurtling down onto the promenade if they were accurate, just about anywhere else if not.

'Wouldn't catch me doing that,' grumbled Monica. Rosie didn't reply.

Being well away from the hotel, apart from the occasional paraglider, there was nothing to disturb them. There was nothing to moan about at all, in fact, but

Monica still managed to do it. Monica Kerridge was a new friend; the neighbour who had bought the semi-derelict house next door at about the same time as Rosie was beginning to renovate hers. It had been good to share progress reports over the fence in the early days. Later, as winter had drawn in, the problem sharing over delayed plumbing and tricky electrics had moved into the pub in the evenings. The friendship had gradually developed into one which Rosie greatly valued. Monica's abrasiveness could often be funny, a foil to Rosie's milder nature. Her way of pointing out the obvious while Rosie still dithered around the finer points of a thing, was healthy and cheered her up considerably, but this constant crossness was beginning to grate.

One problem with the beach for Rosie was that she wanted to swim but was terrified of the sea. It was hardly surprising really, after what had happened to her parents. The beach was pleasant, but the poolside felt safer and all the music that wafted from it, even the shrieks of the children as they played in the pool, reached Rosie's ears across the sand like a siren's song. As the hours of that first day slowly passed, Rosie wondered with increasing regularity what she might be missing.

By the second evening, dinner was served outside since it was now mid May and just about warm enough. Their table was set at the edge of the terrace, overlooking the now peaceful, darkened pool, with an uninterrupted view of the majestic, shadowed mountain. Only a few tiny points of light, glowing like the ends of cigarettes, showed on the mountainside, its peak only slightly darker than the night sky above.

The music on the terrace was more subdued now. It was gentle, with the lilting arrangement of Turkish pop, and against this background the friendly waiters went about their business, deaf to Monica's string of complaints. She didn't like the food any more than she did the music, asking them several times to turn the volume down. They smiled, nodded and ignored her requests.

And then, quite unexpectedly, spilling its light like fiery butter over the mountain top, the dramatic presence of the rising moon made itself known. The brightness, the solemnity, the grandeur of it, left everyone speechless as it spread its light across the crags and scrub of the mountainside. For a moment, even Monica was quiet, pausing in her flow of complaints. The music from the giant speakers seemed to hush as everyone's attention was drawn to the spreading molten glory that was emerging from the mountain.

It was a moment of magic. When the silver disc of the moon had completed its steady emergence from the crags and rocks, lifting imperiously into the night sky, the mood on the terrace seemed to have changed. Monica said little and when she did speak, her comments were less barbed, her humour somehow improved.

Incredibly, she made no real objection the next morning to Rosie's suggestion that they spend part of the day by the pool. Luck played its part in this. The weather had become cloudy, meaning that the animators had dug out their winter clothes again, shuffling gloomily about the place in voluminous sweaters and trousers. They kept away from the pool, not bothering anyone to play games. To them, this cloudy yet warm weather was far too inclement for any activities. It was truly the best sort of day to begin what Rosie hoped would become a new habit; sitting by the pool. She swam in peace, sharing the water with only a few toddlers in rubber rings.

That evening she pushed home her advantage, moving the focus on to the nightly show in the amphitheatre.

'Think I'll give the show a try tonight,' she commented casually, 'Why not give the animators a bit of support?'

'I can think of quite a few reasons. They're paid, aren't they? All right, I'll join you but I am *not* joining in with that ridiculous Club Dance afterwards. As soon as I hear that demented music I'm off!'

Despite such proclamations, by that evening both girls were beginning to feel a bit more relaxed. The beginnings of a tan and wearing summer clothes after months of grunge and double layers of everything made Rosie feel better, even slightly glamorous. She'd had her dark brown hair cut before they'd left and it seemed to suit her, swept back from her face and just reaching her shoulders. Monica had shed her pallor too, though her evening wear still consisted of the same dark jeans and a variety of black or grey T-shirts. Her moaning was becoming less vehement and she was laughing more. Gradually, the working world at home was slipping away. Things that had seemed important a week ago hardly mattered now.

Sitting on the terrace over dinner, Rosie was contemplating how much more restful it was now that Monica was beginning to lighten up. So, it was with perfect timing that the clown arrived.

He was shuffling on huge red shoes beneath a pair of spotted pajamas. His make-up was already showing signs of wear, the white paint on his face badly streaked and lines of it running into his big, red lips. Trickles of black ran from his kohl-painted eyes like big tears and he peered at the girls through the red nylon spikes of his two-tone wig.

'Oh, please,' snorted Monica, not trying very hard to keep her voice down.

'Hello!' cried the jolly clown, 'My name is Berkant and I am here tonight to welcome you to Comic Clips Show tonight. At half past nine. You will come? We are animation team and five peoples. If you want to know some things, ask me. My name is Berkant.'

Rosie was grinning, trying to say that they'd already decided to watch the show, but she was too late. Berkant and his shoes had already moved on, tripping over the table and spreading joy to the rest of the assembly.

'I can't believe we've agreed to see that thing!' spluttered Monica.

But they went. Sitting on the cold concrete of the amphitheatre steps, they waited for the show to begin. Darkness had fallen and a string of small white lights was glowing in the olive trees to the right of the amphitheatre. Beyond the stage stretched the dark shape of the pool and the rows of colour-washed bungalows. Their pale forms gradually blended with the night as a breeze stirred up from the sea, agitating the tree lights and bringing with it the scents of pine trees and someone's barbecue.

Music from the steps behind the amphitheatre burst into life, pounding and relentless, and the Comic Clips Show began. It had all the corniness of naughty seaside postcards and was trying to please Germans, English and Turks all at once. Predictably, no one found it all that comical, though the audience still laughed, just in all the wrong places. Berkant had shed the clown suit and was dancing manically with a tall lad in a red beret who kept shouting something unintelligible. There was a third man, smaller than the others and by far the best dancer, who somehow managed to keep a Mexican hat on his head despite his energetic dance moves. When it was all over, Lili, the glamorous and athletic team leader, strode on to the stage wearing fishnets and a red circus ringmaster's jacket, and introduced her team. There was Berkant, once again sporting the clown suit, Yasim the good dancer and Zeynel, the one in the beret who shouted a lot. Lili's female helper was a sweet, smiling girl called Esra.

Monica clapped politely but darted off as soon as the Club Dance music began, leaving Rosie to copy everyone else's moves as she went along. Since most of the dancers were doing the same, nearly everyone was more than a beat behind. It was a total mess, which made it all the funnier. Rosie was soon laughing, joining in with the general chaos and loving every moment of it.

The next day, the weather had improved and they returned to the same sun beds by the pool, snatching the chance to read in the rare moments of peace between spurts of pool activity. They declined the eleven o'clock darts, the midday Club Dance and the two o'clock aerobics. With each interruption, Monica's mood descended further into bristling irritation and she buried her nose pointedly in her paperback, shutting her ears against the din.

Rosie, however, was happy to be distracted. Her book became less and less interesting as she kept an idle eye on what was going on around her. Now and then, when the pool was quieter, she went for a swim. At other times she was content to gaze up at the huge mountain that seemed so close she could practically make out individual olive trees. The place was gradually working its magic on her. It made her feel like a child again, but without the old fear and nightmares. Everything seemed so very innocent and protected.

Later, she would look back on that moment and find it remarkable that she had still been her usual, fairly uncomplicated self. Had anyone asked, she would have said she was happy enough, but then the events that would next shake her world were yet to happen. The peaks and troughs of her happiness were never far apart and the contentment she felt was perhaps just a benign form of dullness.

After what was to happen, the old peace would be gone forever. The peaks and troughs of her emotions would be jolted right off the scale.

But right then, in that tranquil moment in the sun, there was nothing to worry about, nothing more serious than the glass of pineapple juice she was sipping through a candy-striped straw. By her side, Monica was quiet, though still looking irritated.

'You want play water polo?' shouted a voice very close to Monica's ear. Neither of them had seen the owner of the voice approaching and the question, delivered with all the subtlety of a firework going off in your pocket, was enough to send them bolting out of their skins. Zeynel, he of the manic voice and the Comic Clips, was standing just behind them, hugging the parasol support and looking at it intently, as if his shouted question had been addressed to it. The red beret, that had controlled his hair the night before, had gone and without it his dark hair flopped forward like soft cloth over his eyes.

'Water polo?' repeated Rosie, slightly perplexed.

'Yes, in five minutes we have d'water polo. Do you want play?'

'Well, I er…'

'Look,' snapped Monica, finally losing the last scrap of her patience, 'Do we look like we want to play water polo? We do not wish to play darts, table-tennis, water polo, bungee-jumping or anything else you may care to think of. We wish merely to be left in peace!'

The tall animator looked faintly surprised, understanding only the tone of her voice, none of the words at all. He gave a little smile, still more directed at the parasol than at the girls.

'OK,' he said in a slightly quieter voice and with admirable good grace. 'Does not matter. See you later,' and with that, he had gone.

'That,' complained Rosie, rounding on her, 'was a bit much! He was only doing his job. He only asked!'

'Yes,' Monica responded through tight lips, 'and I only replied. He'll know to leave us alone in future.'

Such a future seemed surprisingly depressing to Rosie, who decided to go for a walk before they really fell out.

She left the poolside, wandering onto the coarse grass of the lawn. The grass was typical of that region of Turkish Western Anatolia and seemed to be sown wherever a lawn was required. From a distance, it gave the impression of a neatly tended garden, but this grass was disastrously over-watered. It looked as if the gardeners were leaving nothing to chance, watering it religiously whether it needed it or not and giving it an oozing, evil smelling, bog-like quality. As Rosie's flip-flopped feet began to sink into it and the thick, black slime began to squelch between her toes, she realised too late why no one else ever walked there. With her head down to watch her feet, she was completely unprepared for what happened next.

A man fell out of the sky. He almost landed on her head.

There was a sudden rushing of air and a yell, the two things storming her senses at once. All around her was an avalanche of heavy falling nylon that almost knocked her over, turning the world yellow. The stiff yellow fabric engulfed her, attaching itself to her head and pulling at her hair before collapsing into giant folds on the grass. She was fighting her way from under it, knocking metre after metre of the yellow parachute to the ground, when she became aware of the man who had landed right in front of her, coming to earth with an undignified thud. Everything; the surprise, the yellowness, the total strangeness of it, hit her at once, time catapulting her from an ordinary moment into a truly surreal one.

The man who had fallen out of the sky, however, showed no sign of distress. With astonishing calm he removed his dark glasses, his movements slow and relaxed, as if falling on people from a great height was an every day event. With equal slowness, he took off his helmet, a bright red lacquered dome which appeared to take a strenuous effort to remove, and which left his brown hair standing on end like a rough halo around his head. He was still attached by a number of cords to the parachute.

'Sorry about that!' he called out cheerfully, 'Misjudged it a bit. Haven't been going solo for long, so I was lucky I didn't end up in the pool really.'

'*You* were lucky!' she muttered under her breath, but he didn't seem to hear.

'Ever tried it?' he went on conversationally, huge brown eyes pinning her down with their glance. Nice voice. Monica might even have accused it of being posh. Self consciously, she raised a hand to tame her hair which was still alive with static electricity from its brush with the parachute. Realising that her coiffure was standing on end like a bottle brush, she gave up.

'Can't say that I have,' she smiled. Loud and panicked voices reached them from across the grass as two very straight faced Turkish instructors ran towards them, the whiteness of their trainers easy prey for the black splashing mud. They began pulling cords and pieces of equipment from their pupil, like slaves attending a sultan.

'What happened?' one of them demanded, 'You missed d'beach. You had trouble with d'wind?'

The man gave them a quizzical look and Rosie couldn't stop a childish giggle erupting. She put it down to the strangeness of the situation. The instructor turned to her.

'He says he's OK to go solo, but I think he needs more days. He with you?'

'No,' she laughed as the three men began walking away from her, carrying the expanse of yellow between them, 'he's definitely not with me.'

As the man turned away, she could have been mistaken, but she thought he muttered, 'Pity!'

Later, Rosie stood before the full length mirror in the twin room she shared with Monica and for the first time in ages examined her appearance. Things were not that bad, she considered. The slowly developing tan was helping to make her look healthier and she was just about keeping the weight down. Her dark hair was behaving itself tonight, staying where it ought to for a change, and her make-up didn't look over-done, just mascara and a smudge of grey eye-liner framing her blue eyes. But the clothes were all wrong. The dress would have to go. What had she been thinking when she'd packed so many terrible floral dresses? They made her look over fifty. She needed something a little more sophisticated tonight. Perhaps the pencil skirt...

'What's all this, then?' laughed Monica, emerging from the bathroom in her dressing gown.

'Nothing! Just time to change the boring old image.'

'Nothing to do with the Flying Man, then?'

'Absolutely not.'

She had completely forgotten her earlier irritation with Monica, returning to her immediately after the strange incident on the lawn and telling her all about it. She'd not really found the Flying Man all that attractive. It was just that it had been so sudden, so strange. So why was Monica finding this so hilarious? More to the point, why was Rosie suddenly interested in not looking like Doris Day?

She found her cream silk blouse on a hanger over three pairs of trousers at the back of the over-stuffed wardrobe. Despite the creases, the blouse didn't look at all bad with the black pencil skirt. Though she was tall, she still liked to wear heels, and her black stilettos as she stepped into them, finished the look. Monica stuck to her habitual jeans and dark T-shirt with just the tiniest bit of make-up, but at least tonight the shirt was one of her newer black ones. Thanks to her dark hair, hazel eyes and small, slim figure, the affect was quite a good one.

Before dusk obscured the view of the sea, they took up what had become their customary seats on the terrace by the bar. Drinks in hand, they watched the soft light falling on the deserted sand and gently lapping waves. Such calm, such peace and beauty, was something they'd not expected to find amongst the general din and manic activity of the Melek Hotel. The early evening peace, watching the sea from this vantage point, was something they'd begun to include in their simple daily agenda. It was the perfect blending of the day's activities into evening.

The mood that presented itself after dinner came as a complete contrast. Music began bashing its way out of the bar speakers; an assortment of European pop that was anything but appealing. Whatever entertainment had been promised for that night had to be something special, because the bar was packed with expectant looking people. Many of them were non-resident strangers and the girls' usual corner table had been invaded by a stag party. The group of ten, their voices loud and getting louder with every beer and margarita, was dressed in a variety of Hawaiian shirts and straw trilby hats. As they swayed around and toasted each other, their pineapple and sunset festooned shirts gaped to display sunburned chests that glowed an angry red.

'Should have packed your Ambre Solaire, boys,' quipped Monica as she narrowly missed collision with one of their San Miguel swigging elbows. The girls found another table, which they had to share with three teenage girls who looked as dissatisfied as they were.

'Whatever this is,' stated Monica, 'it had better be good.' One of the teenagers chewed on a freshly painted nail and stared at her grumpily in what looked like agreement. The European pop medley faded and died, the big speakers crackling in momentary relief as they prepared themselves for the next onslaught.

Then, with a great drunken cheer from the stag party boys, the entertainment began. Insistent drumming and exotic, flute-like music was snaking its way out of the speakers, introducing the belly dancer. She made her appearance on the top terrace, moving her sinewy body in time with the music and smiling her unwavering, knowing smile. The stag party boys stood up and wiggled their rounded, sunburned bellies back at her, punctuating the music with more cheers. Other men were pushing paper money into the dancer's sequined bra as she passed by and everyone seemed to be enjoying themselves. Even Monica was laughing.

'Look at that lot!' she said, pointing to another group of sun burned shaven heads and big bellies nearby. One of them had a python tattoo that slithered its way down the centre of his back, its head disappearing between rolls of fat and down the back of his low-slung jeans. Rosie hoped the tattooist had had a strong stomach.

A ripple of laughter moved through the crowd as the belly dancer began pulling people to the floor to get them dancing. She heard Monica groan, 'No way,' and she laughed in agreement, but already her attention was wandering.

Maddeningly, ever since they'd first arrived on the terrace that evening, she'd been aware of the Flying Man's presence. She'd located him immediately. He'd been with a large group on the other side of the crowded terrace and

33

didn't appear to have noticed her. He had moved away from the group shortly afterwards and she'd lost sight of him for a while, but then she'd tracked him again, standing with some other people at the bar. Trying not to be obvious, she'd trained her newly discovered fine-tuned antenna onto him, following him wherever he went without having to move her head too much. It was a very bad sign. She knew when he went to the bar and she knew when the dancer dragged him to his feet. She even noticed the exasperated look he threw the poor woman. The dancer, however, had seen these looks many times before and knew how to out-manoeuvre every objection. In the end, Rosie observed, he'd not been able to avoid laughing and was obviously enjoying himself.

'Him?' cried Monica, 'You've got to be kidding. He looks like somebody's dad!'

'Mmm, dances like one too!' Rosie had to agree and they both dissolved into giggles. The giggles soon faded, though, when they noticed a blonde woman joining him. She looked about his age, forties, Rosie guessed. Perhaps he really was someone's dad. No reason why not. Why was she even bothered, she asked herself? He was either quite a bit older than her or very old for his age. Or both. She didn't understand why she was so interested.

'Do you think that's his wife?' Monica went on, 'Ah, no, you're all right. The blonde has her man sitting right there...ooh, but look at the cheek of her, she won't leave the Flying Man alone!'

True enough. They were arm in arm now, attempting some strange version of the belly dance, laughing hilariously together. Rosie's mood was becoming distinctly jaded, but mercifully the music was already fading away. The dancer was waving a theatrical farewell to a raucous round of applause and cheers.

As people began to drift back to their seats, Rosie turned to talk to her friend but was astonished to see that she was no longer alone. The clown was sitting there, or at least she thought he was the clown. Without make-up and the wig it was hard to tell, but, yes, this was Berkant the Clown. And he was chatting up Monica! Obviously, he had no idea what he was taking on.

'So,' came a voice from behind her, 'What are you drinking? I think I owe you a drink after what happened earlier and certainly an apology.'

There was no mistaking the voice, the confident, assured sound of it. Desperately trying to scrape together some cool, Rosie turned in her seat to face him. The heavy iron chair rocked sideways, completely destroying the sophisticated approach she was hoping for. But at least the blonde had gone.

'You do?'

'Certainly. For nearly breaking your neck today. I'm afraid I still need a lot of practice...so would a drink help?'

'A gin and tonic might,' she smiled, 'Thanks!'

He went to the bar, taking a few minutes to compete with all the other customers before bringing the two gins back to the table. When he spoke it was as if the flow hadn't been broken.

'So, why don't you have a go yourself?'

'Paragliding? Not my sort of thing. How long have you been at it?'

'Two years, or at least two holidays here. It's one of the best locations in the world, so once you discover it you just tend to come back. Last year I took the course, was hooked and kept going until I had my beginner's licence. Having that means I can jump solo, but as you saw, there's still plenty of room for improvement.'

'Don't you bother much with just, well, lying around in the sun and reading, like normal people?'

He grinned.

'Not my sort of thing! And anyway, when the weather's good I just want to be up there, making the most of it...what the hell *is* this din?'

'Turkish pop. Don't you approve?'

From behind Rosie came the unmistakable sound of Monica trying to suppress a giggle. The rotten bugger was listening.

'Approve? Do I seem that bad? I suppose I *am* a bit old fashioned when it comes to music. Born at the wrong time, I think, which reminds me how bad my manners are. Name's Henry. Henry Blanchard.'

Rosie suspected that Monica was laughing again but a quick glance told her that her friend was listening to Berkant with angelically rapt attention. Rosie suppressed her own smile and had to admit that in thinking up a more suitable name for Henry, you'd be seriously challenged.

'Rosie Stone,' she replied, both relieved and faintly surprised when he didn't shake her hand. Instead he began talking about the area of Turkey they found themselves in, and how much he liked the nearby town of Fethiye. She found she liked him. Looking at him more closely, she guessed he was mid-forties, a little younger than she'd thought at first, but he had charm and formality that seemed to belong to an earlier age. He was easy and interesting to talk to, with warmth that made her want to draw closer.

Time seemed to speed by, marked now and then by fresh drinks or by someone joining them briefly before leaving them again in peace. The night club atmosphere, which the girls usually tried to avoid, took over the bar about midnight without them really noticing. When Rosie next looked at her watch, it was two o'clock. The strobe lights from the bar were being switched off, the few remaining dancers flagging. Berkant had gone to join Zeynel and the other animators, who were slumped in a tired huddle at the end of the bar, quietly smoking Marlboros.

Henry, Monica and Rosie walked back to reception to collect their keys. Rosie was swaying a little, knowing that she'd had too many gins, but didn't care a lot. She did care, though, that quite suddenly he was gone. Turning back from speaking to Monica, she went to say goodnight, only to realise that he had disappeared.

'I don't believe this man!' she wailed as they reached their room, 'I didn't even ask him how long he's staying!'

'You mean you actually care? I've heard of centenarians with younger attitudes!'

'Perhaps I just like old people,' grumbled Rosie, but Monica was long past paying attention, having fallen into bed with a quick swill of her face, and was already unconscious.

At breakfast, Henry was nowhere to be seen and Rosie assumed that on such a perfectly wind-still day he would be paragliding. She lazed around the pool with Monica and talked of taking the communal minibus, or dolmuş, into Fethiye in a few days' time. Henry had made the old town sound well worth visiting and Monica was keen to see the area. By late afternoon, Henry had still not appeared, so Rosie assumed he must have booked two jumps for that day. Perhaps she'd see him at dinner.

But she didn't. Monica wasn't much company either, scouring her guide book and making plans to take trips out and to see as much as possible while she had the chance.

'We could see the rock tombs and the Roman Amphitheatre while we're in Fethiye for the market tomorrow,' she was commenting, 'but we must see Ephesus too.'

'Ephesus? But that's miles away, and on these roads...'

'No problem. It's a three day trip,' replied Monica tartly, 'so distance is irrelevant. We'll see different places of interest on the way there, too, so it's really worth making the effort. Shall I book it?'

'Er...'

'Oh, I see! You'd rather just hang around here all day, every day, in case Mr Oh-So-Bloody-Dashing-Flying-Man deigns to come down from his mountain and throw you a crumb of attention.'

Put like that, it did sound pathetic, but still Rosie spluttered her indignant protest. As she'd found several times before with Monica, if she failed to fit in with her plans, she was quickly made to feel at fault. Yet, this was her holiday too, and if her choice was to wait around, being pathetic, so be it.

'Well!' concluded Monica crisply, 'No need for us to live in each others' pockets. I shall go anyway.'

'OK,' Rosie smiled, determined not to give in to bad feeling, 'I'll just stay here and practise my water polo.'

That evening must have been the night off for most of the animators, because the planned entertainment was a game of bingo at the bar.

'Over my dead body,' snapped Monica when Esra, the youngest of the animators, politely asked. She took it as a no.

By the following lunchtime, Henry had still not reappeared and Rosie began to suspect that he'd simply gone home. She hated caring that he hadn't said farewell. She hated the fact that he had the power to spoil even a small part of her holiday.

The girls took the little dolmuş into Fethiye, crammed elbow to elbow with locals and tourists alike. The minibus made its grinding, slow, horn-tooting way up the hill towards Hisarönü, hailing more passengers, no matter how stuffed the vehicle became. Having started their journey at the terminus, the girls had seats, but they were beginning to wonder how they'd ever get off again. With every mile, the vehicle became more crowded and the aisle ever more blocked with swaying passengers. The word dolmuş, Rosie pondered, which meant "stuffed" in Turkish, described this kind of communal transport perfectly.

Staring through the hot glass at the rocky landscape, they passed rows of square beehives on the hillside and pine forests full of spindly trees. Whenever they came close to a village, they saw troupes of children in neat blue uniforms, trotting to school along the roadside in cheerful single file. After a while, the dolmuş reached the straggling outskirts of the town with its scattering of tumbledown concrete dwellings and sun-baked scruffiness.

Gradually, this gave way to more solid buildings as they neared the centre. Big shop signs with trailing black electrical wires, as attractive as dead spiders, dominated the street scene. Here and there, a single vegetable shop displayed its colourful produce and men sat at rickety tables before barber shops, playing Backgammon and smoking. In one place, a group of women were chatting at the roadside while one of them scrubbed energetically at a carpet that was stretched out on the concrete. Despite the dust and the general scruffiness, there was a feeling of making the most of everything and of cheerfulness. When at last the dolmuş reached the centre of Fethiye the driver yelled something, cut the rattling engine and everyone trooped obediently off. There'd been no need to worry about disembarking after all.

Fethiye Market was a delight. It was a huge canvas-covered world of colour, noise and scents. Big smiles, with the hailing and pestering of every likely customer, were relentless. When no sale resulted or they were politely put off, even ignored, the smiles hardly faded. Often, Rosie found her apologetic refusal earned her an 'OK, have a nice day anyway.' It was easy, very easy, to like these people.

Once past the outer area of toy camels, curly slippers, Turkish Delight and belly dancer outfits, the atmosphere changed noticeably. In this inner tented world of dim light and comparative quiet, the locals shopped amongst stalls that overflowed with spices, fruit, white cheese displayed in huge animal skins, bright silks, clothing and farm tools. The tools seemed to come with a choice of rusty or shiny. And shoes. So many, many shoes, all in various states of dustiness, to suit every taste. The air was filled with the scents of leather, flowers, perfumes and spices and as a background to it all was the haunting mixture of oriental music, sales patter and general chaos.

Monica was making herself completely at home, buying a less than averagely dusty pair of shoes and a bright yellow T-shirt. Rosie found this choice of colour astonishing, but said nothing. She bought several boxes of Turkish Delight and a big bag of apples before they left the market for the peace of the rock tombs.

The climb up to the tombs didn't look too onerous from the ground, but once they had started, they realised what an illusion that had been. The heat made things even more challenging and by the time they reached the top they felt like wrecks of their former selves. Sitting in the shade of the ancient tombs, they ate apples and listened as all the mosques of Fethiye joined in the call to prayer. One would start, joined by three more from across the town, then another would begin, until the whole of Fethiye was joined in the chanting of this strangely beautiful lamenting sound.

They walked along the harbour with its many boats moored stern-on to the quay and its myriad bars and fish restaurants. The salespeople were out in force here too, advertising boat trips for all they were worth, but the whole experience was wonderful, perfect in the sun.

By the time they arrived back at the hotel they were exhausted and hot. Monica headed straight to their room and Rosie meant to go too, to take the shower she was yearning for, but she found herself drawn to the amphitheatre, where some sort of rehearsal was taking place. The music was exotic, attracting her with its Pied Piper magic. She saw that the stage had been decorated with flowers and balloons and about twenty children, faces painted with tiger stripes, were learning dance steps from Zeynel and Lili. With unfailing patience, the two animators demonstrated each small step while Berkant looked on. Every few minutes one of them would pause to holler rapid instructions in Turkish to the unseen presence operating the music system. Remembering the posters she'd seen about the place, Rosie realised that they were practising for the forthcoming Kiddie Show.

Putting down her bags, she leaned over the back wall of the amphitheatre to watch. The children finished their dance and moved with fluid grace to form a semi circle around a small, pretty blonde haired girl, aged about five.

The child looked completely free of nerves, her little tiger's chin raised proudly as she drew breath to sing.

Rather than the anticipated sweet singing, however, all the child managed to deliver was an indignant squeal. Small hands on hips, anger clouding the pretty face, she stormed over to where a few children had begun to whisper. Her small eyebrows shot up indignantly towards her hairline.

'Quiet!' she demanded, her voice ringing out imperiously, aided by the natural acoustics of the amphitheatre, and her small foot stamping hard on the marble stage, 'Quiet, while Dollie sings!'

Rosie laughed to herself.

'Not exactly introverted, is she?' remarked a voice from behind her, speaking her thoughts exactly. Why did he always have to creep up behind her? Rosie must have spun round in a millisecond, if only to confirm that this truly was him. At last. He was there, smiling, his hair standing up on end again, as if he had just pulled off his helmet. He was still wearing a jump suit.

'Still at it, I see,' she smiled, as they began to walk towards the hotel.

'While this good weather continues I thought I should get a few jumps in,' he explained, 'They're talking about high winds over the next few days and there'll be no paragliding at all if the weather does change. By the way, I wanted to ask how long you were staying. Not planning on leaving yet, I hope?'

'Over a week yet. You?'

'I've still two weeks left out of the four, I'm happy to say. This is the second year that I've managed a full four weeks away. I find it takes a good two weeks of holiday to wind down and leave all the grunge of everyday life behind, so having four weeks is perfect. Had to get a locum in, but I'm sure I won't be missed that much!'

'Must be nice,' she murmured, 'to have such a long break.' He didn't reply and in comfortable silence they

walked to reception. Collecting keys, they said their
farewells and began walking away in opposite directions.

'I was just thinking,' he called after her, 'I think we
should see how well little Dollie sings after such a build-
up. The kids are putting on their show tomorrow night.
Will you be there?'

'Yes,' she called back, 'I'll be there.'

Perhaps her response had been too eager, but she was
smiling, not caring a bit. She was grinning ear to ear in
fact, and walking quickly down the corridor so that he
wouldn't notice.

Chapter Four

Rosie. Sunday 18th January

When the dull pain in her head dragged her to some sort of consciousness on Sunday morning, the January sky was still completely dark. The digital panel on the oven downstairs read seven o'clock, but the only light admitted when she opened the curtains on the ground floor was the pale yellow glow from the street lamp opposite Monica's house.

She felt far too fragile for bright overhead light, so she used the tiny light on the cooker extractor hood to show her around the kitchen as she made tea. Her movements were sluggish, the throbbing pain in her head making her wince as she tried to work out how such a small amount of wine had created so great a hangover.

It hadn't, she decided. It had been the nightmares that had caused this. The old terror was back, that nightmare of sinking, drowning, ankles caught in long tendrils of seaweed and being dragged downwards. This had always been what happened when she allowed the past back in. All that self-indulgent recalling of past events was always going to demand its price and now she was paying with the inevitable nightmares and pain.

Her favourite Mickey Mouse mug warming her hands, she padded into the dining room on her slippered feet, wrapping her old dressing gown around her as she collapsed on to the window seat. Half dozing, she sipped the tea while watching the light of a new day seep into the garden, illuminating the yew bushes and gleaming on the frosty path.

Her head was still full of the night's dreams and the drowning nightmare was just one of them. Fragments of other dreams, no more than disjointed images now, were melting away with the darkness, but there was one that remained clear, its details refusing to fade.

A dream of being marooned in the wrong place and being so very alone.

She'd been in a house that was totally unknown to her, a grand and immaculate home that gleamed and sparkled with care and attention. There had been people everywhere. However much she'd kept moving, she just hadn't been able to escape them, their loud, boozy voices following her wherever she'd gone. She'd felt vulnerable and out of place and had kept trying to find a way out, but the right door had continued to elude her. Panic was rising within her as she'd blundered from room to room. Most people were unaware of her, which was a blessing, their eyes sliding lazily past and through her. But there'd been just a few individuals whose eyes hadn't drifted past, but had locked right on to her, hostile and unwelcoming. Their drinking had saved her most of the time, however, their cold, drunken eyes sliding away without comment, back to their beer and over-fed stomachs.

But then there'd been the woman. As tipsy as the rest, with her steely, determined eyes she had stared long and hard at Rosie and then, quite unexpectedly, she had smiled. For some reason, the smile had been even more alarming than the coldness, and there'd been no escape from her. Rosie had kept on meeting those piercing, friendly eyes until at long last she had found the door and escaped.

Recalling it all from her window seat in the gradually increasing morning light, she knew this had been no mere dream. Clear, detailed, night time wanderings like this had been part of her life for as long as she could remember. With their crystal clarity, they always lingered in her memory, every detail remaining with her throughout the following day. At a very young age she'd tried speaking to her mother about these happenings, but her mother had had no personal experience of anything like it. As hard as she'd tried, she hadn't been able to help. When Rosie was older and living with her grandmother, she'd tried to learn about what was happening to her, reading every book that

44

touched on the subject. To start with, she hadn't even known which words to look up, but eventually she'd found something about research on "Astral Travel" or "Out of Body Experiences". What they described sounded very familiar. With time and the coming of the Internet, more information had become available, and what she'd found out gave her a little comfort. She wasn't alone after all.

She wasn't the only one, it seemed, who had these disturbing experiences. There were others out there who would know what she was talking about. She would have loved to be able to meet some of them, to ask the many questions she needed answers to. For example, did the people who were able to see her during these nightly wanderings remember it afterwards? Would they recognise her, if, say, she met them in the street? But it was no good. The chances of ever meeting another person who understood were very small and it was getting to the point where talking to almost anyone would help. Since that talk with her mother so very long ago, Rosie hadn't discussed it with anyone. It was time she did.

But it was still the weekend, a hopeless time for trying to see friends. Those she had in Peterborough were all married and on a Sunday would be with their families. She didn't have anything in common with her work colleagues, so that was no help. There was, of course, Monica next door. On a Sunday she was usually at home, but this weekend she was away at a wedding. Anyway, Rosie wasn't sure that Monica's often fractious common sense would take this seriously.

Her tea finished, she unfurled her reluctant body from the window seat and went to pour the cold tea dregs into the sink of her tiny, yet beautifully new and gleaming kitchen. Going upstairs to take her shower, she didn't relish the thought of another long, solitary day.

She had only just finished breakfast, the cups and plates neatly washed and put away, when the doorbell trilled. She had been planning a quick drive to the car boot sale, something to break up the solitude, but whatever diversion the doorbell brought would be welcome.

'I thought you were away until tonight!' she cried, seeing Monica's short stature and big smile lighting up the doorway.

'I was, but I came back last night instead. Wedding receptions that go on into the evening…well, they're easier for couples, let's say.'

'I know just what you mean…fancy a walk round the car boot? You might find the plates you've been looking for.'

They went, driving in Rosie's frost covered silver Mazda MX5. As she made her way through the slow Sunday traffic, she wondered several times about bringing up the subject of dreams. Every time she composed the right sentence in her head, though, Monica began talking about the wedding she'd just been to or the decorating she was still doing in the house. It was obviously not the right time to discuss it.

The market was lively and noisy, busy in the frosty, bright morning air. Rosie forgot her troubles while she and Monica hunted down the items they wanted for their homes. Monica had recently bought a second hand dresser for the end wall of her dining room. It was not terribly old but had the right look for the house and she wanted interesting plates and dishes to decorate it.

'You're hardly going to find anything eighteenth century around here,' observed Rosie, as she sorted through a washing-up bowl of cracked and dusty 1970s ceramics.

'Apart from the road surface, no,' agreed Monica, as she withdrew her foot from a badly filled-in pot hole. She did find a couple of items she could use, though. She paid a pound for a chipped and cracked tiny dish that she said was an early Worcester tea bowl, and slightly more for a pink lustre plate. They were both so damaged that they were practically worthless, but Monica didn't care. On her dresser, chips turned towards the back, they would look just fine, she said. She loved seeking out little treasured things from the past. Her work as curator of a small local museum was more than just a job; it was a passion. Rosie found Monica's love for her work quite enviable.

Rosie found a bag of old fabric that she could make into cushion covers, so the morning was useful for both women. It was good to escape the worst of the cold for a few minutes and head for the covered area near the fruit and vegetable market where they could buy a cup of coffee and sit down.

It was just as noisy inside the make-shift shelter as it was outside, and almost as chilly, with the draft blowing in under the large awning, but they huddled themselves into white plastic chairs around a wobbly metal table and drank their coffee to the merry background sounds of the market.

'GET your bananas! HALF price now, ladies! Chuck you in a couple of apples as well with that, me luv. There you go. HALF price on the satsumas! Only a few bakin' spuds left now, luv, I'll throw you in these leeks an' all...'

The girls grinned, oddly at peace with the world. Rosie noticed that her headache had gone. It was good to be out and laughing again.

'Not much like Fethiye Market, is it?' she giggled.

'I thought you didn't like talking about that!'

'Well, I don't really, but since we are, have you heard from Berkant lately?'

'I still get the odd email from him.'

'Really? He's still keen then. I couldn't believe the change that came over you when you were with him. You seemed so happy, always having fun. I seem to remember you even deigned to do the dreaded Club Dance once.'

'True, though it's a terrible thing to admit to. Yes, it was fun, but you can't live your whole life like that. I decided just to let go for a bit,' she smiled broadly.

'You certainly did that. And Berkant's still interested...'

'I'm not getting carried away about it,' she stated predictably, 'I'm sure he enjoys quite a lot of flings in that job of his, but, yes, I am pretty surprised that he keeps in touch. In fact...'

'Yes? In fact what?'

'He reckons he's coming over in the summer, visiting some relatives in London, then coming up here to see me.'

'What? Why didn't you say? That's really nice news!'

'Because you didn't want to talk about the holiday, that's why.' She paused for a moment, rubbing a ring of coffee from the table top with a thin paper napkin from a container next to the ketchup bottle. 'I think you were right to put it all behind you, though, after what Henry did. You haven't heard from him, then?'

'No, and I don't expect to. It wouldn't be hard for him to find me if he really wanted to, with us both working in financial services. It just confirms what I knew all along, that he wasn't all that interested. I found him easily through the Internet; Henry Blanchard of Mason and Blanchard in Downham Market. A smart little outfit, apparently, and just a few miles away, can you believe? There was a picture of his shop front on the website; a sweet looking Georgian building. You'd love it!'

'Honestly, Rosie, for someone who was going to put it all behind her, you've found out quite a lot!'

'Not really. It was just a quick search. Henry's company obviously likes to advertise, so it was easy to find. He could have found me just as easily, but he clearly chose not to!'

'You don't know that. Perhaps he's just being sensible, like you. I feel I made things worse for you too. The worst thing I did was to go on that trip to Ephesus, leaving you behind with him.'

'No, Monica, whatever you did, it was always going to happen. Some things are meant to happen, whatever the consequences.'

Chapter Five

Henry. Monday 2nd February

'Good morning, Mason and Blanchard!'

Julia had grabbed the telephone, answering it before its second ring, but had managed to drop her filing and upset the overflowing waste bin in the process. Clutching the phone in one hand, she started to gather up paper and old tea bags with the other, stuffing them back into the bin. Meanwhile, the coiled telephone wire, which seemed to have developed a will of its own, managed to wind itself around her open desk drawer. Her calm telephone voice carried on smoothly, giving nothing away and answering the caller's questions in her usual flawless manner, while one hand abandoned the mess on the floor and began working to free the wire. With perverse abruptness it sprang free, catching the pin tray on her desk and scattering paperclips over the floor.

Henry arrived at his premises on that cold morning just in time to witness this scene, but he wasn't really aware of it. Shaking off his coat and blowing on his hands, his thoughts were far away, already working on the report he had to write. He called out a careless greeting to Julia before continuing towards his office, oblivious of her crawling around on the floor and flinging tea-stained debris into the bin. He had reached his door, his hand turning the smart brass knob, when it finally sank in that Julia's telephone voice had stopped and that her silence was heavier than usual. He turned to see her still crouching on the floor behind the counter, staring at him expectantly.

'Sorry, did you say something?' he enquired with an amiable smile.

'Yes, Henry. Good morning. I just said the fund value you requested has arrived.'

'Ah, excellent, I'll need that for the report.'

He opened the door and entered his inner sanctum with its oversized mahogany desk and bookcase. The walls were papered in dark green, the same shade as the long velvet curtains that framed the sash window overlooking the small car park behind the building. Decorating the walls were paintings by local artists. One was in oils of Ely Cathedral on a rainy day, the artist cleverly showing reflections of the ancient building in shimmering puddles in the foreground. There were a few figures on the pathways, little flashes of colour with bright umbrellas that contrasted with the sombre stone of the cathedral. The other pictures were water colour Fenland scenes; pollarded willows and flooded low-lying ground with winter sun breaking through waving grasses. They were all things of beauty but he had bought them more because he'd thought them appropriate than because he truly liked them. He was trying hard to get used to living in the Fens and was determined to keep up the good work of running this business in Downham Market. The paintings reminded him daily of the landscape he was trying so hard to like, but it was difficult. He missed his native Dorset and one day, one day, he'd pack up this business and go home.

In the meantime, he had his immaculate, pleasant office and this room which was entirely his own. His old partner, John Mason, had died three years earlier and despite several attempts at recruitment, no one had seemed right to replace him. These days, Henry used John's old office, easily accessed via a communicating door between the two rooms, to interview his clients in. Working alone suited Henry in a way; he had enough long-established clients without having to look too hard for more, but he missed John's companionship and being able to discuss the business and the more complicated client problems with him.

Business-wise, things were going pretty well, helped in no small way by the highly efficient Julia. She fielded non-urgent phone calls, kept him supplied with tea and coffee, did all his administration and even kept the place neat. She had obviously been tidying up that morning, because his desk was free from yesterday's clutter. The only objects decorating the dust-free surface were his pens, telephone and the two silver framed photographs that always sat there. One was of his father standing by an immaculately restored Austin Seven and the other showed a particularly well groomed Antonia, her hair three shades blonder than usual, and her eyes staring directly into the camera, as if keeping a close eye on his working life. The fountain pen, biro and retractable pencil had been a Christmas present a few years ago from a client. Each item was beautifully designed in green enamel and gold, sitting in an elegantly crafted stand of the same green enamel. Henry loved using them. He still wrote with the fountain pen for less hurried work, though having to keep refilling it from the bottle in the drawer created a bit of a mess.

This morning, however, there was no time for looking at paintings or refilling fountain pens. He had to get on quickly and complete this report. Scrabbling for scrap paper from the desk drawer and picking up the biro from the stand, he began to write. It was hard to concentrate. All too often he'd find his attention had wandered to the view of his black Jaguar. It sat in its usual parking space next to Julia's little red Peugeot, just outside the window. Even the car park was neat, he noticed, as tidily swept as the pavement in front of the premises. Julia must have arrived even earlier than usual for work. She never seemed to expect any acknowledgement, let alone thanks or payment for all these extra hours and Henry was not always good at remembering to thank her. Yet he did appreciate what she did. He knew he would be completely lost without her, and once a year he tried to show his appreciation by buying Julia a rather nice Christmas present and paying her a decent bonus. It would perhaps be appropriate sometimes to take her out to lunch as well, to show her how much she was valued, but Antonia would never approve. He would never hear the last of it.

There was a movement at the door and he looked up as Julia struggled to enter the room with a small tray.

'Coffee, Henry,' she said cheerfully, placing the white porcelain cup and saucer on his desk with a tiny matching plate of ginger nuts. No mugs in this office. Had that been her idea or his? He couldn't remember now.

No sooner had he thanked her than she was back again, this time with a pile of dog-eared blue client files. She had been keeping computer records for their clients for years now, but Henry refused to have a terminal in his own office, considering such things pointless monstrosities. Because of this, all the notes were duplicated on paper and kept in these blue, ragged files.

'Not much post today!' she sang brightly, as if cheering up a hospital patient. She placed the pile at his left elbow and he gave it a disgruntled look.

'Good thing,' he muttered. 'I have to get Ronnie Barnstone's report finished. He's coming in at twelve!'

'Half past eleven, actually, but if you get the pages through to me by half past ten I'll make sure it's ready. Then you have lunch at one o'clock with Mrs Ellis, and Anna Sobers, the City Life inspector, is calling in at three.'

Henry let out a long groan.

'Whatever was I thinking of, booking in so much for today?' He covered his face with his hands, looking exhausted when he took his hands away. Julia glanced anxiously at him, thinking how worn out and miserable he looked these days.

Just for a moment Henry thought she was about to speak, but then she seemed to change her mind. There was something about her glance, about her whole manner, that worried him on some level, but he hadn't the time to think about it now. The report had to be written. Fortunately, the awkward moment lasted no more than a couple of seconds and she was her brisk self again, bustling from his office to leave him in peace.

He opened Ronnie's file, looked up a figure and began writing again, his thoughts at last flowing logically and well. His pen flew over the paper, the report taking shape as he detailed his advice. Within thirty minutes he had reached the concluding paragraph and had almost finished.

He was aware that he was probably one of the last remaining people in the country to write reports long-hand and then have the luxury of someone to type it for him, but he couldn't work any other way and Julia was good like that.

Julia. Again he groaned. Could Bruce be right? Could it really be true that Henry's secretary had a crush on him? Surely she knew that he wasn't interested? Henry had to admit, though, that he wasn't one of life's more observant people when it came to other peoples' feelings. Antonia often accused him of being inconsiderate and insensitive. He supposed she was right because he certainly didn't intend to offend the people she said he did. Apart from her mother, that was. That bit was always intentional.

Was it possible that he just hadn't noticed the effect his behaviour was having on Julia? Was she somehow misreading his friendliness and genuine respect for her as something deeper?

He knew he ought to be more careful how he spoke to her in future, for her sake as well as his own. If gossip ever reached Antonia's ears about Henry and an imagined relationship with his secretary, he could well imagine the consequences. Life with Antonia, whenever she grew suspicious about his activities, was hardly worth living. Perhaps, to be fair, she had good reason to be suspicious. Over the years, Henry had struggled with fidelity. Each time Antonia had found out about some little indiscretion he had paid for it with weeks of silences, pierced here and there by poisonous remarks. He couldn't face all that again, especially when for once he was innocent.

Especially not after last time. Even now, he failed to understand how he had given the game away so easily last summer. Returning from his Turkish idyll, he'd thought he was being so careful. He had talked endlessly about the joys of paragliding and the delights of Turkey, but somehow she had known. Greeting his words with that slate-hard, cynical look of hers, she had seen right through all he said. Though she never discovered any facts, for weeks she airily informed their friends, right in front of him, that Henry had been 'at it again.' There had then followed weeks of silences, separate bedrooms, threats to leave, threats to stay and many, many insults.

But Rosie, the woman who'd been at the root of all this, was part of the past now and that was where she had to stay. She'd made it quite clear on that final morning when she'd walked out on him in Turkey, that she wanted no more to do with him. He'd made himself forget her and move on, coping at the same time with his caustic domestic situation.

All that had been eight months ago. Even Antonia said little about it these days, though he suspected his paragliding days were at an end. For the sake of his own sanity he had to keep Antonia sweet. He could not afford any misunderstandings about Julia on top of everything else.

He pulled himself together with a jolt and resumed his writing with a determined scrawl. He finished the last sentence and began reading the report through. When the phone on his desk rang out with shrill urgency Henry cursed loudly, his concentration exploding into tatters.

'Antonia for you, Henry.'

'Oh, tell her I'll get back to her after my meeting, would you?'

'I did suggest that to her, Henry, but she says it's urgent.'

'It's always bloody urgent. You'd better put her through.'

But it was Antonia's voice, not Julia's, that answered him and it was impossible to tell at which point her ear had tuned in.

'Stop being so pompous, Henry. Have you done it yet?'

'Done what, Antonia, for...'

'No need to snap. We discussed it at breakfast. Invite Julia, of course! I must know the numbers for the party today so that I can tell the caterers. You promised to phone me.'

'I've been extremely busy...anyway, the party isn't until March. What's the hurry?'

'They aren't just any old caterers and they get booked up very quickly. I must confirm the booking and let them have the numbers today.'

'So why didn't you just ask Julia when she answered the phone?'

'Because, as we discussed, she's your employee. And I would like *you* to do it!'

She rattled on for a bit longer and he found himself looking at her photo on his desk. The image seemed to be speaking to him, the lip-sticked mouth moving in that bossy way of hers, while the bleached hair remained rigid and lifeless. Her voice still pounding in his ear, he snatched the photograph and threw it into the desk drawer, slamming the drawer shut with a loud thud. From the other frame, his dad smiled.

When at last her voice had gone, he let out a ragged sigh. This was all he needed. He would have to be extremely careful about how he invited Julia. He couldn't afford to give her any ideas. But, he reminded himself once more, all that would have to wait. Time was getting on. Yet again, he turned back to the report, trying to concentrate as he finished reading it through. It was a quarter to eleven already and Julia still had to type it.

Striding to the door, he opened it swiftly, peering over his glasses as he handed the report to his secretary.

'Er, Julia, you don't happen to be free on 21st March, do you? It's a Saturday, apparently.' She was gazing up at him, brushing her fair hair back from her forehead with one hand, as if nervous. He noticed with alarm that she was blushing, colour spreading rapidly across her cheeks. He rushed on, anxious to repair any damage. 'What I mean is, Antonia's throwing a birthday party for herself on

March 21st and she wants to know if you can make it. It's her fortieth, you see.'

If the last sentence was a disappointment to her, Julia was quick to disguise it.

'Yes,' she was smiling, 'Yes, I'm sure that date will be fine. I can't think there's anything yet in the diary for March. Will you thank Antonia for me?' She glanced at the scrawled pages that Henry had passed to her and added, 'Must get on if I'm to finish this in time...'

With relief, Henry made a hasty retreat into his office, forcing himself to concentrate on Ronnie Barnstone's file.

Once the door to Henry's office was safely closed, Julia smiled to herself. There was nothing flustered or blushing about her now, just a full-blown, beaming smile. She glanced at the familiar hand writing on the pages in front of her and began to type, her cool, confident fingers flying over the keys. With efficient speed she transformed the scribble into neat paragraphs and columns of figures and all the time in the background her mind was working on something new and delicious.

With five minutes to spare she printed off the pages and clipped them neatly together. She strolled confidently into Henry's office and handed the report to him with a triumphant gesture. He was poring over the Barnstone file and didn't raise his head as she entered the room, his eyes peering at her instead over the steel rims of his reading glasses. His fringe flopped forward in its usual undisciplined way. It was hair that seemed to defy all haircuts, carrying on regardless after any attempt to control it, and even this tiny detail pulled at something inside her. He didn't need to be handsome, she thought. He was attractive as he was, unbearably so. Henry was just Henry. He was thanking her now, his mouth managing to twist itself into a look she couldn't quite read. She loved that too, the way his mouth could express cynicism, tolerance or humour, with just a simple twist.

Back in the safe haven of the reception area, Julia was free to smile as much as she liked as she indulged herself with exciting new thoughts. As law abiding as she was, Julia's morals encountered no obstacles where Antonia was concerned. That over-manicured woman, who was too self-obsessed to peel a potato, didn't give a damn about Henry. Likewise, Henry was clearly not in love with her. In fact, it was obvious that he could barely tolerate her and he hardly bothered to pretend otherwise. So surely, there was just a glimmer of hope for his faithful secretary?

The wonderful thing was that Julia was going to another party at Henry's. She had been to these things before, of course, but she and Henry seemed to be growing closer with every passing week. One of these days, or party nights, he would realise that she could be so much more to him. It was immaterial how many other people would be at the party. It would still be her chance to shine, to be close to him and to be herself. She could shed the guise of secretary and be the flirtatious, vivacious woman she truly was.

Julia leaned back in her chair and planned the purchase of a new dress. It would be something in black, maybe a little seductive but not too obvious. She would have her hair done too. No budget was too big for this campaign of hers, because you just never knew when another opportunity might come your way. Such happy, hopeful thoughts and a new event to plan deserved a celebration.

She reached into one of the drawers to the right hand side of her chair. It was one in a row of low, wooden filing cabinets that fitted neatly beneath the long counter-top desk. All Henry's blue files were stored in alphabetical order in rows of cabinets like this; tall ones against the back wall, shorter ones beneath the counter. They formed part of Julia's office within the reception area, neatly separated from the visitors' section by a long, curving counter. This counter, with its lockable gate and lifting hatch, was the barrier behind which Julia sat and from where she ruled her small empire. Apart from the odd times when Henry found himself alone and had to search for files, this area was Julia's alone. She could have found her way around it in the dark and now, her eye checking the main entrance, she slid her hand between the file dividers in the drawer. Her fingers searched for a few seconds before closing around the cool, comforting shape of a bottle. Withdrawing it deftly, she lifted it to her lips and drank. The gin glugged lazily into her mouth just as she glimpsed a movement at the entrance door. Quickly she replaced the bottle cap and dropped it back behind the divider, sliding the drawer shut behind its neatly typed label, 'Hi-Hz'.

Julia's mask of efficiency was neatly back in place in plenty of time to greet Mr Barnstone, who was looking very dapper that morning in new Harris tweeds. Slightly late, as usual, Ronnie offered no apology. He and his brother Malcolm were two of Henry's best clients, and fully aware of this, he strode into the waiting area with his loud voice and overbearing self-importance. Julia lifted the hatch and went to meet him, taking his coat with her usual smooth smile and showing him into John Mason's old office. Henry was already there, waiting to shake his hand and offer him coffee. Julia could hear Henry's welcoming voice ring out as she closed the door.

'Ah, Ronnie! Good to see you again!'

Left alone, her most urgent work of the morning completed, Julia had time to daydream and to plan in peace.

It was something she had become very good at.

Chapter Six

Rosie. Monday 2nd February

Twenty past five, and outside the tall office windows it was completely dark. Rosie closed the web page she'd been working on and logged out. She had checked more than enough files for one day and had brought the compliance records up to date. Outside her office door she could hear the two clerks, Jenny and Alice, packing up for the day and whispering about something.

The boss was out of the room so they were most likely discussing him, though it could equally be Rosie. She didn't really care. As the compliance officer with her own small room, she had never been "one of the girls". Despite this, she, Jenny and Alice were the only three women working in a firm of male financial advisors and their portly chairman, so they made a token effort to be friendly to each other. As the three of them arrived each morning, they exchanged a few polite comments and a little lifeless conversation. Sometimes it stretched as far as a scrap of lame gossip, but nothing more. Compliance officers were fairly solitary figures. Their job was mainly to keep the office records up to date and to make sure the advice given to clients complied with the ever-changing regulations. None of this made her very popular, though Rosie tried hard to apply common sense to it all, knowing that the advisors had a living to earn and were all trustworthy individuals. She understood that they did their best for their clients, but still she frequently had to ask them to make corrections or rewrite items, when all they wanted was to be back out on the road, seeing people and earning money.

Jenny's and Alice's indifference towards her had very little to do with her job, however. They simply had nothing in common with her. They loved television and practically everything on it. They avidly watched programmes that

Rosie had never heard of and whenever they asked if she'd seen something on some weird new channel, they found she'd been watching something else, or even worse, hadn't bothered to switch the thing on at all. She was a huge disappointment to them.

Alice looked up as Rosie closed her door behind her, switching off the light.

'All done, Rosie? Seen Raymond?'

'Not for hours. Why?'

'We think he's having a mid-life crisis. He's been out this afternoon to buy himself a new image.'

Rosie smiled. At least she knew now what all the whispering had been about. Alice pulled a small mirror from her bag and peered into it, patting her neat auburn bobbed hair and tilting her chin to check her make-up.

'Put the alarm on, Jenny. Time to go!' Raymond's jovial voice called from the hallway as his large, balding head peered round the doorpost.

Jenny called out a cheerful reply and Raymond's head disappeared.

'He's hiding them,' hissed Alice and both girls giggled, hands over their mouths like school girls with a crush.

'Hiding what?' asked Rosie, knowing she'd have to find out in the end.

'Come on ladies!' chided Raymond, who was pulling on his coat in the doorway, his generous form coming into full view. A new pair of vivid, custard yellow corduroy trousers flowed from the sturdy belt that circumnavigated his generously sized belly. Even Rosie found herself staring. The yellow was so bright, especially when combined with his winter clothes and shoes, that the trousers seemed to light up the hallway. Behind her, Rosie could sense that Alice was still sniggering.

'Ah, I do see,' she muttered and the giggling exploded again. Poor old Raymond. He was a decent boss and a good chairman and of them all, Rosie found him the easiest person to work with.

Alice led the way out of the office and down the stairs while Raymond searched for the big front door key. The two girls threw a careless farewell over their shoulders as they walked away, hardly pausing in their flow of chatter, but Rosie lingered, waiting as Raymond completed his locking up for the night.

'Bad day?' he asked pleasantly.

'No, not really. The winter's getting to us all a bit, I think. It'll be good when we can walk home in the light, that's all!'

'Very true. Book yourself a holiday, Rosie! It'll cheer you up. I just have; we all need something to look forward to.'

Rosie was surprised by his comment, unaware that she looked gloomy enough for him to notice. The thought of holidays was the last thing to cheer her up, but Raymond could hardly be expected to know that. With as cheery a farewell as she could muster, she walked towards the town bridge and turned into North Brink.

There was hardly anyone about and very few cars passed her, going along the one-way system on the Brink. Across the river however, on the main road through town, there was plenty of activity; car lights gleaming and turning, slowing at the traffic lights, then accelerating away. There was confusion for a while and a temporary hold up as an emergency vehicle of some kind tried to make its way through the traffic, its siren wailing and blue lights flashing. The lights; blue emergency, green, amber and red of traffic signals and the pale, moon-like beams of car headlights rippled and shone, reflected in the tidal river below as it flowed out to the sea.

To her right, safe in the comparative peace of this side of town, noble town houses stood soberly in the lamplight. Their tall presence was somehow reassuring, even though most of their windows were unlit. She passed the stately Peckover House, set back from the pavement and secure behind its black railings, shutters closed in preparation for a new National Trust visitor season. Rapidly moving past the Quaker Meeting House and a row of high, handsome terraced homes, she hurried through the cold and damp towards home and a solitary night.

She contemplated her situation as she made her way along the Brink, breaking into a trot every so often. She didn't hate her job, she considered. It was always better when the advisors came in, even if she wasn't their favourite person. At those times there was banter and liveliness in the place, people to talk to. No, she didn't hate her job, though it gave her little happiness. What was really dragging her spirits down was the thought of an evening alone, with too much freedom to think. Ever since that wallowing in memories a couple of weeks earlier, she'd managed to keep herself occupied and avoid more remembering, but it was inevitable that in the end her thoughts would return to the past and finish what she'd started.

Chatting to Monica that Sunday at the car boot sale had been nice, but her own words had kept playing in her mind, over and over again, ever since; that what had occurred in Turkey was always going to happen, whatever the consequences.

Whatever the consequences. So, she would allow herself to continue recalling it all, but it would be for the very last time.

Arriving at home, she put frozen chips and a big fish cake into the oven. She watched the News while she ate, hardly listening, hardly tasting.

By the time she had washed up and settled down she was back again. She was back in that other time and place.

Dollie, the child star of the Kiddie Show, did in fact sing very well, and since by then Monica had left for Ephesus, Rosie watched the show with Henry. She'd eaten dinner alone, watching as the animators dashed about on the stage below, preparing for the show. She'd felt ridiculously nervous, wondering whether Henry would let her down or whether he would appear at the last minute, pulling off his helmet as he had before. But he'd done neither of these things, simply falling into step beside her as she left the terrace.

They watched the show from the amphitheatre steps as the last glimmer of gold faded from the mountain top and the tiny electric lights began to glow from the olive trees. As the darkness gathered, the lights grew in strength, gleaming ever more brightly until the branches of the trees had been swallowed by the night and the lights seemed to hover by themselves, like swarms of stationary fireflies.

Rosie and Henry were used to the format of these shows by then and waited patiently as each of the short scenes was followed by an over-long interval of frantic backstage activity. As the last sketch was cleared away and the next one prepared for, the darkened stage would come alive with a number of shadowy figures. With a strangely stooped posture, they swept up debris and mopped up water before fleeing the stage in the same bent-over way, perhaps thinking it made them invisible. Then, at last the lights would flood back on, the music system would blare out something abrupt and deafening, and the next sketch would begin.

Henry and Rosie watched it all, show and intervals alike, with the same level of amusement, needing none of it to be entertained. Already, they felt completely natural in each others' company. Rosie sensed that he was as easy with her as she was with him, but then he had to go and spoil things. Perhaps he thought it was better to get such formalities out of the way, but whatever his reason, Henry chose one of the intervals to blurt out the inevitable question.

'So, are you married, then?' His words cut the air like a bark from a snappy dog. He had probably been preparing the question for so long that it came out uncontrolled and harsh.

'No, divorced. Are you? Married, I mean.'

He paused before replying, holding his beer glass up to the night sky and using it to magnify the cluster of lights in the olive tree, as if this study of light through beer were crucial to his answer.

'No,' he said at last, 'No, I'm not.'

Too many negatives and too long a delay before speaking. For perhaps a micro-second, Rosie *did* let these things cross her mind, but the moment was far too happy, too carefree to bother with troublesome doubt or with digging too deeply. Ever since Monica had departed in her air-conditioned coach, all Rosie had been able to think of was meeting Henry that night. All too quickly she was losing contact with common sense. The hotel, already beautiful, was fast becoming a jasmine scented paradise to her, and the music she had once considered to be mere noise had become the perfect setting for this heavenly place.

That was, of course, with the exception of what they were listening to at that very moment. The pretty songbird, Dollie, had taken centre stage and the introduction to her song was pounding and thumping out of the speakers. Henry was screwing up his face in distaste and Rosie grinned as Dollie bounced and skipped coquettishly across the stage. Though she couldn't have been more than four or five years old, she seemed to know all the right moves. Giving full vent to her powerful voice, she hugged the microphone and bellowed out her song.

'Very nice, I'm sure,' whispered Henry drily, 'but you could so easily hear a bit too much of Dollie.' He had found Rosie's hand in the darkness and they sat more closely together in the shadow of the amphitheatre steps. Dollie's time in the spotlight went on for another few minutes before she was prepared to hand the microphone to one of her supporting cast. At last, Zeynel walked onto the stage wearing a battered top hat, an old vest and not much else, and brought the show to a close, with huge rounds of applause for the children.

The introductory bars of the Club Dance pounded the air, blended with Henry's protests as he made for the bar. Zeynel and Esra spotted him and brought him back like a child escaping from a play pen. Henry tried valiantly to join in, stepping right when everyone else was going left and generally getting in everyone's way, but it only made the whole thing funnier. As the days passed, fewer and fewer guests were refusing to take part. Monica had managed to escape the dance for three more days by going to Ephesus, but in the end, even she would probably cave in. She still looked down on this sort of organised activity as being for 'sad' people forcing themselves to be jolly. No one here, though, looked either sad or to be forcing themselves. In fact, an uncommonly good feeling was spreading across the amphitheatre, and everyone, including Henry, was laughing as the dance ended and they made their way up to the bar. The world, considered Rosie, could do with a lot more of this 'forced' jollity.

The bar staff worked like dervishes to cope with the sudden demand for drinks after the show, but gradually the crush subsided and the staff began to relax. Mustafa, the sober head waiter, took to the dance floor, his serious Ottoman features untouched by a single flicker of a smile. He moved with natural grace, his polished leather shoes kicking up the dust as he danced, his red silk tie swaying against the confines of his gold tie clip. One of the waitresses took his cue and parked her loaded tray of empty glasses on the edge of the bar before grasping the arm of one of the waiters. They swung each other round in an abandoned dance with none of Mustafa's sobriety.

'I don't believe it!' complained a bloke who was waiting for his glass to be refilled, 'Nobody can get a drink around here. Bloody waiters are always dancing!' But even he was smiling.

Henry and Rosie bought a bottle of wine and took it to the terrace of her ground floor room. The wide, terracotta paved terrace was hidden from the garden by a huge oleander bush and climbing bougainvillea. They sat there for a long time, listening to the waves and the cicadas, sipping wine and talking quietly and later they lay down in her narrow bed. By five o'clock, when the first call from the minaret echoed down the valley, Rosie had still not slept. It didn't matter. Nothing mattered. How could it? She suspected that very prematurely she had fallen for this man. Perhaps he felt that way too. Perhaps. He never said.

The pale morning light arrived gently and brought with it a breeze that blew in from the sea, scattering petals and leaves on the terracotta tiles of the balcony. A jay swooped low in a flash of pink and blue, perching momentarily on a litter bin before its rapid flight carried it onwards. In the distance the first tentative notes floated from the breakfast terrace and the music drifted on the breeze over the water-logged lawn. Rosie heard and saw all this, yet was truly aware of none of it, lying in the narrow bed next to the man she had met less than a week before. From where she lay, she could see the far away mountain. She thought of the two arms of rocky headland that stretched out to the sea, immovable and indifferent, and how she was here between them, a fool who had offered her heart for breaking. And Henry, like the mountain, would probably never know.

The day passed. They ate, drank and slept together and as evening came they danced and laughed and stayed up late. They played water polo because Henry wanted to and because Rosie was keen to oblige, though she was terrible at it. Always off-side, frequently dunked by the other team and rescued by Esra or Zeynel, she was always relieved when the game ended. She still volunteered the next time, though, because Henry was good at persuading her to. In this languorous, lovely way they spent the three days of Monica's absence. Of course, Rosie knew how little her friend would have approved. She would think her a fool for being carried away like a teenager over a mere man, and of course she would be right.

Time was passing quickly, but unusually for Rosie she felt no desperate need to hold on to each second. This was because she had discovered that back home, in dear old England, Henry lived and worked near her. Incredible, really. Usually, people she met abroad had never heard of any of the Fenland towns. Henry, however, had not only heard of them, but *lived* in one of them; his home and office were in Downham Market, less than half an hour from Rosie in Wisbech. Even more of a coincidence was that Henry too worked in financial services.

She imagined him as a financial advisor of the old school, sober and professional, greatly respected and admired. The firm she worked for was a much larger and very different kind of enterprise, with twelve, mostly young, advisors looking after a much wider spread of clients. Even so, she and Henry inhabited the same working world in the same region. It was a very strange coincidence, but then everything seemed beyond belief at that time. He had told her about his working life one evening as they strolled along the sea front, and in her happiness she hadn't asked him much. She had been too busy getting over such a coincidence and apart from the plain facts, he had volunteered little. She had hardly noticed, happy to let this new knowledge comfort her and remove any sadness about the rapidly passing days. She was encouraged by the thought that the end of the holiday needn't be the end of the romance.

By the time Monica returned from Ephesus, Rosie was besotted beyond redemption. To her mild surprise, Monica didn't complain much about Henry's constant presence. She was sun tanned, happy and full of enthusiasm about the ancient city of Ephesus and everything else she had discovered on her trip. When Rosie admitted to her who had been sharing their room while she had been away she only smiled and shrugged her shoulders.

'As long as he gets his rubbish out of my wardrobe in the next ten minutes, who cares?' And of course he did.

Monica soon picked up her easy going friendship with Berkant again, joining in with so many of the hotel's activities that Rosie began to wonder whether she had had some kind of personality transplant. In the space of two days, she had won an eyelash tinting session at the local salon and a boat trip, by coming first in a table tennis competition. Even more incredibly, she'd managed to beat fifteen teenage girls to the top prize of a gold necklace (from head waiter Mustafa's cousin's shop in Fethiye) in a dancing competition. In between these frenzies, however, she reverted to the same, steady Monica that Rosie had come to trust, her regular caustic comments still managing to bring her friend down to earth. For both girls the holiday was becoming as close to perfect as they could have hoped for and the days were passing with astonishing speed, bringing them all too soon to the very last few hours in the hotel.

On that final morning Rosie awoke early and alone in her single bed in the room she shared with Monica. Out of consideration for her friend, she'd declined Henry's suggestion that she move into his room, so it was not this solitude that was behind the unease she felt as soon as she opened her eyes. The pale, early morning light stole timidly into the room, not yet coloured by sunshine. Through the French doors she could see the first glimmer on the mountain top and she watched as the light moved with the passing minutes, stealing across the dark ravines, ticking away time, moving it rapidly, relentlessly forward.

The uneasiness she'd felt on waking suddenly came to a head as she was reminded with a jolt how quickly time was running out. The feeling of security from Henry's proximity at home was no longer enough. Still he'd said nothing about seeing her again. It was ominous and she had to face the truth of it.

True, she had said nothing about seeing him again either, but the old fashioned side of her believed that such things should come from him. It had to be discussed, brought out into the open and it had to be done now. She was out of bed in a single movement, swilling her face and body at the basin and pulling on clothes. Monica did not stir.

The morning air that touched her face was still cool as she made her way to reception. For once, she was too bothered by her fears to notice the usual waking sounds of the place; the harsh cries of the garden jays, the clatter of laundry trolleys on the stone pathways and the rhythmic sweeping of brooms in the courtyard. She barely noticed the scent of flowers that wafted in through the open doors, greeting her like an old friend she was about to leave.

A movement caught her eye as she entered the airy reception hall and Zeynel strolled in from the garden. For someone who habitually stayed up so late, he emerged impressively early in the mornings, his clothing showing more of the strain than his face. His creased T-shirt was crumpled over shorts of a washed-out tomato colour and both items were daubed with blue splodges where a child had attacked him with poster paint a few days earlier.

Seeing Rosie, he came to meet her in the doorway, his face unusually devoid of a smile, but his eyes far from unfriendly. There was something else in his expression that she had no time right then to think about.

'Rosie,' he muttered with uncharacteristic quietness, 'Letter for you this morning. Look, I took for you.' She was confused, wondering why he should have picked up her post and why he was looking at her so strangely. Was it sympathy she saw there? She certainly hoped not.

Hesitantly, she thanked him and took the letter. Noticing the scribbled room number in the corner of the envelope, she started to say that it wasn't hers, but Zeynel had gone, seeking his breakfast.

No, not hers at all; Henry's.

She was left alone in the empty hall, holding the blue air mail letter. Afterwards, she was unsure how many fractions of a second it had taken to understand quite what it was that she held in her hand. Hardly aware of where she was going, she had wandered into the courtyard, her eyes still riveted on the elegantly penned address on the envelope. It was written with a fountain pen, wide-nibbed in turquoise ink. Flowery. It may as well have been sprayed with perfume. She knew then. She knew.

A wave of misery swept over her. She leant against a pillar in the courtyard, her body almost engulfed in the climbing bougainvillea while she did her best to recover her dignity. Her pride did its best to kick in, scolding the weak, careless person she had been, in falling for his charm. How had she not seen this coming?

She crossed the courtyard and his door was in front of her. No sign of life yet. She knocked and waited.

Chapter Seven

Rosie. Tuesday 3rd February

'Morning Rosie. Good grief, you look terrible!'

Jenny hung her coat on the rack. She paused at the door to the compliance office, one hand smoothing her long, dark hair, her face a picture of concern.

'Thanks,' croaked Rosie with an attempt to smile, which hurt. She walked to the window, opening the blinds to let in the muted, clouded light of the Fenland winter's morning. Her computer stuttered into life, playing a few fractured notes of some unrecognisable melody, and she headed for the coffee machine. Paracetamol was doing nothing to ease the pain in her head, but coffee might help.

'Here, have a biscuit,' offered Jenny, 'They're double chocolate with caramel.' Rosie thanked her and accepted one. The girls could be all right sometimes.

She clicked her way through several screens on the computer, entering passwords and trying to settle down to work, but the text kept jumping and the screen dazzled her with its brightness. She could hardly bear to look at it. Memories of last night's terrible dream were still lurking in her mind; the fear and panic of drowning, the long limbs of seaweed that reached up from the sea bed to drag her down. The horror of this old nightmare hadn't lessened with the years and this time, when it had woken her so early in the night, she'd been reluctant to go back to sleep in case it returned. It wasn't as if she hadn't understood the consequences of letting in the past and now she was truly paying for such self-indulgence.

She sipped her coffee and ate the chocolate biscuit, letting her gaze wander around her small office. There was no view through the window from where she sat, apart from a sullen, dense sky above a few chimney pots, where cold pigeons roosted, wings folded, as if waiting for a bus.

On the wall opposite her desk was a dog-eared and frameless print of a Picasso, faded, tatty and depressing. For the hundredth time Rosie wondered why she'd never replaced it. "Guernica" may have been a very clever painting with all sorts of analytical remarks to be made about it, but it was her predecessor's taste, not hers. She needed something far more comforting on the wall than battle-slain bodies and suffering. She needed something calming, like a forest or the sea, or...

'There you go, Rosie, not much post today.' Alice had appeared at her elbow, looking as concerned as Jenny had. Perhaps they thought she had a hang-over. Alice placed a few letters and life office bulletins on the desk and peered kindly at her.

'Why don't you go home? You don't look at all well to me.'

Rosie looked up at her.

'Maybe I will. I didn't get much sleep last night and this headache is pretty bad. I don't think I'll be able to work like this.'

Yes, maybe she should just give up and go home, she thought. Idly, she leafed through the post, picking up a brightly coloured flyer for a compliance workshop in April, to be held in King's Lynn. It sounded like a good idea. She liked to get out of the office sometimes and talk to other people. Besides that, she needed to keep up to date with the regulatory changes that were forever taking place. She put it on one side, meaning to have a word with Raymond about it sometime, but for now she was taking Alice's advice and going home.

'See you tomorrow, Rosie,' Raymond called out as she left his office. She noticed that he'd gone back to more sober winter trousers this morning, though he was sporting a red and black spotted bow tie. She wondered what the girls would make of that.

She closed the heavy front door behind her and walked out into the dense and clammy morning air. On the bridge she paused for a moment to look down at the sluggish

72

brown water flowing out towards the sea, the pain in her temples relenting a little.

She had been doing all right, she considered. She'd been plodding along slowly, but doing all right. And then she'd given into temptation, insisting on revisiting those memories. But it was almost over now. There remained just one nasty little episode and then it would be done with. She would go home and finish it and then she would go out for a walk in the orchard. She would sleep well and then it would be over. Tomorrow she'd return to work with a clear mind. Perhaps she could even consider a new start, another job. She was free to do whatever she wanted, but first she had to finish this, to put the bad memories back into the past where they belonged.

Back in the solitude of her cottage, she made coffee and took her Mickey Mouse mug to the window seat. She was already back there in her memories, leaning against the pillar in the courtyard of the Melek Hotel, swathed in purple bougainvillea.

She crossed the courtyard and his door was in front of her. No sign of life yet. She knocked and waited.

He answered the door in a white bath robe, his arms reaching out to her and pulling her into the room, blissfully unaware that anything had changed. She let him hold her at first, let him laugh and talk carelessly on, and she wanted so much to collapse into him, to go on believing in him. The thought crossed her mind of pretending the letter didn't exist, of destroying it unopened.

Perhaps, she considered, she should wait and see what he suggested, if anything, about their future.

His room was in chaos. Clothes were strewn over every surface; some fresh and laid out for wearing, others thrown into heaps and needing the laundry service pretty badly. He seemed unaware of the mess, apparently quite comfortable in this small, malodorous and untidy room. He obviously hadn't noticed that she'd tucked the letter hastily into her pocket. He was kissing her, kissing her peacefully and languorously, as if they had all the time in the world and she were not going away that morning and leaving him.

'Maybe I could look you up when I get back,' he was murmuring, 'and we could perhaps meet for lunch....I could drive over to see you in Wisbech....'

It wasn't exactly the proposal of the century, but it was something, and Rosie moved a step closer to forgetting her purpose and the envelope in her pocket.

'Or I could phone you at your office...' she added enthusiastically. A flicker of something like panic crossed his face, leaving him looking distinctly nervous.

'Of course...my secretary could always take a message if you said you were....nice girl, Julia,' he managed to say, eyes darting around the room, over Rosie's head, as if searching for a way out. He blundered on. 'She's a good secretary, Julia...thinks I don't know about the drinking, but still a very good secretary none the less, and if you...'

His words were rambling almost as wildly as his panicked thoughts. His arms around her slackened as he fought his fears and pretence and searched desperately around in his mind for something positive to say. She pulled back from him, her disappointment turning to anger, her patience snapping. The last shards of happiness were falling away like beads from a broken string, scattering all over the floor, and there was nothing she could do to save them. After all they had shared in the last ten days, he could only suggest 'perhaps' meeting for lunch, and then only on his terms. It was suddenly perfectly obvious that he was far from free, that he had been lying to her, that every moment of the last ten days had been nothing but a lie. Her anger and hurt left her in no mood to spare his feelings.

'What is it? What's the matter?' he asked as his panicked monologue finally petered out and he noticed the expression on her face. Very slowly, she pulled the folded letter out of her pocket and handed it to him.

'Ah.' It said just about everything, that little sound. He looked stunned and sat down heavily on the bed amongst the piles of dirty laundry. He gave the letter only a brief glance before rolling it into a tube and twisting it between his fingers as he stared at the blank wall before him. He looked utterly defeated.

'Don't let me keep you,' she said coldly,' Go ahead and read your post from England.' He moved his head very slightly, lifting his face and peering up to where she stood by the door. For once, the sight of his big, appealing eyes failed to make her heart lurch. Instead, everything inside her tightened with anger.

'I'm sorry,' he sighed eventually, 'I should have explained the situation at home. It's true that I'm not married, but that's hardly the point, is it? We live together, have done for a very long time. We've never got around to marrying, but neither have we managed to split up, which is what we should have done years ago. I should have told you the truth. We wouldn't have had this time together, but I should still have been straight with you.'

'Yes, and I should have seen through you. It must be great, getting away from the little woman at home for weeks at a time, while enjoying all the comforts of your dull, settled life for the rest of the year. In a place like this it must be so easy for you to pick up women. You do this often, do you? Coming to think of it, you soon dropped the paragliding!'

He frowned, his face sunken and clouded with remorse. His head in his hands, he didn't reply. She looked at his bent head, seeing him clearly at last without the fog of romance getting in the way. He had deceived her deliberately. As the days when they'd become so close, so incredibly good together, had passed, he'd still made no attempt to come clean and tell the truth. He had just let the lie run on for day after day, cheating her and cheating the other woman too. Presumably, he would lie just as easily when he returned home, showing the other woman photos of his paragliding pals and talking about the weather and scenery. At least now Rosie understood why he'd never had a camera when he was with her.

'There's no excuse, Rosie. I'm so sorry. I just knew you'd have nothing to do with me if you knew the truth…'

'You're right there.'

'…and I couldn't take my eyes off you. Honestly I couldn't….something about you. And no, this hasn't happened before on holiday. It really hasn't. There've been other people in the past, but never like this. Antonia and I….I don't know what to do about it.'

'What were you going to do, Henry? Would you ever have told me? Would you have phoned me from home and let me down gently? Or am I still being naive? Perhaps you never intended to speak to me again. After all, there's no place for me in your dull life with…Antonia?'

'I don't know, Rosie, I don't know,' he was rubbing his eyes with the heels of his hands, as if he hadn't slept for weeks. The screwed up, unopened letter had dropped to the floor, having done the job it was probably sent there to do.

'I suppose I should be glad that I found out before I left,' she went on, more to herself than to him, 'Thanks to your Antonia I'm leaving at midday without any illusions. You'd better thank her for me…' she stopped short. Everything suddenly seemed so pointless and getting even angrier and hurling abuse at him wasn't going to help. He wasn't even trying to defend himself, still sitting with his head in his hands on the bed.

'Rosie,' he said quietly at last, 'I wanted to go on seeing you when we got back, I just hadn't figured out how. Can't we meet when we get home? Just once? We can't leave things like this.'

'Goodbye, Henry. Go home and sort your life out.' As she left his room her voice was quiet, no edge of anger or sarcasm to it, just dull acceptance. In the end, their holiday romance, which had seemed so perfect, had finished without shouting or the slamming of doors. This relationship, which had been so very passionate, had ended in a way that was devoid of all passion, a love affair that had been faultless in everything but its honesty.

Rosie wandered along the still deserted paths towards the swimming pool. There was no one around as she went to stand by the water's edge; even the bar was still closed, the coffee machines silent. A dusting of sand that had blown in overnight still covered the wooden bar top. She looked across the smooth, blue surface of the pool, watching it shimmer as a swallow swooped low to scoop up insects. They had had such fun here; Monica, Berkant, Henry, Rosie. The pool in its heavenly garden had become an oasis of beauty to her, but now, with all her illusions smashed to powder, the pool was just a pool. It was a man-made concrete hollow in a man-made concrete hotel. For all its scented attractiveness it was suddenly and quite unfairly tainted. She could bear it no longer. It was time to go.

She saw Henry just once more. As she and Monica waited in reception for the car that would take them to the airport he came to her with the same apologetic stance and large eyes. Monica, surprisingly gentle about all this, went off for a walk to give them space, but nothing was said that made any difference. When Monica returned, it was with Berkant, who had come to say goodbye. They hugged each other, laughing easily without any tears. At least one of the women would take home memories without regrets.

Rosie's last sight of Henry was as he stood in the porch of the hotel, watching the car pull away. The car climbed slowly out of the village then up the long road to the top of the valley. As it turned the corner, the view opened out for one last glimpse of the Melek Hotel. Even from that distance, she could see that he had gone.

And she had never seen him since. Her pride and anger, together with her refusal to wallow in memories, had been her allies in the months that followed. Relying on that stiff backed, shoulders-straight attitude she had inherited from her grandmother, she had coped with the long, aching absence of joy that faced her. But now the anger had died. Only pride and discipline were there to keep her head up, to keep her sane and prevent her from phoning him.

But she would not break her resolve. Life would get better. It had to.

Chapter Eight

Rosie. Thursday 19th March

Late February and early March brought snow to the Fens. It arrived with a Sunday afternoon blizzard and renewed itself every few days with a new, heavier coat, filling the drainage ditches and lying thickly over the ploughed acres. Rosie and Monica carried on with life pretty much as normal, walking to work along the slippery, compacted ice on the pavement of North Brink, but many people living in more rural areas didn't risk the journey to work. In some cases, village and out-lying roads became blocked with snow drifts or were treacherous with ice, and in some areas it was impossible to reach the main roads. Few people came into town, the shops remaining empty but for a few hardy salespeople who stared forlornly out of the windows. It felt like life in suspension, like a lull in cricket when rain stops play. It was almost comforting, as if you could step off the treadmill of life for a rest and no one would notice.

Once the ten days of snow came to an end, the weather warmed considerably, beginning the thaw. Soon the snow was no more than a memory and a few dashes of white caught between the ploughed furrows and lying beneath the trees in the orchards. It was light in the mornings when Rosie awoke at seven and it felt as if winter was at last releasing its grip.

By mid March there was a perceptible feeling of optimism in the air. Rosie welcomed the early morning sun as it beamed in through the long yellow curtains that covered her window seat. She was thinking again of holidays, of applying for a more interesting job and sorting out the garden. Everything seemed possible to her and even the job she still had felt more bearable. She drove over to Peterborough several times, to visit old friends, and this new energy affected everything she did. Even the usual walk home from the office in the evenings had become a cheerful stroll, her steps more fluent, her thoughts usually positive. The longer hours of daylight helped, with darkness not falling now until almost six o'clock.

She was just drawing the curtains as she reached home one Thursday evening when she heard Monica at the door. Arms full of wallpaper and fabric samples, Monica had managed to drop most of them when she tried to ring the doorbell, but was still looking cheerful as she tumbled into the hallway. Rosie helped her gather the rest of the samples from the pavement outside.

'Got a minute?' Monica asked, pushing the hair back from her eyes, 'Only I need some advice about the dining room. Don't want anything too glitzy...'

Rosie grinned and welcomed her in, pleased to have a visitor.

'Why don't we just go to your house and look at the situation?' she suggested, picking up some of the samples and stepping into the court shoes she'd worn to work.

Monica's house was set out as a mirror image of Rosie's, both their front doors opening straight onto the pavement. In the days when the two homes were one farmhouse, it had stood beside a dusty cart track that followed the river out of town. The track had long ago been widened and surfaced, so that now the building stood far too close to the road, leaving no room even for a tiny front garden. There were gardens at the back, though, so it was a small price to pay for such a peaceful location.

Monica's dining room, like Rosie's, was at the back of the house and had an identical window seat, but the view of the garden was missing. A giant yew, which had been allowed to grow too close to the house, blocked the light and, in Rosie's opinion, much of the cheerfulness. She certainly preferred her own home.

Monica looked like she'd changed out of her work clothes more hurriedly than usual, pulling on any old item that came to hand. A washed-out black polo, stretched out of shape and faded to grey, was pulled over her paint-smeared black cords, but she looked relaxed and happy. Rosie was feeling over-dressed in her navy work suit, but she kicked off her shoes before working through the pile of samples with Monica, holding each one up against the walls and window so that her neighbour could make a decision. In the end, Monica decided to forget wallpaper altogether and go for paint instead.

'This pale green would be all right for the walls. Not exciting, but OK,' she nodded, 'then your idea about the darker green striped fabric for the curtains looks good. The old carpet can come up and I can restore the floor boards. A rug would be nice. What I save on not having a fitted carpet could go towards the curtains.'

Rosie gave her a slight, thoughts-elsewhere type nod of the head, pulling the chosen samples out of the pile and stacking the rest in the corner. She sat down on the floor, resting her back against the wall.

'Do you fancy a holiday again this year?' she asked tentatively, her finger tracing patterns on the threadbare carpet, 'Perhaps try somewhere a bit more exotic...' She paused mid-sentence as Monica sat down heavily on the window seat, looking faintly embarrassed.

'What's the matter?'

'I'm sorry. With all the trouble last time and you refusing to discuss anything remotely to do with holidays, I booked something for myself. I thought it was for the best. I'm going to Sydney at New Year! I've always wanted to go and I thought that, with England playing Australia for the Ashes again this winter, I could get tickets for the final test in Sydney. It's costing so much that I won't be able to afford a holiday in the summer as well...'

'Of course...' Rosie said, recovering quickly and smothering her disappointment, 'you and your cricket! Of course, you're right. I've been terrible company lately and Australia will be wonderful for you. I'll probably just go on a bargain break to Great Sludgeford or a coach trip to Brazil or somewhere. Don't worry about me!'

'I *said* I was sorry!' giggled Monica, glad that she was taking it so well. She hadn't anticipated this improvement in Rosie, let alone her sudden desire for another holiday.

'I can hardly expect you to make your plans around me,' continued Rosie in a far more sober tone, 'but I feel lately as if things are better, that I've moved on. Finally. I'm sorry I've been such a pain. At last, I'm just about safe to be let out again on my own, so I'll have a browse through the last minute bargains, maybe do something daring and dangerous. Or just go to Great Sludgeford.'

She was looking through the window at Monica's unruly garden as she spoke, peering around the oversized bulk of the yew tree to the sticks and stalks of last year's hollyhocks in the leaf-strewn beds. It was even worse than her own garden.

'Maybe I was a bit of a hypocrite,' she added suddenly.

'Eh?' Monica looked confused, 'I thought you were about to lecture me again on cutting back that tree.'

'What?' Rosie gave a small smile, 'No...I've been thinking a lot lately and have started to see things differently. I know now that the reason I was so mad with him was because he made a fool out of me. It wasn't so much that he already had a partner, but that he'd lied. Lied by omission, I mean. He'd deliberately kept me in the dark. But at the time, when he'd been found out and had to tell me, I gave him a hard time, gave him all the moral high ground stuff. Now, I can't help wondering whether, if he'd just told me the truth from the start, I'd have gone along with it anyway...'

There was no need to explain who she was talking about. So much effort to avoid mentioning his name for so long, had made Henry's place in Rosie's problems as obvious as an elephant in the corner.

'You've never forgotten him, have you?' Monica's voice was kind.

'No, but now I've admitted the truth to myself, I can stop being so angry with him and move on from this self pity.'

'Great Sludgeford had better be ready, then!'

Fish and chips and a glass or two of cider later, Rosie left Monica's and returned next door. She was happy, far happier than she'd been for months, so perhaps all that digging up of the past had done some good after all. Maybe bringing it out into the open had destroyed some of its power to hurt.

Idly switching on the TV, she watched the last few minutes of an old repeat of Poirot. David Suchet as the great detective was busy with his summing-up routine, circling the library and pouncing on wary and protesting well-to-do 1930's characters. It was still early when the programme ended but Rosie felt suddenly tired. She tidied the room quickly before going upstairs and getting ready for bed.

She fell between the sheets and read a little before giving in to her tiredness. Sleep came easily. So did dreams, wheeling her from scene to scene with a host of easily forgotten nonsense, until they settled her in one particular place where she became suddenly conscious of every detail.

She was in a garden at night, in some kind of circular clearing, surrounded by tall, straggly shrubs. It was difficult to see very much; the night sky was dense with hardly a star to pierce the cover and there was no glimpse of the moon. The only light came from the weak glow of a few fading solar powered lights, set unevenly around the clearing, but as her eyes became accustomed to the darkness she began to make out a few details. In the centre of the space she could see the pale shapes of aluminium garden furniture. She moved slowly towards them through the long grass, their ghostly white forms consolidating into four chairs and a table as she grew nearer. Even in the dark, she could tell they were heavily covered in green lichen, their surfaces rough and dirty. The chairs were

83

tumbled about anyhow on the long grass, as if abandoned long ago, pushed back as their last occupants had risen to go, and left there, never tidied. The whole area had a strong feeling of neglect. The untended grass, sodden with damp and thick with thistles, reached high against the tree trunks. Drifts of papery autumn leaves patterned the ground beneath overhanging bushes, left undisturbed in the long months since they'd fallen.

Moving to the edge of the clearing, she realised that light from another source was making its faint way through the trees. From quite close by, light from outside house lamps was stealing through the garden, broken by leafless branches into honey coloured beams. She stepped carefully between the tall bushes until suddenly the wide view of a lawn opened out before her. In contrast with the part of the garden she'd just left, the lawn was well lit. It was so unexpectedly bright, in fact, that she shrank hastily back into the trailing ivy and briars of a small thicket. She could see that the lawn had recently been mown, but judging by the spiky ridges that stood up between the lanes of freshly cut grass, whoever had mown it had been in a hurry.

She knew that she was dreaming and this awareness brought her calm and reassurance. She turned away from the light, wandering to explore the fenced confines of the large garden. As she walked, she heard the rustlings of hedgehogs and other small mammals in the tangle of undergrowth, and from overhead, the cry of a barn owl. They seemed unaware of her, unmoved by her presence as she trespassed in their garden. But for some reason, with the black cat it was different.

Around the corner it strolled, from between the elder and the tall holly. Confident and alert, the small cat was completing the final security check of its territory before bed time. Then it froze, ears pressed back against its head, its whole body shrinking backwards as it assessed the threat presented by the stranger in the shadows. Rosie froze too, staring back into the cat's big, green eyes before she had time to recover from the shock of being seen. She crouched down on the leaf littered earth, a couple of metres away from the animal, her eyes avoiding contact now with those all-seeing eyes. She began to speak softly to the cat, murmuring nonsense she hoped would reassure it. But the cat was anything but reassured, its spiky little teeth glinting as it wailed a low-pitched protest. It backed off, eyes pinned on to the human, its body primed and ready for flight. Then, in an instant it had torn away, darting through the bushes towards the lawn and the safety of home.

There was another sound then; the scraping of a swollen wooden door as it opened and caught on the frame. There were voices outside in the light, people standing on the patio.

'Polly?' came a woman's voice, loud and commanding, 'Is that you, sweetie?'

Rosie edged through the bushes, finding a good vantage point between a laurel and a cotoneaster, and watched as the dark shape of the cat streaked up the wide steps to the patio, its tail carried low from the horror of its encounter with the stranger.

'There you are darling!' sang the woman, reaching down to caress the cat's back. The tail rose as the small animal smooched around its mistress's legs. 'What is it? Did something frighten you?'

'...the matter?' Another voice joined the woman's, male, muffled and low, and then there were several people, all standing at the edge of the patio, staring out into the garden. Alarm jarred through Rosie, robbing her of the power of movement. All she could manage to do was shrink back into the unrelenting bushes.

Her eyes were drawn to the woman who now leaned against the stone balustrade, holding the black cat in her arms. Well groomed, as if she'd just returned from the hairdresser, her shoulder length blonde hair framed a perfectly made-up face that was attractive in an expensive, high maintenance way. A tall man was muttering something into her ear and she was shaking her head. As Rosie tried in vain to draw back further into the bushes, she felt the distinct and extremely uncomfortable sensation of eyes peering at her, of being seen.

'Who's there?' shouted the tall man, 'Come on, out!'

And then she was out, out of the dream and at home, in bed.

Opening her eyes, she could make out the shadowy outline of her bedside table and she groped for the light switch. Blinking in the sudden light, she read the display on the little plastic alarm clock. Half past midnight. She had been asleep for barely an hour and a half and she was exhausted. The peace she'd felt in the early part of the dream had long passed, leaving her with the feeling of being, however unintentionally, a nasty little stalker. And of being caught out.

And there was something else. Somehow, and she didn't understand how, she just knew the scene she'd witnessed was connected to *him.*

All that confidence and bravado when talking to Monica the evening before seemed a joke now. Emotions flooded back, bringing an age-old longing with them. She eased herself up on her pillows, eyes closed, battling with her thoughts. Getting to sleep after this was going to be next to impossible. With a groan, she dropped her feet to the ground, reached for her dressing gown and stumbled down the stairs to make tea.

Chapter Nine

Henry. Thursday 19th March

'And how is the lovely Antonia on this fine spring evening?'

Bruce was leaning over the patio wall, his palms flat on the stone surface, his eyes peering into Antonia's sun-bed tanned, expertly made-up face. She glanced back at him and for a second or two managed to maintain her look of icy superiority, but despite all she'd had to say about Bruce Ryan earlier, she was visibly melting.

'It's hardly a fine evening, is it? In fact it's darned chilly out here, but I'm well, thank you, Bruce,' she stated with a reluctant smile.

'I don't know how you do it,' he continued in the same flattering tone, 'Here we are again, once more enjoying your hospitality, and as ever you've made everything perfect. I bet you're working flat-out to be ready for Saturday and yet you look fantastic. The house looks like a show home...what a hostess!'

There was a suppressed sound from behind them that sounded half way between a sneeze and a hiccup as Henry joined them by the patio wall. Antonia ignored him, unsure whether he was laughing at her or at Bruce. She was no fool. She knew Bruce was teasing her and that he deserved one of her sharper retorts, yet for some uncanny reason she found herself patting him playfully on the shoulder instead, mumbling something about the hospitality being no trouble at all, and almost forgetting all the things she'd said a couple of hours ago.

Henry had not forgotten, however, and was watching Antonia in mild disbelief. She was actually dimpling in a silly coquettish way that was quite unlike her, and for heaven's sake, with Bruce, of all people! Her earlier torrent of abuse still rang in his ears. Could this really be the same woman who on his return from the office that evening had ranted on and on because, 'that crowd of old cronies' was coming round again? Why, oh, why, she had demanded, when she was to entertain them at her party on Saturday, did they have to come round on Thursday night as well?

Henry had been feeling extremely jaded from a long day in the office and was in no mood for one of Antonia's tirades. He had just come out of a meeting with one of his clients, a certain Mrs Pettifer. Like many of his long-term clients, she was having trouble adjusting to the new, largely commission-free financial services world. In the old days, it was usual for a client to take hours of an advisor's time, soaking up free advice without doing any business at all. Advisors like Henry had always put up with it because if or when they finally managed to place a contract for the client, they would be rewarded with commission from the life office or investment company. These days, however, with commission turned into a dirty word by bad press, then practically disappearing altogether, most things had to be done on a fee basis. Try explaining that to the Mrs Pettifers of this world, who thought nothing of gassing for hours about their financial affairs, flicking through every company's literature and boring him silly with photos of cute grandchildren, before declaring that they were not yet ready to make a decision. He'd tried sending her a bill for these consultations, but she'd just posted it back.

This pointless meeting, together with the daily struggles of running his business, had left him exhausted and frustrated. Antonia's loud complaints about the trivial, pampered world she occupied were the very last thing he'd needed that evening.

Perhaps on this occasion, though, she did have a point. It was all too easy to give in to one of Bruce's bright ideas, and Henry was in the doghouse for giving in to yet another one of them. In the pub earlier that week, when Henry's mind had been elsewhere and he'd just wanted to be left alone to munch his cheese and onion crisps, Bruce had been waffling on as usual. How nice it would be, he'd been saying, if they could all meet up before Antonia's party for a chat and a few drinks. Pamela had quickly joined in, of course, going on about helping Antonia to plan the party. And somehow, as always seemed to happen, Henry had found himself being swept along with it. Before he'd even finished his crisps and started to pay proper attention to what they were saying, the venue for this informal little soiree had been decided on as his house. As bloody usual. With free drinks and nibbles for all, of course. Of course.

'As if I need help with planning my own party!' Antonia had exploded, 'They're acting like a load of school kids! That darned Bruce Ryan! Who does he think he is? He'll have moved in soon, and I bet you'll even help him unpack! Don't these people realise I have everything planned already? I have the caterers organised, the golf club are sorting the drinks, the florist is delivering at five o'clock, the…'

'The florist?' Henry had interrupted, staring at her incredulously, 'Why on earth do we need a florist?'

'For heaven's sake, Henry! Flowers for the house, that's why! This is my fortieth birthday party and I have my friends from the golf club coming. Do you honestly expect to impress them with that lone dandelion you tend so lovingly in the patio planter? Anyway, let's not digress. The point is that, as usual, without consulting me, you've invited that lot of freeloaders again…'

'Oh, come on, Antonia,' he'd protested wearily, 'There are only three of them and you know we'd have a pretty dull social life without them.'

'Henry, we have a pretty dull social life *with* them!'

'Well, that doesn't say much for the hairy crones you play golf with, does it?'

And so the quarrel had continued, resolving nothing, and was only abandoned when the telephone blasted out. Fortunately, the caller had been one of the hairy crones, because Antonia was able to vent her anger into a sympathetic ear instead of shouting at him, and he'd made good his escape, leaving behind the sound of Antonia's angry hissing into the telephone.

When he'd showered and changed into chinos and a light sweater and descended again to face her mood, Antonia was nowhere to be seen. The kitchen had been left just as before, Antonia refusing to lift a finger to help with any preparations for the evening. Grudgingly, he'd begun to prepare a few items himself, ham-fistedly stabbing bits of crumbly Wensleydale and the remains of a tin of pineapple with a few cocktail sticks, and emptying crisps and peanuts into mismatched dishes. Searching the fridge in desperation, he'd found half a jar of pickled onions and a suspicious looking pot of olives, which must have been in there for ages. Screwing up his face in distaste, he'd poured the viscous, cloudy brine into the sink and fished the brownish olives from the pot into one of the dishes. From upstairs, he could hear the shower running. Antonia would take her time before appearing, carefully reapplying her make-up and selecting something suitably dressed down to wear for the evening.

Yet now, as Henry watched the refreshed and newly pampered Antonia chatting to her unwanted guests, he could almost have believed that this whole thing had been her idea. He heard her laugh boisterously, her head thrown back without disturbing a single hair of her spray-plastered coiffure, as Bruce fed her an olive. Good thing, thought Henry with the nearest thing to amusement he'd felt all day, that neither of them had seen the sell-by date on the olive container.

He threw himself into sociable bonhomie, joining Pamela and Sylvia at the scruffy oak table at the end of the patio. He realised too late that he ought at least to have wiped off the bird droppings before his guests arrived.

'Come on, you two. You're frozen. Let's all move indoors.'

'Actually, darling,' replied Pamela, her mouth full of pickled onion, 'we were hoping you were going to suggest that. We've got more goose pimples than a plucked chicken and I've got something horrible on my sleeve.'

'I'll get you some kitchen paper,' muttered the host, 'sorry about that. Bloody pigeons are everywhere.' Sylvia smiled, catching Henry's eye as he departed, and was rewarded with one of his satirical looks.

As her visitors entered the house, Antonia supervised their foot wiping on the heavy sisal mat with hawk-like attention. She closed her eyes in long-suffering despair when Bruce's size nines missed the mat entirely, treading mud and half a dozen old beech leaves on to the kitchen floor. Bruce was oblivious of her pain, throwing himself into an antique mahogany chair in the sitting room and almost doing himself an injury on one of its elegantly turned arms.

'So,' he shouted enthusiastically, 'What do we all need to bring on Saturday? A bottle? Bag o' crisps?'

'Bruce,' cut in Antonia icily, 'Everything, and I mean everything, is arranged. There is absolutely nothing for you to…'

'I could bring over my Jimmy's game of Twister,' he continued, 'There's nothing like it for livening up a dull party. And I could borrow his old CDs. He won't mind, he'll just use his...'

'For heaven's sake, Bruce!' Henry finally cut in, 'Antonia has everything arranged!'

'What, even the music?' he persisted, his anxiety about the dire state of Henry's record collection rendering him fearless of the thin ice on which he was skating under the frost of Antonia's stare.

'Even the music. That's my department. Always is,' said Henry with an air of finality. Pamela met Bruce's look and sniggered.

Antonia left her seat and trod majestically into the kitchen, where she could be heard noisily loading the dishwasher. The remaining four made an effort at conversation, Henry doing what he could to relieve the tension that was invading the atmosphere like a bad smell.

He had to admit that a little background music would help at times like this, even the sort that Bruce liked. He offered them more drinks, but the supplies in the living room had run out and clearly no more were on offer from the kitchen.

'Any more beer in that fridge o' yours, my love?' Bruce called out to Antonia in the kitchen. Henry winced. Did this man have no idea of when to leave well alone?

'I'm not your love and you've had your lot,' shouted the lady of the house, her brief flirtation with Bruce well and truly over. Henry levered himself out of his chair and paced into the kitchen. He opened the fridge without disturbing Antonia, who was turned away from him, pretending to look out of the window. The patio lights had been left on, but even so, there couldn't have been much to look at. He prised a can from a four-pack, walking back to the sitting room and handing it to Bruce.

He heard the kitchen door open with its usual swollen protest and he left the others talking, joining Antonia on the patio. The outside lights had thrown the garden into deep shadow and he felt as if they were standing in a bubble of light, like an illuminated fish bowl. He could smell her perfume, heady and expensive, and a sudden wave of hopelessness hit him.

'It's time for them to leave,' she hissed, 'I've just about had enough.'

'Oh!' he spat, '*You've* had enough, have you?'

She turned her head to face him, her look poisonous. They heard the others behind them now, following them outside. Probably in search of more beer, Henry thought. They had most likely heard Antonia's comment, but Henry was almost beyond caring. As he turned to them with an apologetic look, there was a movement in the garden that caught his eye and Antonia seemed aware of something too. A long, low wail and a loud rustling came from beyond the lawn, from the laurel bushes.

'Polly? Is that you, sweetie?' Antonia was staring into the garden, eyes combing the dark shapes of trees and shrubs. A dramatic rustling was still going on somewhere in the darkness and then the cat came hurtling out of the bushes, flying on to the patio as if the hounds of hell were on its tail.

'There you are, darling!' Antonia bent down and stroked the cat's back, scooping the animal into her arms and crooning in a strange way that seemed to calm it.

'Wha's the matter?' Bruce asked, striding forward to stand beside Antonia. All irritation with him forgotten, she leaned her face towards him, one hand still stroking the silky head of the cat in her arms. Henry heard them muttering together, their voices cautious, wary. Bruce was pointing towards the bushes where there was a movement; a shape of something or someone.

Something or someone. Henry couldn't quite make it out, but a darker patch of shadow seemed to be moving between the bushes. As his eyes gradually adjusted to the darkness, the figure, which was almost absorbed by the shadows, seemed to move just for a moment into sharper focus. He frowned to himself, trying to make some sense of what he saw.

'Who the…' he muttered under his breath.

'Who's there?' demanded Bruce, 'Come on, out!'

But then, with only a tremor of shadow, there was no longer anything there. For a few seconds more, the group on the patio continued to stare into the garden, but still there was nothing. Someone laughed; a release of tension.

'A trick of the light, that's all,' came Sylvia's voice.

'Yes, come on in, everyone,' Antonia was saying, 'Polly was probably just picking a fight with the neighbour's cat. I'll put some coffee on...'

But Henry, left alone for a while on the now silent patio, continued to stand and look into the shadows of the garden. He knew things had been bad lately, that he was more miserable with his lot than he'd ever admit to anyone, but now he was seeing things. For a moment, for just the tiniest, fleeting moment, he'd thought he had seen Rosie in the shadows of his garden.

Chapter Ten

Henry. Saturday 21st March

When consciousness prodded Henry's frail constitution that Saturday morning, it came with slow, rhythmic waves of throbbing pain. He groaned loudly and rolled over to find a cooler place on the pillow, his eyes refusing to open.

'Ah, good morning!' trilled an excessively jolly voice into his delicate ear. Opening one eye, he could make out the blue silk draped form of Antonia, already sitting up in bed, sipping coffee and doing a lot of rustling.

He grunted something unintelligible and rolled over again.

'Charming!' she trilled again, the rustling getting louder. 'Ah! Here's one from Margie! How sweet of her to remember! Really must get a game in with her soon…oh, and one from Eugenie and Ted. Didn't know you could still find cards like that…'

Hell, thought Henry, giving up all hope of any more sleep, it's her birthday. With a supreme effort he opened both eyes and rubbed them. The room was a blur of lamplight and birthday cards.

'What time is it?' he muttered.

'Six-thirty. I've made coffee and thought I'd start looking through my pile of presents and cards. Look, I've twenty three cards already and the postman hasn't even brought today's yet. Then, there'll be even more tonight!'

'Happy birthday,' he managed to utter, though it was said without any conviction and he knew he would have to try harder. With a further effort he dragged himself into a sitting position against the pillows and tried to smile convincingly. Against his temples the pain readjusted itself into stabbing violence and his smile collapsed into a wince.

'Headache, darling? Well, if you must down half a bottle of Glenfiddich in an evening, what do you expect at your age? It was the same Thursday night and I dread to think how much you'll get down you at the party tonight. Drink your coffee.'

He grunted again, fumbling around on the bedside table until he located the cup and saucer, lifting it gratefully to his lips.

'Thanks,' he acknowledged as he drained the cup, 'As you say, it's self inflicted. Happy birthday!' This time he managed to maintain a smile and she softened, leaning towards him and kissing him sweetly on the forehead. If it hadn't been for his sore eyes, he'd have been certain that she was fluttering her eyelashes at him. He had the feeling that something was expected of him.

'Do you have something for me?' she asked teasingly. These days he didn't see much eyelash fluttering from Antonia and even in this dehydrated state it was gradually dawning on him what it was she was after. He reached out again to the bedside table.

'Of course. But wouldn't you rather wait until after breakfast?'

'Oh, no! I can hardly wait! Where have you got them hidden?'

'Them? How many presents did you expect?'

'Oh, I mean... Oh, come on Henry, don't tease me!'

'All right, then. Here you are. Once again, happy birthday, Antonia!'

He picked up the small, brightly coloured package that he'd hidden behind the alarm clock on the bedside table and presented it to her with a flourish. He'd had it gift-wrapped in the shop and it looked suitably expensive, but even so, as expected, he saw the brightness fade from her eyes. Disappointment already, and she hadn't even opened the present. She was still smiling, but the smile no longer quite reached her eyes and it was maintained out of good manners, rather than anything genuine. She pulled at the yellow silk ribbon and the stripy golden paper collapsed to reveal a tiny red leather box. Gently she opened it, peering inside at the crimson velvet cushion on which rested a white golden loop, fashioned into a small tied knot and finished with a single diamond in the centre. It was a beautiful item and Henry felt quite proud of his choice, having spent a long time in the shop selecting it. It was just the right size and shape, he thought, to look good on some of Antonia's clothes. She was making little comments of appreciation, but he could still feel her disappointment.

The postman brought no more cards, so she only had Henry's to open at breakfast. It was one of those cartoon cards, which he thought was quite funny, but Antonia didn't really get the joke. Her earlier bounciness was visibly diminishing and she was buttering her toast with little irritated, jerky movements.

'So, how will you spend your day?' he asked pleasantly, 'Bearing in mind of course that you'll need a couple of hours to beautify yourself for the party.'

'What's that supposed to mean?' she snapped, then thought better of it and smiled. 'I thought I'd have lunch with the girls at the club. Margot and Dottie are meeting me at twelve-thirty.'

'Ah, yes, the Whiskered Twosome,' grinned Henry. She smiled reluctantly.

'They're coming tonight, so for goodness' sake don't let that name slip out! Anyway, I assumed you'd go out for a lunchtime drink with Ronny and Malcolm or Bruce.'

'Yes, I suppose I shall.'

It was polite, strained talk, more suited to two casual acquaintances waiting for too long at a bus stop, than a couple who'd shared years together. Both of them were making an extra effort to avoid spoiling the day. Things between them had been even more strained than usual lately and they both knew that some effort was required to maintain a semblance of peace in the house.

He was relieved when at last she left for her lunch and he had an hour of solitude in which to nurse his hangover before Bruce arrived. They'd made no plans to go to the pub, but he just knew that Bruce would turn up. And turn up he did, with a heavily revving engine and a squealing of brakes.

Offers of a lift to the pub from Bruce were rare and Henry gratefully accepted, brushing most of the old sweet papers and cigar ash from the passenger seat before he sat on it. He leaned his throbbing head against the neck rest, painfully aware of the music that trumpeted from the old Vauxhall's CD player. There was a lot of clever electronic sound, plenty of languorous lamenting, and it was making his headache worse.

'Haven't you any Matt Munro?' he asked predictably. Bruce leaned across and depressed the "off" button.

'Been hitting the whisky again, mate? No wonder your head hurts!'

'Yeah, I know. I've had a couple of bad nights, but it'll stop now.' A couple of bad nights, unable to stop thinking about the figure in the garden. A figure that looked so much like Rosie that he'd been sure he was going crazy.

Early spring sunshine bathed the road as they drove out of Bridgewell in companionable silence. Bridgewell was too small to be called a village really; just a few houses scattered on both sides of the river, linked by a narrow bridge of crumbling Victorian brick. You could say the place was more of a hamlet, boasting a defunct petrol station that sold used cars and did MOTs, a dilapidated and long abandoned church, and a farm shed that sold vegetables. There was no pub, no shop, just the old Well Creek that flowed through the centre on its way from Outwell to Downham Market.

Bruce took the back way out of the hamlet, crawling along a road which was hardly more than a cart track. At some point in its history it had been tarmacked, though the surface was well worn now, cracked and breaking away at the edges. From both sides of the road the view was endless; nothing to greet the eye but vast dark acres of furrowed earth, the potato crop not yet showing through. The road was bordered on both sides by drainage ditches, the water in them at a low level following the recent dry weather. The ditches were invisible from the car, the only sign that they were there at all being the lines of feathery-headed fen grasses that moved in the breeze.

Sometimes the car slowed for dog walkers or a rider on horseback. On mornings like this, when the sun was shining on the fields and illuminating the tall grasses, Henry could forget for a moment the beauty of the Dorset coast he missed so much and his life in Fenland didn't seem so bad.

In silence, he watched the constantly changing pattern of light and dark on the ploughed earth. A cloud was making its hurried way across the sky, followed by its shadow on the ground. The shadow deepened and advanced across the earth, spreading like a frown and darkening every hollow and furrow. Then, with the passing of the cloud, the tentative, wavering, golden sunlight seemed to shiver before racing across the ground and reasserting its authority, touching the grasses and filling the furrows with warmth.

He understood what Bruce meant when he sang the praises of this atmospheric landscape with its no-nonsense towns, such as the one they were approaching now. You were as likely to see shoppers in wellies here, as in stilettos. And the wellies, as Bruce was fond of emphasising, were usually thick with mud and accumulated grime from hard work on the land, not nice clean, expensive ones worn by people who wouldn't know one end of a hoe from the other. This, Henry knew, was a dig at the places he imagined Henry came from, some kind of up-market, "twee" village, where ladies carried tiny shopping baskets and teetered around on tiny heels. Henry tried to explain that it wasn't like that at all. His home town of Wareham was quite small and rural, not unlike Downham in some ways, just set in a kinder landscape, and peoples' wellies certainly saw a lot of hard work. Bruce's mind was made up, however. No amount of explaining was ever going to convince him.

They'd entered Downham Market now, its cheerful, narrow streets alive with shoppers. Henry watched them in continued contentment, his headache receding to a more manageable level.

'Dog and Duck?'

'Might as well.'

Bruce manoeuvred his dented Vauxhall into the car park that was already filling with the assorted vehicles of the lunchtime crowd. Many were serious looking four-by-fours, built for hard work, and judging by the amount of dried mud patterning most of them, doing a lot of it. With a sudden sense of freedom Henry followed his old mate into the lively atmosphere of the bar. There was liberty in honesty and with Bruce he could enjoy being as honest as he liked.

The interior of the pub was more comfortable than smart, its cream paint turned to a grubby shade of beige and its carpet worn thin in several places. The bar was simply furnished with a hotchpotch of mismatched wooden tables, chairs and benches, and a few framed photos on the walls of long dead publicans and long forgotten past events. The place had a good feel to it, though, making it very popular, teeming with drinkers most of the weekend and enjoying a respectably good turnout on most week nights.

'Well, then,' began Bruce as soon as they'd settled with their pints and packets of crisps, 'Does she know yet?'

Henry, who had let his thoughts wander back to his private fascination with the figure in the garden, looked confused for a second.

'Oh, about the present you mean!' he replied at last, light dawning.

'Yeah, the golf clubs. What else would I mean?'

'Oh, no, she doesn't know yet. It won't hurt her to sweat a bit. It'll do her good to think I might not have picked up on her heavy hints about new clubs for her birthday. They're in the office at the moment and Julia's going to bring them over tonight. I'm going to wait until the party really gets going and then make a little presentation of them…' He paused when Bruce's loud laughter drowned him out.

'Blimey, mate, that'll be leaving it a bit late, won't it? Your name will be mud by then. As soon as she gets with the Whiskered Twosome this lunchtime, news of your meanness will have spread throughout the golf club, the village, and most of Norfolk.'

'Meanness?' Henry spluttered as his beer went down the wrong way, 'That brooch was white gold and the diamond wasn't exactly a midget!' His voice gasped into a full blown coughing fit and Bruce waited patiently until order was restored.

'Henry, I was being sarcastic. Why you put up with her demands I just do not know.'

'No,' admitted Henry thoughtfully, 'I don't either. There were good times in the past. I used to like her sense of humour and we had a lot of fun, but things have deteriorated since we moved up here. She hates the Fens and if it wasn't for that golf club of hers she'd be even more impossible to live with. Why I keep putting up with her I don't know. She clearly doesn't like me any more than I can stand her. And what's the worst that could happen? If we went our separate ways we would both lose the house and she would expect a huge pay off, but so what? I could get a smaller house and be a lot happier on my own. Things can't stay as they are. I'm going to have to do something...Ah! Jeanette!'

The landlady, Jeanette Radley, who hadn't been on duty when they arrived, seemed to materialise out of nowhere. Henry noticed her far too late and struggled hopelessly to change the subject, trying desperately to appear full of Saturday afternoon cheer. He had no idea how much she'd heard.

'Good afternoon, boys! How are you both today? Can I interest you in any bar food? I'm doing the All Day Breakfast at half price and there are some nice beef pasties or cheese and onion ones, all with chips.' She had started

100

to clean their table, removing old crisp bags with one hand and manoeuvring her cloth with practised efficiency with the other, wiping away damp rings from long-emptied glasses.

'No thanks, duck, we're saving ourselves for tonight,' answered Bruce cheerfully.

'Oh, yes. I can't wait! I've managed to get cover for tonight, so I'll be able to stay for the whole party. Not easy to get anyone to work on a Saturday night, but the effort's worth it! See you later, then boys!'

'Was she having a laugh?' asked Henry when she had gone.

'No, mate, she's serious. She actually enjoys your parties. Someone has to.'

'But why does she have to keep calling us boys?' grumbled Henry, 'And why does she have to sneak up like that, especially when I'm moaning about Antonia?'

'Let's face it, mate. It'd be difficult to sneak up on you when you *weren't* moaning about Antonia.' Henry gave him a funny look.

'Damned woman! She'll have heard the lot and I bet she found it pretty entertaining, too. I just hope she keeps quiet about it.'

'She won't say anything. She loves your parties. She loves sucking up to the pair of you too, even though Antonia makes it pretty obvious that she can't bear her. She's hardly going to gain favour by gossiping, is she?'

'I suppose you're right,' nodded Henry, but a sense of gloom had returned, replacing the contentment he'd felt earlier.

'Another?' offered Bruce brightly, 'I'm on the orange juice now 'cause of the driving but I think I'll have one o' them pasties after all. What about you?'

'Why not? I'll go for the cheese and onion.'

'Didn't think you liked them.'

'Oh, I do, it's just that Antonia really hates it when I eat them. Moans like hell about my bad breath.'

Henry was still dwelling on his problems when they stepped out into the bustle of the market town street just under an hour later. Downham was a pleasant town with a purposeful air about it. There were still plenty of shoppers about and the shops were, although as varied as in most towns, mostly of the genuinely useful kind; hardware, chemists, home furnishings, shoe menders, grocers and butchers. There were the supermarkets too, of course, but the smaller shops also seemed to be doing a decent trade. Above the colourful shop fronts, the buildings gave clues about the town's age. Plain yet elegant Georgian house fronts were interspersed with more elaborate Victorian ones, with a few early twentieth century buildings thrown into the mix. Some parts of the town were older still; the Crown, where the men sometimes drank their Saturday pint, was a sixteenth century coaching inn and the Swan had an interesting history too.

'Yeah,' nodded Bruce as they drove out of town and Henry was mentioning the historical side of things, 'King Alfred or somebody stayed at the Swan once, I think.'

Henry laughed, forgetting his sorrows for a moment.

'You've a real grip on local history haven't you? It was Charles I, you idiot. They say he stayed there in disguise when he was escaping from the Roundhead army.'

'How did they know who he was, if he was in disguise?' asked Bruce innocently.

'How would I know?' Henry spluttered, 'I don't know! Maybe his wig slipped after a few pints! Who knows?'

Henry shook his head and grinned. Bruce had cheered him up and had listened to him moaning on about his problems. He knew he could trust him, but just discussing things wasn't going to get him out of this dead end. The time was fast approaching when he would either have to take action, or decide to do nothing. Doing nothing meant shutting up once and for all about his problems and living with them. Was that truly an option?

With such thoughts, that night's party was going to be even more of a nightmare.

Chapter Eleven

Julia. Saturday 21st March

David Bowie's "Absolute Beginners" was playing on the radio, an old favourite of Julia's. She knew all the words, every note and every pause by heart, and like an old, trusted friend it spoke words of encouragement to her as she drove along. When, just as she was approaching Bridgewell, its opening bars had pounded from the radio, she'd taken it as a good omen. But now she had arrived, slowing down outside his house on the riverside road, and the song had come to an end, taking with it its confidence boost.

She parked the little Peugeot neatly by the kerb in front of the Blanchard house and very slowly unfastened her seat belt. The driveway was already packed with cars, but it didn't matter. She would rather be parked out on the road. After all the excitement and anticipation, the thought of this party was suddenly unnerving and she wasn't at all sure how long she would stay, how soon she would need her car for escape. Her fantasies about being swept into a passionate embrace by Henry right under Antonia's nose seemed a bit silly now, not to mention far-fetched. However, she had promised Henry she would deliver Antonia's present and she rarely failed on a promise. Especially not one made to Henry.

With a decisive movement she opened the car door and teetered out on to the pavement in her new stilettos. She felt ridiculously uncomfortable and self conscious in the new dress and shoes she had treated herself to. Her earlier excitement and confidence had evaporated, leaving her feeling anxious and wondering where all that positive feeling had gone. In the spring sunshine she'd felt so good, strolling into the shiny-floored Queensgate Shopping Centre in Peterborough and enjoying being part of the Saturday shopping crowd. Breezing from one gleaming shop to the next, she'd eventually narrowed her choice of dresses down to two. One was a conservatively chic little number and the other was a rather short creation with a low neck line which left little to the imagination. They were both black, but that was where the similarity ended. She'd tried them both on, but in a crazy rush of confidence there had seemed no real competition. She was tired of being conservative and the glamorously daring little black dress made her feel seductive. It had seemed the very thing to make her irresistible to Henry. So why, after all the time she'd taken to get ready, did this micro-mini, cleavage-advertising creation feel more tarty than glamorous? Even though she'd added a little black jacket to tone down the effect, the vampish Julia that had gazed defiantly back from the mirror was hardly recognisable, even to her.

Never mind, she told herself as she tottered on the heels past the parked cars on the dark drive, it was done now. At least, in a dress like this she was less likely to be ignored. The concrete drive was uneven and cracked, with holes in it here and there where the surface had worn away and tussocks of grass peered through. There was no street lamp anywhere close to the house and the driveway itself was unlit, as was the front of the house. The darkness made the perils of navigating her way past the cars even worse. She had to watch her step very carefully, keeping her eyes down as she wobbled precariously on the impossible stilettos. One way she did not want to draw attention to herself was by falling in a heap on the driveway before she'd even arrived.

She had almost made it to the front door when she became aware of an odd assortment of noises coming from above. She ignored them at first, being too busy with watching her feet, but a loud squeaking, followed by tapping, finally made her peer upwards. In the darkness she was unable to see at first where the noises were coming from, but the tapping was becoming more insistent.

'Psst! Psssst!'

Still peering through the gloom, she realised that one of the upstairs windows had opened and that Henry was leaning out, tapping on the glass for all he was worth.

'Julia!' he whispered hoarsely, 'At last! I've been waiting for you!' Despite being well aware that all he was waiting for was Antonia's present, she couldn't help the happy glow these words brought. 'Where are they? In the boot?' he continued, 'A bit later I'll give you a nudge and we'll go out and swap them for Antonia's old clubs, OK? Where've you parked?'

'On the road, behind Bruce's Vauxhall.'

'Good, see you later!' With that, his dark form at the window had withdrawn from sight. With another squeak of the sliding sash frame he had gone, leaving her to ring the doorbell and wait on the doorstep.

Seconds later, a very cheerful Antonia was opening the door. She was dressed in an expensive looking mauve chiffon creation that, unusually for Antonia, didn't suit her at all, its loosely fitting shape hinting at far too many curves.

'Helloooo, Julia! Do come in! Let me take your coat. My, my, that's quite a dress! Have you met my golfing friends? Ah, well, let me get you a drink and then come through and I'll introduce you…'

Emerging from the kitchen with a gin and tonic grasped safely in her hand, she was following the rapidly moving hostess through the crowd when Henry came down the stairs. There was something in the way he paused in mid step as he saw her, something in the way his eye travelled almost imperceptively down, then up her black silk attired body, that made her heart stop. Perhaps the dress wasn't such a mistake after all. He smiled and then, as if referring to their conversation at the window a few seconds earlier, he did something quite out of character. He winked.

Julia coped fairly well at first with meeting the golfers, even though she had absolutely nothing in common with them, because she was still glowing from that small encounter with Henry. There were nine golfers; six of

106

them in couples plus two unattached ladies called Margot and Margie and a single, bored looking man who introduced himself, without making eye contact, as Cyril. The two single ladies seemed pleasant enough, but Cyril made no effort to be sociable, keeping both hands stuffed in his pockets and saying nothing. One of the married men seemed incapable of tearing his gaze away from Julia's cleavage, while his wife, the woman Antonia had introduced as Dottie, had clearly taken an instant dislike to Julia, the owner of the cleavage.

'Do you play any sport at all, dear?' she enquired in a chilly tone.

'No, Dottie!' cried her husband loudly before Julia had the chance to reply, 'Glamour girls like Julia do not put their pretty feet into those hob-nailed things you wear, though... let me guess...' he bent forward, his face uncomfortably close to Julia's front, 'I bet you ski, don't you? You'd look magnificent in a pair of ski pants, eh, my dear?'

'Reggie,' laughed one of the other men, 'Leave the poor girl in peace.'

Julia, who was extremely embarrassed and was wondering how soon she could slip away, was relieved when Bruce Ryan joined them.

'May I say how fantastic you're looking tonight?' he asked loudly, announcing his presence. Though he was hardly more subtle than Reggie, Julia was glad to see him and used this opportunity to escape with him into the hall.

'I should watch that lot,' said Bruce, suddenly serious, 'Poisonous as hell. I thought you might need rescuing.'

'Thank you!' she enthused with sincerity. At that moment the doorbell rang again and Antonia rushed to it, ushering in a blue taffeta-clad Eugenie.

'What, no Ted tonight?'

'No, sorry, Antonia. He sent his apologies and would have loved to come, but had a last minute darts match. Couldn't get out of it! Anyway, I was cleaning out the freezer today and found some prawns that had reached their use-by date. I thought we could have them tonight. I found a jar of that pink sauce as well, you know, the sort you mix with them...'

Antonia hardly had time to introduce Eugenie to the golfers, throw the prawns and sauce into the waste bin and suck on her bleeding finger where she'd cut it on the prawn bag, before the doorbell rang again. This time it was Sylvia Farrah and some other friends of Henry's, all of whom had to be introduced to a few people. Shortly afterwards, Pamela Ayling arrived from down the road, but Pamela needed no introductions, being already well acquainted with everybody. The house was filling fast and there was a good atmosphere, backed by unusually lively music. Julia had noticed while trying to escape from Reggie that there was an incongruous looking blue plastic, bulbous object plugged into the wall by Henry's coal scuttle. Scattered around it was a huge collection of CDs.

'My lad Jimmy wouldn't let me borrow any of his new stuff,' Bruce explained, 'so I fetched the old CD player from the attic instead. Henry didn't want to borrow it, but I insisted. I don't think anyone could take much more of his battered old vinyl. Anyway, I intend to enjoy myself tonight because at last I've had a bit o' promising news about a job!'

'Oh, I am pleased! What sort of job?'

'Nothing too exciting, but a job's a job. A mate of mine knows a bloke who needs a mechanic. His business specialises in repairs to tractors and farm equipment and a lot of the machines they repair are old. He needs someone who understands old machines and that's me, duck. I saw the man today and he says he's got a few other people to see but that he'd let me know for sure in a couple o' weeks or so. I feel right about this one, though. We got on well; my sort o' bloke. Speak the same language.'

'Well, good luck Bruce. I really hope it works out for you.'

'Come through to the dining room, everyone!' Antonia was calling, 'We'll eat soon and we have some corks to pop!' She was still sucking on her bleeding finger, too distracted to bother with finding a plaster.

Pamela appeared at Bruce's elbow at that moment and steered him away. He managed a quick 'be back in a minute' to Julia before disappearing into a corner of the hall with Pamela for what looked like quite an intense discussion. Julia resisted the call into the dining room, staying alone to nurse her drink. It looked like Antonia was expecting speeches and toasts, perhaps to be showered with more gifts, with her none too subtle mention of popping corks. Julia wasn't greatly attracted by the thought of all that jollity. She gulped her drink nervously, watching a few guests file past her into the dining room.

Her solitude didn't last long, however. Malcolm Barnstone, brother of Ronnie and one of Henry's best clients, spotted her on his way from the kitchen and barged through the crowd to join her.

'I say, that's a fine frock you have on there, Miss Turner. Is that your new office uniform? The old dog! How he manages to keep his hands off you all day in that little office is a mystery to me!'

'No doubt,' said Antonia very coldly as she returned to the hall to round up her disobedient guests, 'but I trust Henry has more sense and taste.'

Malcolm spluttered and almost spilled his pint over the hostess' mauve chiffon.

'Aw, come on, old girl, you know I was only jesting! After all, Julia doesn't have her lovely legs on display when she's at work, now does she?'

At least it was her legs this time, rather than her cleavage, Julia thought bitterly. She'd become mute with anger, frustration and embarrassment and could only stare wordlessly at the pair of them. So far, this appalling gathering seemed to consist of old lechers and bovine women in hideous chiffon. One more comment about this dress, she seethed, and she'd go home and change. Or just go home.

When Bruce returned he'd brought her another drink and they followed the others into the dining room. They stood by the high sash window, looking out at the well lit garden.

'Having trouble?' he asked her gently.

'It's this dress,' she complained. 'I must have been crazy to buy it, let alone wear it to a thing like this! Normally, no one takes any notice of me, yet tonight I've had nothing but seedy comments and insults!'

'Jealousy,' he smiled, 'Take it as a compliment. And believe me, Julia, many people take a lot o' notice of you. It's just that tonight they see you in a... well... different light! You've got Antonia's feathers ruffled! Serves her right!'

Julia laughed, warming to him. His kindness tonight was very welcome. She took another mouthful of gin, leaning her hand on the window frame and feeling at peace. For the first time that night she'd forgotten to wonder where Henry was.

'I should think we'll be eating soon,' continued Bruce in an easy tone and she murmured something in reply.

'Come on!' hissed a voice at her elbow, 'Now! While the coast is clear!'

'Oh for heaven's sake, Henry, can't you see this young lady was enjoying a moment's peace?' complained Bruce, 'What's the hurry, anyway?'

'Antonia's clubs! Quick, while she's still out of the room!' whispered Henry to them both.

'Let her wait,' replied Bruce. Henry simply looked impatient.

'You know Antonia never waits,' he sighed and walked purposefully away, leaving Julia to follow.

Bruce watched them go with a shake of his head. Henry, he thought, was living under such a cloud that you could almost see the darkness of it hovering over him. Julia, despite Henry's obvious disinterest, followed him everywhere in miserable devotion. Bruce had been nuts about Julia for ages, though she hadn't a clue about it,

110

being blind to everyone but Henry. And none of them ever told Antonia what they really thought of her. It all seemed totally pointless to Bruce, yet he knew it could continue that way forever. Unless something drastic was done to break it up.

Julia caught up with Henry by the time he had reached the front door, where he turned and smiled at her.

'Sorry this is all so cloak and dagger, Julia. Nice of you to help, anyway. Come on, let's get the birthday girl's present!'

'But Antonia's gathering everyone together in the dining room. You're going to be missed very soon!'

'It'll take her ages to get that lot together in one place! When I last saw her, she'd been trapped by Reggie in the pantry.'

'She has my sympathy there at least.'

They walked out together, down the uneven drive, avoiding the parked cars. This time, though, Julia paid less attention to her feet because of her complete obsession with the man at her side. He was obviously in no mood to prolong things, however, striding hurriedly towards her car and waiting impatiently while she fumbled through her handbag to find her car keys. She unlocked the boot and leaned inside, trying to haul the huge bag over the lip of the boot.

'Come on, let me do that!'

'Why does it have to be so heavy? However many clubs does she need?' asked Julia in bewilderment, 'How can anyone need so many?'

'No idea. Never played golf, but apparently, they need a lot of these things,' he replied quietly. She loved his voice when he spoke like this at low volume. All the brusqueness was gone from it and it seemed gentle. He lifted the huge bag down to the pavement, following it with a second black bag which was not quite so large or heavy, but was unwieldy.

'Do you think you could manage the trolley if I carry this lot?'

'This thing is a trolley?'

'Yep, she needed a new one to cope with the extra weight of the bag. Can you manage it? Sorry it's so damned awkward.'

Their progress up the drive was a lot slower than their march down it had been. Finally reaching the front door, Henry pushed it slowly open and peered cautiously inside like a spy in a bad movie, beckoning her in behind him. Luckily, everyone seemed to have vacated the hall. From the dining room came the staccato sound of group laughter. Had anyone still been hanging about in the hall, Henry had explained earlier, Antonia's presents would have had to be left on the doorstep, but apparently they were in luck. All this secrecy seemed to Julia as silly as it was amusing and she couldn't help laughing to herself as she pushed the trolley bag through the hall towards the large broom cupboard next door to the lavatory. Henry was in the cupboard already, hastily dragging out all Antonia's old equipment and pushing it into the hall. Even with it gone, there still wasn't enough space in the overstuffed cupboard to accommodate the much larger new equipment and Henry grunted impatiently, well aware of the raised voices and laughter coming from the dining room. He grabbed carelessly at a few cardboard boxes that littered the cupboard floor, pushing them into Julia's arms and finally making space for the new items. She placed the boxes, which appeared to be full of all sorts of discarded nick-nacks, against the skirting boards in the hall.

'Hurry up!' she whispered unnecessarily, 'They'll be looking for you!'

He closed the cupboard door, snatching the old bag of clubs while Julia picked up the old trolley, following him back out to the drive and closing the door behind her.

Her strappy shoes were biting into her feet through her tights as yet again she made her way over the concrete, following him to place the old equipment in the Peugeot's boot. It would stay there now until she took it to the office on Monday.

'What will you do with these old things?' she asked.

'Depends on Antonia, really. If she doesn't want them I could drop them into the charity shop.'

Henry was moving back to the house, walking far too fast for Julia in her heels. She was disappointed that the highlight of her evening, this silly, shared secrecy with Henry, was coming to an end so quickly. He had reached the door and was about to open it, when suddenly he seemed to think better of it and paused to wait for her.

'Thanks again for your help, Julia,' he whispered, and then to her amazement, he leaned forward and kissed her on the cheek, 'You've been marvellous, as usual, oh and…' he grinned suddenly, 'I'm sorry, but I've just got to say it…that's one hell of a dress!'

She had no time, either to be flustered or flattered by this unexpected attention, because there was a sudden shriek behind them and Jeanette Radley's shape came looming out of the darkness, up the drive towards them.

'Sorry I'm late, darlin'! Couldn't get the relief barman to come in any earlier. What are you two doing out here, anyway? Bit parky for all that, innit?'

Henry managed a strained half smile and pushed the door open for her.

'Evening, Jeanette. Go inside and I'll get you a drink in a moment.'

'Hell!' he groaned once she was safely out of earshot, 'I wonder what she thought she saw? It could all so easily have been misinterpreted!'

'What could?' Antonia's voice was pure ice as she opened the door and stood on the step, glaring down at the pair of them, her eyes travelling with disdain from her partner in life to the girl in the dress and back again, 'I'm trying to organise drinks and speeches in the dining room. I'd just about managed to get everyone together when I realised you'd buggered off!'

'For heaven's sake, Antonia!' replied Henry with surprising and refreshing crossness, 'If you'd just hang on

113

a minute you'd see there was a pretty good reason for my buggering off!'

Julia slipped away, leaving the couple to their hissing and snarling, and found herself another drink in the kitchen. After a few solitary minutes, she made her way to the dining room where everyone seemed at last to be gathered. There was plenty of loud laughter and she was astonished to see Henry and Antonia in the centre of the crowd, smiling at each other with such feigned pleasantness that it would have been impossible to guess how different their mood had been a few minutes earlier.

'So I'd like to propose a toast...' Henry was declaring, smiling chivalrously, 'to my dear Antonia on this great occasion where she marks the crossing over the hill to the great age of forty!'

'Hey!' she objected, but this time with a tolerant smile, as everyone cheered and downed their glasses of bubbly. There was general chaos for a few seconds with too many loud voices bantering at once, but as the noise died down, Bruce's voice broke through.

'Now, come on, Antonia,' he was calling, 'You keep spending all these hours at the golf club. Isn't it about time you showed us all what you're made of?' Julia assumed this little speech was all part of the act, planned earlier with Henry.

'Yes, absolutely old girl,' called Reggie, (was he in on it too?) 'I keep saying to Dottie that it's about time we saw the pair of you in action! Cyril here has a couple of plastic practice balls in his pocket...'

'Good for old Cyril!' interrupted a male voice from somewhere.

'...and we're determined that you and Dottie show us what you can do!'

The bored looking golfer whom Julia had met earlier came forward and with a grimace that was probably meant to be a smile, deposited a bag of perforated, yellow plastic balls onto the edge of the dining table next to the smoked salmon canapés.

'Oh, really Reggie, Cyril, but I couldn't! It's a party! We can't bore everyone with our golf swings!'

'Of course you can, Antonia,' joined in Henry, 'You can be as boring as you like at your own party! In fact I think it's a marvellous idea. You and Dottie can each have six balls and we'll see who can hit one the farthest. Why don't you go and get your clubs? Come on, everyone, out through here to the patio!'

'But the buffet!' protested Antonia lamely, almost knocked over by the sudden surge of guests heading for the patio. 'We were about to eat!'

'We can do that straight afterwards,' Henry smiled. 'Go and get your clubs!'

She took no more persuading, happy to oblige with anything to do with golf. It wasn't long before the guests who waited on the chilly patio heard the anticipated excited exclamations coming from the hallway. Seconds afterwards, the birthday girl herself burst through the door to join them.

'Oh Henry, Henry! How absolutely, utterly marvellous! Oh, you shouldn't have!' She threw her arms around his neck and he laughed a little awkwardly, but was obviously enjoying the fact that something had gone right for once. Everyone applauded and gathered around in the cold March air to admire the impressive looking birthday gift. Julia shivered, wishing she'd remembered to collect her coat from the hall. All the other guests looked equally cold, wrapping their arms around themselves, but seemed to be enjoying the moment, laughing at in-jokes and keen to get the mini contest between Antonia and Dottie started.

Unnoticed, Julia slipped back inside, seeking the bottle Bruce had found earlier in the kitchen. She could still hear them outside. The competition was obviously very entertaining, judging by the chorus of guffawing that broke out every few seconds. From Antonia's regular shouts of delight, it sounded as if she was winning. Naturally. Julia could hear Eugenie's voice too, joining the chorus of onlookers, even though she usually showed no interest in

115

golf. Only Julia, apparently, had stolen away and she found the temporary solitude a relief. She located the bottle, partly hidden by stacks of empty glasses next to the sink, and she helped herself, making the most of this peaceful interlude.

She wandered into the hall where, minutes earlier, Antonia had discovered her new clubs and trolley. She'd left the door wide open in her excitement and all sorts of rubbish had spilled out onto the parquet flooring. Julia pushed the bags and boxes back with her foot, closing the door with a satisfying thud. It was then that she became aware of voices, or rather whispers, and she froze, realising that she was not, after all, the only one to have crept back inside. The whispering seemed to be coming from Henry's study, the small room at the front of the house, and one of the voices was most definitely his. The study door was not fully closed, but neither Henry nor his co-whisperer seemed to have heard her. She knew that skulking around like this in someone else's house, listening at doors, was shameful, but her curiosity outweighed all that.

There was also something in his whispered tone that set her inner alarms ringing. It was that hushed, gentle tone of voice that she loved so much, except that now it was mingled with a teasing flirtatiousness. Every so often the soft, chuckling voice of a woman would break in. They both laughed suddenly, not a loud, throaty laugh, but a far more intimate sound, the sound of a secret shared.

Unable to help herself, Julia moved so that she could see through the partially opened door, gaining a view of the couple that stood by the fireplace. Their bodies were close together, as if dancing to slow music, her hand on his shoulder, his cheek against hers. They were totally unaware of anyone and everything else. Julia recoiled in horror, backing away from the door and slopping some of her gin on to the oriental rug. She had only retreated a few steps when Antonia flew out of the dining room and almost collided with her.

The contest was clearly over and the radiant look on the hostess' face confirmed that she'd won. She smiled openly at Julia, probably forgetting her earlier remarks.

'Where's he slipped off to this time? Ah, don't tell me he's in the study again! We're going to eat at last and I need him in there...Ah, there you are! Oh, for Heaven's sake, put Sylvia down. I don't know why you put up with him, Sylvia!'

Julia blinked in disbelief. A few seconds later, she watched the three of them stroll gaily from the study with absolutely no tension between them. Fair enough, this was Sylvia Farrah, a long standing client and an old family friend, but did family friends usually behave like this? They certainly didn't in Julia's previous experience. Sylvia was undoubtedly a beautiful woman and the fact that she was older than Henry didn't seem to matter at all. Her hair was such a perfect silvery tone that it looked expensively coloured. Julia could not, for the life of her, understand why Antonia, who seemed permanently engaged in sniffing out Henry's misdemeanours, was so unruffled by this. Perhaps she was just used to it. Perhaps she knew that there was nothing in it beyond a few smooches. Antonia was hardly one to disguise her feelings, so it was clear that she was not worried. But Julia, left alone once more in the hall, most certainly *was.*

The hall was dimly lit and Julia was glad of it. She had finished her drink somehow, though she didn't remember drinking it, and was just contemplating the idea of helping herself to a refill, when the dining room door opened again, spilling Reggie and Cyril into the hall.

'Hello again m'dear,' barked Reggie while Cyril disappeared into the loo, 'Why so alone, eh? Don't you want to eat? Ah, I see! Rifling through the Blanchard silver, ha ha! No, don't worry m'dear, only old Cyril would do a thing like that, ha!'

Julia looked at him in dull puzzlement until she followed his eyes down, not to her cleavage for once, but to the box on the parquet that she was almost standing in.

She'd pushed it there earlier when helping Henry with the clubs and hadn't even noticed it in the dim light. Reggie was bending down, placing his beer on the rug a little precariously, and peering into the box.

'Ah! Fancy old Henry keeping an out of date sat nav like this! Not much use now, eh? I bet it doesn't even show motorways, ha ha.'

Julia had moved cautiously out of the way, but seeing that he was harmless when engrossed in the contents of the box, went to look at the gadget he was examining.

'Henry hates new technology,' she explained, 'I should think he hid it away without even using it.'

'Very true, very true. Gawd! Who saves half-used candles these days? And faded old cotton reels? This vase has seen better days too...'

'That's what I keep telling him,' boomed Antonia, who had entered the hall, sucking her finger again, 'but it was his mother's and he won't throw it away. Look, all you people, please go through! No one's eating and we ought to start the dancing...but I really must get a plaster for this finger, darned thing won't stop bleeding!'

Despite her apparent hurry to start dancing, she took the battered brass vase that Reggie was holding, turning it over in her hands.

'I suppose we could find a use for it in the ladies' changing room at the club,' she mused, 'but I don't imagine Henry would hear of it...' she returned the vase to Reggie, picking up the steel cased sat nav instead.

'As for this, I don't know why I bothered. He hardly looked at the thing before tossing it in here.' She dropped it carelessly into the box, clapping her hands together, as if organising fielders in a cricket match.

'Come on, m'dear,' said Reggie to Julia, 'better do as we're told'. There was a flushing sound and Cyril emerged from the loo, still looking miserable.

'Right, Cyril,' Reggie cajoled, 'in we go! First one gets a pork pie, ha!'

In the sitting room all the furniture had been moved back, the door to the dining room left open to reveal the table that still groaned under the weight of so much food. A few people stood around, clutching little china plates piled high with delicacies, their wine glasses perched at perilous angles at the edge of the dining table. Henry and Antonia were already attempting to dance in the centre of the cleared sitting room, fixed smiles on their faces. One of Bruce's CDs was playing, something with a beat far too fast for them to cope with. They were jiggling their feet around in an odd kind of quick step, arms immobilised by what they probably assumed was the requirement to hold on to each other. Perhaps, Julia thought, they'd anticipated a slow dance and had been caught out when the beat changed. Any moment now, she predicted, they were going to collide, chin against forehead and it was bound to be all Henry's fault.

'Want to dance?' Bruce had appeared at her side and she smiled at him. Why not? Anything to take her mind off her obsession with Henry, Sylvia and Antonia. Others were starting to dance too; Pamela with Ronnie Barnstone and one of the golfing couples. Even the gloomy Cyril was dancing with Eugenie, though he was still chewing on the Parma ham wrapped sausage he held in one hand. Julia began to dance too, a little awkwardly at first, with Bruce twirling her round so that she began to laugh and forget her worries. Sylvia, the lady who was causing her so much concern, was quite unaware of it, sitting in one of the big chintz covered chairs, peacefully sipping whisky from one of Henry's best cut glass tumblers.

For an awkward interval, Bruce abandoned Julia, leaving her to dance by herself while he went round the room, pulling everyone to their feet. Some resisted his attempts to get them dancing, but most of them were laughing, giving in to bob up and down and wave their arms about in a half-hearted fashion.

Without warning, the tempo of the music changed. One of the golfers was reloading the machine, creating an abrupt transition to a slow beat. Bruce had moved on to the people around the table, cajoling them to give the food a rest for a moment and join in. Julia lingered awkwardly, dancing on the spot and wishing he'd hurry up.

'Oh, well,' sounded a different voice at her side, 'I suppose it's not such a bad party after all, though I wish Reggie would pack up going through my cupboard. Anybody would think it was a bloody car boot sale.'

'Is he still doing that?' she giggled, 'I thought he'd given up. Perhaps he's hoping you'll give him your sat nav if he goes on long enough about its being out of date.'

'Out of date?' he laughed, 'I suppose it could be, though Antonia only bought it for me last Christmas. Or was it the one before? Can't remember... just couldn't get on with the damned thing! I dumped it in there with all the other rubbish.'

Henry put one hand on her waist, the other on her shoulder and began to waltz. She laughed, half in surprise, half in delight.

'We can't waltz to this!' she objected, 'Its four-four time!'

'Who cares? I won't complain if you don't! And we,' he said in something like his usual workday manner, 'will have to call you a taxi, young lady. Can't have you drunk in charge of old golf clubs!' His words were more slurred than hers and Julia smiled happily, deciding she rather liked this squiffy, easy-going version of Henry.

'But, don't you agree?' he asked after a few minutes.

'Agree with what?'

'That it's not such a bad party after all?'

'Ah, yes, Henry. I agree. It's not such a bad party after all.'

Chapter Twelve

Henry. Sunday 22nd March

'Well, thanks very much, mate!'

Bruce's look was thunderous as he faced Henry across the entrance hall of the Crown on Sunday. Henry, having had to cope with far too many weekend drivers and inexplicable hold ups along the main road, was late arriving and already in a bad mood. He'd had it in the neck from Antonia too and was having to cope with all this anger through the fog of an almighty hangover. He stared at his friend in bewilderment, struggling in vain to understand how he'd managed to offend him as well as Antonia.

'What for?'

'Julia, that's what for. You know, for once, just for once, last night I thought things were going pretty well with her. At last, I thought, if I asked her out she might just accept. But no, I turned my back for two minutes to get *your* guests dancing, to get *your* party warmed up, and when I went back you'd grabbed her! All over her! And yet this is the woman you reckon you don't even find attractive!'

Bruce had started to walk into the bar and Henry followed, his memory trying to reconcile his impressions of the night before with Bruce's accusations. The air in the bar was thick with wood smoke from the wayward fire in the ancient grate. For a few minutes, as new, damp logs were added to the fire, the smoky air hung like a curtain, cut through with beams of pale morning sunshine that stole through the old coaching inn's windows. The place was buzzing, alive with laughter, the wood smoke somehow managing to add to the atmosphere. There was always a feeling in this bar at the Crown that time had stopped still about two hundred years earlier, and it was all the better for it.

Henry carried their usual pints of bitter to a small wooden table by the window, the bar itself being fully occupied by the locals. His mind was still sifting through random memories and struggling against the jabbing pain in his temples.

'What did I do? Afraid you're going to have to tell me.'

'Nothing serious,' replied Bruce drily, 'you just hogged her and completely ruined my chances. After three dances with you she was so badly groped we thought she'd need first aid. And your Antonia was so livid she ended the party right there and then, chucking everybody out in that subtle way of hers. You were nearly chucked out with the rest of us, let me tell you. More importantly, I'd lost my chance with Julia, so thank you very much!'

'I suppose that explains Antonia's mood this morning.'

Bruce grinned for the first time that day.

'Sometimes I really love your Antonia,' he said gleefully, 'She gives you the hell you deserve.'

'I'm sorry. I can hardly remember any of it. I do recall dancing with Julia for a couple of minutes. It was only because I was grateful to her, you know, for helping with that ridiculous birthday present business. Surely it was only a couple of minutes? Must have had a bit too much champagne...' He groaned suddenly, his sore head collapsing into his hands as another thought attacked his slow functioning brain.

'What the hell am I going to say to her? She'll think...'

'That's right.'

'Oh hell. How did she get home anyway? Surely she didn't drive?'

'You called her a taxi. Have you even forgotten that? Antonia couldn't wait to bundle her into it. Didn't you notice the Peugeot on your drive this morning? I had to move it last night after everyone else had gone. Thought I'd better not leave it on the road. Julia's probably back at your place to pick it up right now, expecting your hugs and kisses and getting dear old Antonia's wrath instead.'

'Oh hell.'

'What's up with you these days?' asked Bruce after a brief interval, 'You seem more miserable than ever and I've never known you have so many hangovers. And why did you have to make things even worse for yourself? Can you imagine the rosy glow around poor Julia today? She's nuts on you and you've just handed her the encouragement she's been waiting for on a plate. Why? Was it because for once I was getting somewhere with her? Couldn't you bear seeing something start to work out for me? Or was it just that you couldn't resist the feeling of power? It must be great to be able to click your fingers and see her running to you.'

'No, no, none of that. I just didn't think at all. I'm sorry, Bruce, I really am. I've got to sort this out with Julia. What the hell do I say to her?'

'I could make a few suggestions, but you won't listen, so I'll just predict what you'll do. You will hurt her even more. You will do that by being your usual arrogant self. You will lecture her on the folly of taking things that happen at parties too seriously. You'll remind her that everyone had had a touch too much to drink. You'll insult her intelligence, lecture her like a child, and she'll feel smaller and more miserable than ever. If Julia has any sense she'll find another job. That would serve you right.'

Henry swallowed a mouthful of bitter, thinking that now wouldn't be the best time to remind him about the gin problem and her prospects of finding a more understanding employer. But, to be fair, Julia's drinking didn't seem to be affecting her efficiency, at least not yet. Bruce was right; he was a fool to risk losing her.

'Look, I won't lecture her. I'll admit I behaved like an idiot... I just hope things don't turn nasty today when she turns up for her car.'

'There's nothing you can say that'll help her take this well...' Bruce was muttering.

'Well, then. Why don't you just leave it a few days and call in and see her? She can cry on your shoulder and you can spend happy hours calling me names.'

'You'll be telling me you've done me a favour next. Oh, and while I think about it, what's really going on between you and Sylvia? We've all been putting up with your flirting and mucking about for years. Makes us feel like a right punnet o' gooseberries.'

'Oh, nothing's going on. Sylvia and I have always been like that. It'll never go any further and even Antonia seems OK about it.'

Bruce snorted and said nothing.

'Another?' Henry thought that under the circumstances he'd better buy all the drinks today.

'Better make it orange juice. Gotta drive back, both of us,' muttered Bruce gloomily.

Henry rose from the small wooden chair and approached the bar where a dozen elderly men were sharing a joke and laughing loudly, their flushed faces caught in the sunbeams that still slanted through the windows. The smoke had cleared now, the fire crackling cheerfully in the grate, but a pleasant scent of wood smoke remained, adding another layer of atmosphere to the ancient room. The men's laughter rang out again, bouncing back from the low, heavily beamed ceiling. To Henry's bruised senses, the beams seemed to amplify the laughter, setting it against the piercing clash of glasses as the barmaid collected empties from the bar top. She looked up and smiled at Henry, her broad, cheerful face looking tired from too many late nights as she snapped the tops from two bottles of fruit juice and poured them into glasses. He rifled through his pockets for change and dropped it into her hand with as cheery a comment as he could muster.

'Changing the subject,' said Bruce as Henry returned with the two little glasses, 'talking about Sylvia...has she ever seen any more of her spooks and spectres? You were winding her up about it in January. Has she said anything else?'

'Why?' asked Henry, suddenly far more alert, 'I didn't know you were interested in that sort of thing.'

124

'I'm not really. But sometimes I can't help wondering if there's something in it.'

'Well, I haven't a clue whether Sylvia's seen anything lately. Haven't asked her...but I know for certain that I have!'

Bruce stared at him in astonishment. Someone by the bar cleared their throat. Henry's eyes flicked over the crowd briefly, as if cautious about being overheard, but the throat-clearer looked innocent enough, just a farmer telling a joke to a small audience.

'Last week, when you all came over to our house...Thursday I think it was... we went out to the patio because the cat had been startled by something in the garden...'

'That's right, but there was no one there, right?'

'Who knows? But the weird thing is this. When I looked out into the shadowed part of the garden I'm sure I saw someone there. A young, good looking woman, just as Sylvia described before.'

'So she was right! Have you told her? Why didn't you say?'

'Because there's far more to it than that. I know her, or rather I knew her once. I looked out and I saw her face in the garden and yet there was no way she could have been there. No one could have got in. Our fences are too high to climb, the gates are all locked and we were certain that there was no living, breathing intruder in the garden that night. We also knew at my party in January that the woman Sylvia described could not have been in the house. What Sylvia saw then and what I saw last week can't be explained, so we've all done what people always do when they can't explain something. We put it down to imagination. We told Sylvia she'd imagined it, that she'd been seeing things. But now I've had a similar experience. So do we truly have a spirit or ghost attached to the house? And if so, how can it be someone I know?'

'But if this person has, well... passed on like, it's possible, isn't it?'

125

'But she hasn't died. She's a living, breathing woman who happens to work in financial services, like me. I know because I checked.'

'Blimey, mate. You really are a dark horse.'

'Do you remember,' Henry continued, 'I told you last summer about that fling I had on holiday?'

'Yeah, lucky bugger.'

'I'm not sure it *was* all that lucky. Sometimes I wish it had never happened. Don't know why, but nothing has ever been the same since. It made me see life differently. When I came home it was much harder to ignore the rut I was in with Antonia. I know I'd done that sort of thing before...'

'Yeah, just a bit.'

'Yes, well, this was different. I'd always been able to forget a fling quickly and move on, but not this time. I've tried to forget her and sometimes I almost manage to. After all, it's nearly a year ago now. But then I saw her face right there, in my own garden, and it brought it all back. And I seem to be getting everything wrong. Messing about with poor old Julia...I really am sorry I did that and it's even worse that I had no idea what I was doing. It was like everything else I've been doing lately, pointless.'

'Yeah, pointless out of your skull. But this woman; you said she was alive and well, so how do you...'

'I couldn't resist looking her up. She was easy to find in the office directory because she's the compliance officer for a firm in Wisbech. Anyway, on Friday, after the garden incident, I rang her office and asked whom I should address a complaint to if I had one...why is our industry so polite about inviting complaints these days? Anyway, the person I spoke to cheerfully fell on the company sword, very seriously surrendered all the necessary information and told me that I should write to Mrs Rosalyn Stone. Rosie. I remember her telling me she was divorced, so that'll be her. She's alive and well and living in Wisbech. In which case, how did I see an apparition looking just like her in my garden?'

126

Bruce's face took on one of its more thoughtful looks. He no longer seemed angry; rather he appeared to be taking an interest in analysing the information Henry had given him.

'The obvious answer, mate, is that you thought you saw her because you wanted to. What I mean is, you wanted to see her, so you thought you had. Sort o' thing.'

'I considered that too, but it doesn't explain how Sylvia saw someone who fits the same description.'

'I dunno, mate. Bit of a mystery, you could say. But enough o' this heavy stuff, I need a pint!' Bruce scraped back his chair and made for the bar.

'OK, OK, but what about the driving? You can't afford to lose your licence, especially now a new job's looking promising,' Henry protested.

'No, Bruce, you cannot. Now bugger off home while I have a little word with dear Henry here.'

Antonia, vibrant and annoyingly healthy-looking, had materialised at the bar. She looked totally out of place there; a brightly coloured, large mannequin in green and yellow, set against the many hues of brown that surrounded her. The clothing, the cloth caps, the walls, the furniture, even the dogs that sat so obediently at their masters' feet, were brown. Henry and Bruce had never noticed before.

'Antonia,' groaned Henry, not even bothering to hide his dismay, 'I thought you were playing golf.'

'I was, but there was a damned four-ball in front of us that wouldn't get a move on and then one of them landed a ball in the sloe bushes. We were losing the will to play, hanging about like that, and Dottie had to be somewhere this afternoon with Reggie, so I gave up early too and went home. Come on, Henry, buy me a drink. I need a word...'

Bruce was no coward and not normally one to walk away when a mate was in peril, but this time he considered, as he replaced his orange juice glass with a determined thud on the bar, walking away and leaving him to it was perfectly justifiable.

Chapter Thirteen

Rosie. Monday 13th April

It was twenty to nine on a Monday morning in mid April when Rosie drove into Tuesday Market Place in the centre of King's Lynn. She had to drive around the car park a few times before she could find a space, but finally managed to squeeze the Mazda between a builder's truck and a Mini. Strolling over to the pay machine in the fresh spring air, she tried to keep calm, but was having trouble controlling another attack of nerves. She stuck her ticket on the windscreen, locked the car and moved away, heading for the front entrance of the pale blue stuccoed Duke's Head Hotel.

She had been to dozens of compliance workshops before. She never minded them, especially since they took her out of the office for half a day. This one, though, was a bit different. This one might just be the time she'd both dreaded and looked forward to for ages. Today just might be the day when she'd see Henry again, for surely Henry Blanchard of Mason and Blanchard had to keep up to date with compliance as much as her own company did?

It had been a long winter and so far the spring had brought little improvement to her mood. She'd hoped that life would be better once the season changed and the weather grew kinder, but instead the same old disappointments, the same feeling of pointlessness seemed to dominate everything.

She hadn't bothered to bring a coat that morning, thinking that her black woollen suit would be enough protection against the chill, but she shivered as she entered the handsome seventeenth century Duke's Head and strode along the corridor. She headed towards the back of the building, to the newer extension, all the time trying to shrug off the nerves that were attacking her stomach.

She opened the glass door and entered the spacious, airy room that had been set out with rows of chairs facing a blank screen at the front. At the opposite end of the room was a long table laden with plates of all sorts of cakes and biscuits; oaten and wholesome looking types as well as the jammy dodger variety. Dozens of pristine white cups and saucers were set out beside a couple of stainless steel urns and a stack of little plates. Rosie headed straight for the table and poured herself coffee, unable to face any of the cakes or biscuits. While busying herself with the milk, she stole a surreptitious glance around the room. There was the usual predominance of men with just a few women, mostly officious looking, hardly a smile amongst them. A few of the men stood in groups, chatting soberly, their dark suited elbows jutting out like coat hangers in an effort to hold their cup and saucer while preventing their jammy dodgers from falling on the floor. No Henry, though. It may have been a long time since she'd seen him, but still one glance was enough to tell her that he was not in the room.

'Hello Rosie, nice to see you!'

She turned to see Anna Sobers, the City Life inspector. Always a picture of poise and confidence, Anna was positively glowing today. Her dark bobbed hair was as perfectly styled as usual and she wore an immaculate white shirt with her charcoal wool suit. Anna Sobers was going places with City Life and she quite obviously wished to get there quickly. She was friendly and outgoing, her big smile managing to off-set some of the steely precision.

'It's good to see so many here,' Anna observed, 'When you arrange these things you're never sure how many will turn up and compliance isn't exactly everyone's favourite topic...' she turned briefly to greet another guest, helping him to coffee before turning back to Rosie.

'I'm one of the lucky ones,' Rosie replied, sipping her coffee. 'I don't have to advise or sell. I can concentrate on keeping everything legal, whereas many people here have to do both.' She knew she was waffling, trying to keep

Anna there while she worked out the best way to steer the conversation.

'True, it's hard to find time...'

Anna's attention was wandering towards the screen at the end of the room, checking her watch. Rosie saw her opportunity slipping away and jumped in hastily before time ran out.

'Yes,' she gabbled, 'especially in the smaller companies. Er...do you visit Mason and Blanchard much in Downham? I often wonder how a one-man-band like that copes with balancing everything...'

'Henry? Oh, yes, I see Henry a lot!' Anna smiled, displaying her very white teeth, 'He's a real charmer! A terrible flirt! He was telling me last time I saw him that he's arranging for outside help with compliance, so I doubt whether he needs to attend this sort of thing any more.'

Rosie forced a cracked looking smile on to her face, trying to suppress her disappointment and the pang of hurt she felt at the thought of all that flirtatious behaviour. She managed to utter something or other as Anna strolled towards the front of the hall, where a colleague was getting ready to start.

Great, thought Rosie. Flaming marvellous. Only a few months ago she would have turned down any invitation that might have brought her face to face with him, but lately something had changed. Everything had changed. She wanted to see him again. The thought was unnerving but still had to be faced. She wanted to see Henry again and she'd hoped so much that it would happen today. But it wasn't to be; all she'd encountered was some conceited woman who'd informed her what a flirt he was.

She found herself a seat in the third row, merging with the sea of dark suited people, her heart as heavy as iron. A few people turned to glance at her and she nodded back, recognising many of them from previous events. She had to make an effort. She picked up the folder of papers that had been left on her seat as a welcome pack and leafed through them, the words swimming before her eyes. At the front of the hall a middle aged, cheerful looking man with a vivid red tie brightening his immaculate appearance, clicked a few keys on the lap top in front of him. The workshop attendees hushed. Behind him, images began to appear on the screen and he beamed at his audience.

'Good morning everyone, and welcome to City Life's compliance workshop!'

The morning passed quickly enough, once she'd forced herself to concentrate. She made notes, contributed to the discussions and the group problem-solving sessions, and by eleven-thirty it was all over. She called out farewells to the men and women she'd been working with and Anna reminded her that she'd be calling in later that week to see Raymond. Rosie's mood had lifted somewhat during the morning. Perhaps some of the positivity and drive that were always a main component of these workshops had rubbed off on her, because she stepped outside to greet the cloudy skies over King's Lynn's ancient market place in a more sanguine frame of mind.

Many of the buildings that lined the market place had been there for at least two hundred years and some, including the Duke's Head, were considerably older. At the far end of the square was an old building marked with the symbol of a heart inside a diamond. The symbol was there as a memorial to the market place's grim distant past, when it had been the site of witch-burnings. The last poor soul to have been put to death by burning here had apparently been a woman called Margaret Read in 1590. Rosie had often looked at the heart inside its diamond, engraved high up on the old house's brickwork, and wondered how this scene of such horrible past events could manage to feel so airy and pleasant now.

Quite apart from the witch-burnings, there had been markets and fairs held here for centuries and perhaps it was these memories which lent the square its good, business-like atmosphere. There was no market today, though. That tradition was saved for Tuesdays, which was a pity. She would have welcomed the distraction and bustle of it. Though it was unfortunate that the number of stalls had grown fewer over the years, it was still a good place to shop.

She followed the traffic out of town, moving slowly through the lights towards the medieval South Gate, unable to throw off the disappointment that had dominated the morning. There was an idea bubbling away in her mind, just below the surface, that had formed about half way through the workshop. She hadn't taken much notice of it, but still it bubbled away, working on her sub-conscious mind, nagging to be noticed. It was a crazy idea, one that would inevitably bring her even more pain, but it had forced its way to the forefront of her thoughts now and she was listening.

She passed under South Gate and the roundabout was immediately ahead. The right hand turn was the shortest route back to Wisbech, back to the office. Straight on would take her to Downham Market. Good sense would take her back to Wisbech immediately, but the crazy idea in her head made her hand hesitate over the indicator switch. She smiled suddenly and changed lane to go straight on. Crazy or not, anything had to be better than this greyness.

She drove through the industrial estate on the way out of town, eventually reaching the Hardwick Roundabout and taking the road to Downham. She switched on the radio, trying not to think too much. She wasn't sure what she'd do once she reached the place, but what would be so bad about simply going in to see him? She was tired of the dullness that had stifled her for so long and the idea of simply walking into his office and seeing him no longer seemed as impossible as it might have done a month ago. After all, what was there to lose?

The one-way system in Downham Market took her further around the town than she'd imagined, but at last she was driving her cautious way along Bridge Street and turning left into High Street. She'd Googled his office address many times, of course, and knew where to find it, but she'd always stopped herself going there before. There was a free parking space on the right hand side of the one-way street, opposite and fifty yards or so past his office. She pulled into the space, switching off the engine and turning round in her seat to look at the shop front. The office was part of a row of Georgian buildings, smart and immaculately painted. There was a coaching entrance to the left of the shop front, large enough to drive a car through. Above a pair of narrow shop windows and a neat door stretched the business sign, which was impossible to read from where Rosie sat. It was the very image of a small but prosperous business.

Stepping out of the car, she paused to allow a stream of traffic to pass, then, as calmly as she could manage, walked across the road and along the pavement. Her hand on the door handle, she paused for a moment, then took a deep breath and stepped inside.

The front office of this smartly decorated business had been furnished with a long, curving wooden counter that served as the receptionist's desk, behind which stood several tall, wooden filing cabinets. The remainder of the room was set out neatly to create a waiting area for clients; four comfortable looking chairs, a healthy array of plants in a large ceramic pot and a coffee table loaded with glossy magazines. The secretary, a good looking, petite woman of about forty with dark blonde, shoulder length hair and blue eyes, was trying to make an appointment with a woman who waited at the counter.

'...Mr Blanchard's diary. Just a moment, please!' The receptionist rose from her seat, lifted a hatch at the end of the counter, and disappeared through a door at the back of the room. There was a pause while Rosie and the other woman waited, staring around the room, before the little fair haired secretary returned, clutching a desk diary. The appointment booking system in Henry's office appeared to be slightly old fashioned and Rosie smiled to herself as she waited, recalling his antiquated taste in music and his old world image. His personality, as she'd understood it in the brief time she'd known him, was confirmed by the decor in his working environment. The dark green curtains, the rather heavy wooden furniture, the neat little prints of Cambridge on the walls, the whole tasteful, restrained and slightly old fashioned theme seemed so very Henry.

The receptionist was discussing dates and times with the other woman in a low voice. Something was entered in the diary and then the visitor left. Rosie walked forward.

'Good afternoon, may I help?' The receptionist was smiling her welcome.

'I don't have an appointment,' she began as boldly as she could, 'but if Mr Blanchard has a few minutes...'

There was a sudden, deafening, plaster-cracking thud behind her that stopped her in mid-sentence. The outside door had swung open, smacking against the wall, to admit a loudly barking golden retriever, his tail wagging as he led a woman on a leash behind him into the office. Hair flying, eyes wild, her arm extended with the dog lead as if driving a chariot, the woman had a kind of Boadicean magnificence about her, riding high in a chariot pulled by some mighty beast.

'No, Arnold! Arnold, sit!' bellowed the woman, trying to hear herself over the din of the barking. Behind her, the street door still yawned open and the receptionist, her face a picture of long-suffering, lifted the counter hatch again and walked over to close the front door. The dog was still barking and refusing to sit, straining on his lead to explore the waiting room. His tail was thrashing wildly, knocking the magazines from the coffee table, one by one. The woman uttered a few token words of protest, bending down to remonstrate gently with the dog, but making no attempt to pick up the magazines. Her blonde hair had fallen back neatly into shape, perfectly plastered into obedience by a ton of hairspray.

'Oh dear, Arnie, what is Mummy to do with you?' continued the woman, looking at the receptionist with half a smile. 'Hardly more than a puppy yet, needs a bit more training...no Arnold, no! Leave the plants alone! Is he in?'

Arnold was still in no mood to take any notice, having discovered the big plant pot behind the coffee table. He seemed especially interested in the tiny spider plants that had been set around the central broad leafed specimen, grabbing them between his teeth and shaking them out of the soil.

'No, Antonia, he's not in. Henry's out with clients.'

'Oh, bother! I was hoping to ask him a favour. Get him to phone me, will you? Just taking Arnold on his usual morning walkies by the river. Arnie, what did Mummy say? Leave the plants alone! Arnold!'

Rosie watched in disbelief as several sorry specimens of plant life were deposited on the carpet, accompanied by a dollop of dark, wet compost. She'd known, even before she'd heard the name, that the owner of this dog was Antonia. She was good looking in a big-boned way, her clothes immaculate even for dog-walking. She'd seen her before, of course, but that was only in dreams. Or something like dreams.

Antonia was leaving at last, the hound still leading the way, still barking. The jarring, booming sound went right through Rosie, bouncing off the walls of the small room and making her long for peace. The door closed at last behind them, but Arnold's barking could still be heard in the street, slowly and mercifully diminishing with distance. Wearily, the receptionist started picking up the magazines, eyeing the disaster zone around her plants before turning to Rosie with a flushed, apologetic face.

'No, don't worry,' Rosie excused herself hurriedly, 'If Mr Blanchard's not in, I'll call another day.' She left the receptionist in peace to repair the damage, shutting the door behind her. She stood on the pavement for a moment, surprised at the relief she felt. She'd been wrong to think that there'd be nothing to lose by coming here and seeing him. His reaction would most likely have been a huge disappointment and she'd have lost the one thing she did have; her unspoilt memories.

Rosie could see Antonia across the road, trying to encourage the young dog into the back of a Mercedes. She watched them for a few seconds, somehow frozen to the spot in front of the building, unable for a moment to make the move back to her car. At last she turned to walk, and as she did so, had a clear view into one of Henry's shop windows. The pretty receptionist had returned to sit behind her desk, her head down as she foraged through a drawer that must have been tucked under the desk top. She pulled out a large, heavy looking object and put it to her lips. Rosie, who was horrified to find herself spying on the woman, hurried away.

She unlocked her car and sat there for a few minutes before turning the ignition key, remembering again that last awful morning with Henry in Turkey. She recalled his mentioning a secretary who drank. But who could blame the poor woman? With the dreadful Antonia calling in when she felt like it, treating her like a servant and letting her dog mess up the office, no wonder she kept a handy bottle in the desk.

It was gone two o'clock when she arrived back in Wisbech and she'd had plenty of time while driving to give herself a thorough telling off about the stupidity of what she'd almost done. Walking unannounced into a man's office after an absence of eleven months, when he was probably up to his eyebrows in work, was no recipe for a happy reunion. She was thankful that events had conspired against her bumping into him there. How could she have been so foolish? This obsession had to stop. She had to put it behind her once and for all and prove to herself that she could move on with her life.

She needed something to distract her; a change of scene, a holiday.

The Wisbech office was quiet as she walked in; no telephones ringing, no buzz of conversation, no giggling from Alice or Jenny. Alice sat alone at her desk and didn't appear to have heard Rosie enter. Her face was down, studying something on her lap.

136

'Afternoon,' breezed Rosie as she strolled past. Alice looked up, as if rudely awoken, from the copy of "Hello" magazine on her knee.

'Where is everybody?' asked Rosie, pretending she hadn't noticed.

'Oh, hi Rosie. Jenny's taking late lunch and Raymond's not in until three, when he's got a meeting with the advisors.'

Good. No need to explain why she was late getting back. Rosie sat down at her desk and switched on the computer, made a few notes in files, but couldn't concentrate. With her screen angled away from Alice in "Hello" land, she typed hastily into the Google search bar, keen to find out where in the world she could take herself at short notice. Once the idea had taken hold, it seemed imperative that she went away soon. She had plenty of leave owing to her and the idea of finding a last minute holiday deal in May seemed very appealing.

A bargain breaks website opened up and she scrolled down the list. Spain, Portugal, Morocco...they didn't really appeal to her. So what did? She scrolled down further. There was a very cheap seven nights All Inclusive in Tunisia and ten nights' self-catering in Turkey. Turkey still seemed the most attractive location to her, but self-catering would be lonely. She returned to the search bar and this time concentrated on last minute deals in Turkey. They looked good at first sight; All Inclusive holidays in Five Star hotels the size of small kingdoms, with family fun, water slides, kiddie clubs and enough entertainment to last you a lifetime. They were mostly in Antalya and Bodrum, big resorts that had been greatly developed for tourism. Unfortunately, though, however bright and enthusiastic the write-up, Rosie felt repelled by them. She knew what it was like to feel lonely in a crowd and with all that family fun going on she was sure she'd feel as alone as in a self-catering villa.

So, where were the smaller hotels? She needed something small and friendly, yet large enough to provide a good mix of staff and guests. At the bottom of the list there were a few Three Star hotels, all offering seven nights in mid-May. She homed in on them, feeling more hopeful. The first was in Kalkan and sounded pleasant enough, but the restaurant in the photo looked more like a works canteen on a Tuesday lunch time. The next was in Bodrum and looked better, but was 'room only.' Once you threw in the necessary spending money, the holiday would no longer be a bargain. The third looked far more promising; Three-Star, All Inclusive, seven nights in a beachside hotel close to Fethiye. She sat back and laughed out loud.

It was the Melek Hotel again.

She glanced briefly at Alice, who hadn't even looked up. It wasn't that she cared if anyone knew she was looking at holidays, but she had no wish right then to discuss it with anyone.

Would it be so awful to return to the same hotel, to the scene of all that had happened before? It was bound to bring back painful memories, but might it also 'bring closure', as the Americans say? She wasn't at all sure, but something about the idea really appealed to her. Some of the staff she knew might still be there, which would help break the ice when she arrived alone. It was a ridiculous idea, perhaps something she would regret, but on the other hand...

She clicked on the icon and a new page opened. She began filling in the boxes, committing herself further with every page.

It was done. She was leaving on May 8th for seven nights. There was no going back now. She would have to go or lose her money.

And anyway, how bad could it really be?

Chapter Fourteen

Julia. Tuesday 14th April

By nine-thirty on Tuesday morning Julia had opened and sorted the post, down-loaded Henry's emails, swept the pavement in front of the office, washed up Monday's coffee cups, put on fresh coffee and finished last night's filing. She had done everything, in fact but heard a single word from her boss.

He was often in late these days and rarely offered a reason for it. Then he hid away in his office for hours at a time, without a word to her. As far as she could tell from ear-wigging at the door, he wasn't speaking to anyone else either. Sometimes he spent whole days away from the office. Of course, days out, seeing clients, had always been part of his normal work pattern, but recently he'd been staying away on other occasions too. Several times lately, when she'd arranged for clients to visit him in the office, he'd phoned in with a terse message, informing her that he'd decided to work from home. That had left her with making apologetic, last-minute phone calls to postpone his appointments and it was getting embarrassing. He'd always been oddly possessive about his diary, insisting that it was kept on his desk, only straying onto hers when she made an appointment for him, but until now he'd kept her up to date with his schedule. Lately, all that had changed and she felt shut out, trying to support a boss she rarely saw and who told her nothing.

Things had been this way ever since the party. Her dreamy happiness, caused by his drunken attention that night, had been extremely short lived. Waking very late the next morning, she'd remembered coming home in a taxi, remembered Henry's kind, solicitous words and understanding smile as he'd phoned the taxi company for her. She'd felt a glimmer of pleasure at that memory, but her heart had sunk at the necessity of retrieving her car.

She knew that seeing any of them that day would be a bad idea. Perhaps things would always be difficult, but that Sunday especially, when all the party debris, recriminations and hangovers were still painfully in evidence, she'd wanted to go nowhere near the place. She'd longed to have the whole of Sunday to enjoy her memories before anything spoiled them, but it was not to be.

After lunch she'd called a cab and returned to Bridgewell. She'd found her car sitting obediently on the drive where Bruce had parked it and she had her spare keys in her pocket. She could simply have driven it away, but it would have been less than polite and anyway, she ought to retrieve her main set of keys. Bruce was bound to have left them with Henry or Antonia. It was no good, she had to ring the doorbell. Even the thought of Antonia's murderous looks or Henry's apologetic ones was not enough to allow her to slink away unseen.

In her flat, very sensible shoes she'd made her reluctant way to the front door, stepping over tall weeds and cracks in the concrete, which looked even worse in the daylight. (The painful stilettos of the night before had been flung into the back of the wardrobe, where they'd most likely stay forever.) She'd paused on the doorstep before pressing the highly polished brass bell that was set into the immaculately dark blue painted door. The pristine appearance of the woodwork stood out in direct contrast to the neglected mess of the drive and front garden, and it seemed strange that the couple paid so much attention to the house and none at all to the outside. It must have been something to do with employing a cleaner but not a gardener.

Antonia had appeared promptly at the door, dressed in green and yellow golfing attire and had stared down at Julia from the imperious height of the door step and her own moral superiority.

'Just removing my car, Antonia,' Julia had uttered as confidently as she could manage, 'I'm sorry it's been here all night.'

'You need to get your priorities right,' Antonia had retorted, her eyelids lowered in self righteousness as she dropped the keys into Julia's hand, 'You need to start thinking about what's more important; your job or the booze.'

Julia had merely nodded and walked away to her car, unsure whether she was more relieved or disappointed that there was no sign of Henry. She'd been prepared for a mouthful from Antonia, so this little speech, loaded as it was with subtle threat, was bearable. She'd unlocked the car and clambered in, her fingers fumbling with the key as they'd searched for the ignition. Beneath the looming glare of the woman who stood in the doorway, the key had at last found the hole and the engine fired. In relief, Julia had released the handbrake and put the car into reverse.

Suddenly, there had been an almighty banging on her side window. She'd taken no notice, ignoring the woman and keeping her eyes on the mirror, ready to reverse the car.

'And just leave him alone! I'm phoning the police, you drunken bitch. You'll still be over the limit and shouldn't be driving even now. I warn you, I'm phoning them. Consider your driving licence history!'

Julia hadn't reacted, keeping her eyes on the mirror as she'd reversed out of the drive. It had seemed to take an eternity, the woman's eyes riveted on to the car the whole time with an intensity Julia could actually feel in her bones. At last she was out, putting the car into first gear, and she was away, on the road towards Downham and home.

She'd fully believed that Antonia would call the police and had been faintly surprised when there was no patrol car awaiting her return. She'd parked the car tidily in the driveway of her small, modern house and let herself in through the neat red front door. All her doors and windows had been purchased in one lot from a double glazing company, so that she'd never have to paint woodwork again. They were easy to clean and kept the house warm. Inside, her home was just as tidy, its modern furniture and laminate flooring a picture of contemporary living. While she admired Henry's beautiful home with its polished antiques, she preferred her own house with its well selected colour schemes and new, energy-efficient appliances.

Something Antonia had said must have hit the mark, because unusually she'd not reached for her trusty bottle as soon as she'd reached the kitchen. Instead she'd made coffee, waiting all the time for a knock at the door and a none too jovial chat with the police.

It had never come. Perhaps Antonia had found other ways to vent her anger. Whatever the reason, though, her relief had been only marginal. The threat still hung over her and she'd still had the prospect of one of Henry's speeches in the morning.

After very little sleep, Julia had been in the office well before nine on that Monday morning. Henry had arrived late. Just one look at his grey face and the bags under his watery eyes had told her how grim his Sunday had been and her usual compassion for him flooded over her as she called out a greeting.

'Good morning,' she'd heard herself say, pleased that her voice sounded fairly cool and professional.

'Morning.'

'Coffee?'

'Ah, yes please,' He'd thrown her some attempt at a smile, but it was thin and tired. His door had closed behind him as he escaped into the sanctuary of his office and she'd gone to make coffee, thinking about the predictability of his behaviour. As expected, he was running for cover; a cornered mouse with her as the cat, pawing at the bushes.

He'd hardly seemed to notice when she'd walked in to place the white porcelain cup in front of him, but something must have stirred his interest because he'd asked where the biscuits were.

'No biscuits, I'm afraid. I couldn't leave the office this morning, being here alone. You're pretty late in.'

'Look, Julia, let's clear the air, shall we?' he'd suggested with surprising energy. She'd looked up, fully prepared for his lecture. 'I apologise for my behaviour on Saturday night. It was unforgiveable and you'd been so kind and helpful about those damned golf clubs. I had to go and ruin it, didn't I?' He'd smiled fleetingly, using his well practised schoolboy-in-detention look.

'It's all right, Henry,' Julia had replied, straight faced, 'I know how these things go. We were both just a bit carried away with the moment...'

'Indeed. One mustn't misinterpret these things, you know.'

'Ah!' she'd almost squeaked in indignation, 'How convenient to be able to do what you like then assume any criticism is misinterpretation! Well, Antonia certainly misinterpreted pretty accurately, didn't she? I saw how easy going she was about things yesterday when I picked up the car.'

Henry had looked faintly surprised. His secretary wasn't usually one for expressing her anger.

'Ah,' he'd replied, 'yes, I'm sorry about that. At least I managed to stop her phoning the police, but I'm well and truly in the dog house. You could say that all the brownie points I earned with the golf clubs have been completely wiped out!' He'd grinned ruefully but she'd stared back at him coldly, her feelings for him hovering close to disdain. She had never shown her irritation before, had always kept her cool, believing a veneer of efficiency and professionalism to be her best protection. But that morning it had been as if all the old rules had become null and void.

'Brownie points, Henry? For heaven's sake! Isn't it about time you dropped the Brownie and Boy Scout games and grew up in that relationship of yours?' She'd noted his look of amazement but continued, taking care not to raise

144

her voice. Her words still sounded calm and as yet she'd not regretted any of them. 'I'm sorry if you think I'm speaking out of turn, but that's precisely how you behaved on Saturday night. With your actions you've involved me in your problems with Antonia. Equally, I should not have invited your attention. You are not the only one at fault here, so let's leave it at that. And thank you for persuading Antonia not to report me. You're a good employer, I like my job and believe that I do it well. Agreed?'

Suddenly he'd laughed and it had broken the tension.

'Good heavens, Julia! However was I lucky enough to have found you? You are such a sensible, nice lady and one of these days you will sort me out as a person!'

'I'll tell you what,' Julia had smiled at last, 'I'll go out and get us some biscuits.'

She had spent the rest of that morning feeling fairly reconciled to her situation. There was no stepping back from the line they had crossed, but having done that, she felt she'd handled the situation well and was once more completely in command of her emotions. She had failed to win his love or anything else for that matter, but in other ways she still had a greater part of Henry than Antonia would ever have. She must simply never make the mistake of flirting again. It was her calm and control he liked. He needed someone he could trust completely and she was good at being that person.

But that conversation had taken place three weeks ago and it seemed to have achieved nothing. Their calm, comfortable relationship, which she'd hoped would gradually be restored, seemed to be a thing of the past. He hardly spoke to her these days and his long, frequent absences were really getting to her.

Yet again, today he was late. He had appointments from eleven o'clock and most likely had preparation to do for them, but he was scarcely giving himself enough time. She knew he still cared about his work, so maybe he really was working from home? Who could tell? She should have been the first person to know and yet he told her nothing. It had to be her he was avoiding. Not his clients, but her.

It was well after half past nine when eventually he strolled in, hanging up his coat with a semi-cheerful greeting, but wasting no time at all on conversation. When she took him his coffee he was already on the phone. This had become a regular tactic; anything to avoid talking to her. She often wondered whether there was anyone on the other end. She left the coffee and biscuits on his desk and departed silently, returning to her own corner of the building to get on with her pile of work.

When the tall, darkish haired man appeared in the doorway it took her by surprise. It shouldn't have. After all, he'd been in the habit of arriving unannounced at the office for as long as she could remember, but something felt different today, and whatever it was knocked her back.

He was smiling that big smile of his, all good manners and boisterousness, and it seemed to fill the room.

'Is he here?' he asked with a grin, leaning against the doorpost and gesturing towards the back office with his thumb. She returned the grin, swinging out of her chair and knocking abruptly on Henry's door. Without waiting for a reply, she opened it a little, peering around it and announcing his visitor. She was usually far more reticent, normally so very careful to fit in with Henry's moods and workload, but suddenly, inexplicably, she was feeling carefree. She ushered Bruce in and closed the door behind him, standing there for a moment to rewind her thoughts and try to identify what had just happened to change her mood.

Although Bruce's visits to the office were commonplace, today she had looked up, seen him there, and felt happy. Suddenly she realised something new and startling. Bruce made her feel happy. How could she have missed that small point before?

In his own room, Henry frowned at the rather abrupt interruption. As Julia's head had appeared around the

146

door, followed by Bruce's whole body, he felt robbed of the power of speech.

'Morning mate,' Bruce hailed from the doorway, 'Still being a pain in your secretary's backside, are you?'

'Bruce, what do you want? I have clients coming in soon and I've work to do.'

'Sorry, mate. Just had to tell you...' he waved a few sheets of paper in the air, 'I got it! The job! I start next Monday!'

Despite Henry's need to get on with his report writing, he sat back in his chair and smiled broadly, feeling genuine pleasure in Bruce's change in fortune.

'Well done! That's excellent news! Told you it would happen soon! We'll have a pint in a day or two and catch up, only I've...'

'Of course, mate. I'm sorry, I know you've gotta get on. Just had to tell you, but I'll leave you in peace and have a word with the lovely Julia...'

He left and Henry smiled to himself. It was good to see Bruce restored to his old bouncy self. His news was the one positive thing amongst the mess of everything that was going wrong. But Bruce's visit had broken his concentration and, try as he might, he couldn't recapture the flow of logic that he needed to finish the report.

From the photo frame on the desk, his father gave him a reassuring smile and Henry picked it up. The other frame, the one with Antonia's photo, was still somewhere in the drawer, where he'd thrown it in irritation a couple of months before. He looked at the image of his father with his beloved Austin Seven, thinking of the long hours his dad had put into restoring the old car. The Austin had been left to decay for decades in his grandfather's tractor shed on the farm and Henry's father had rescued it and brought it lovingly back to life. Henry had even taken his first driving lessons in it at the age of ten, cautiously following the tracks around the farm. The old car was probably still there, most likely forgotten by William, his brother, who had inherited the farm and was working hard to continue the family business. Henry replaced the frame on the desk and found himself smiling back at his dad. He could almost hear his voice gently chastising him, urging him to get on with his work; to care for what mattered.

From reception, he could hear Bruce's laughter, interspersed by Julia's voice. Was she flirting? Would it really matter if she were? He shook his head.

He caught his dad's eye and picked up his pen again. He really had to get on.

Chapter Fifteen

Rosie. Saturday 25th April

There was an old potato basket in the shed, grimy and cobwebbed, yet sturdy and it was very useful when she was weeding. The door of the shed was coming off, screeching against its rusted hinges whenever it was forced to open, and the shed itself was rotting, its lower timbers flaking away close to the concrete base and letting in little shards of light.

She would have to get a new shed from B&Q, Rosie decided. It would have to be a flat-pack, something fairly easy to assemble, as DIY wasn't her strongest point. She squatted down on the gravel path and began working on the flower bed with her trowel, removing stray clumps of grass and deep rooted dandelions, turning the soil over as she worked. There were tiny wild violets everywhere, their tenacious little roots clinging on for dear life. As charming as they were, they were taking over the garden and something had to be done about it. She unearthed their roots and pulled them up by the handful, tossing them into the basket. She was making slow progress, but the garden was beginning to look neat and ready for the new season.

She worked for more than an hour in the spring sunshine, occasionally standing to stretch her back and gaze over the back hedge to the gnarled trees of the old orchard beyond. The sky was an almost perfect pale blue, flecked here and there with hazy little clouds. She felt happy. It was good to be working in the garden, having no plans to change its layout, simply enjoying the restoration of what past owners had created. It was a simple garden, sliced off from its neighbour when the old farmhouse had been divided into two, but its design was pleasant. There was a tiny lawn, surrounded by a gravel path and curving flower beds. In one corner she had cleared an area ready for a vegetable garden and had already planted a bag of "first early" potatoes; Pentland Javelins from the garden centre. She had plans to add courgette and tomato plants later and would probably sow carrots and lettuce too. The work kept her cheerful. She could plan it and work on it without needing anyone else and was often out there, working when the weather was far from perfect.

To rest her back, she sat down on the old bench at the edge of the lawn. It was a comfortable, warm seat, its silvered timbers greedily soaking up the sun as if to ease its tired old bones. From here, she could see the little gap she'd made in the back hedge, the space she'd often squeezed through to get into the orchard.

On a whim, she stood up and wandered over to the hedge, easing her body into the gap. A few hard privet twigs poked into her shoulder and a stray bramble threatened to send her headlong into the nettles, but she managed to squeeze through to the other side without mishap.

The old orchard was a wonderful jungle of ancient apple trees, their boughs sweeping low and their canker-blighted trunks almost hidden by long grass, nettles and briars. Rosie often wondered how long it would be before whoever owned this land decided to uproot the trees and do something profitable with it. But, for some reason the orchard seemed forgotten and it looked as if she was the only one who picked the apples, unless the few dog walkers who ventured this way helped themselves. The path leading from the back lane to the orchard was badly overgrown, almost disappearing in places, so hardly anyone came here these days. The orchard was allowed to remain in peace; quiet and happily neglected, with hardly a soul to disturb the rustlings of the small mammals and birds that inhabited it.

Rosie's gardening shoes weren't sturdy enough to walk far in. The tangle of weeds was just too dense and nettle-ridden, but she managed a few yards of the obstacle course and found her usual fallen, part rotted branch amongst the dock leaves and sat down on it. She leaned back on a tree

150

trunk, wriggling a little to find a less gnarled spot to settle against. The warm April sun reached her through the dark network of branches where the first fragile, pale pink blossom was beginning to appear.

There was nothing on her mind but the simplicity of her surroundings as she drifted into sleep. Sleeping in the daytime hadn't used to be normal for her, but she'd noticed it happening lately when she was physically tired. She didn't try to stop it, just let her mind drift, uncertain of quite when it was that she let go.

She was on a river bank. The water was high; she could see the swift, brown body of it surging against the grassy banks. Tussocks of spiky grass half way up the bank, unused to getting their roots so wet, were getting a ducking for the first time in months and they looked pretty miserable about it. Pieces of twig, old birds' nests, a bread packet and a shoe were caught up for a moment in a whirlpool before being released, bobbling along the river to be washed up unwanted somewhere else.

She heard them before she saw them, the woman and the dog. The dog was leading the woman on the leash again and barking with excitement as he threw himself down the wet, grassy bank towards the water's edge. She heard the woman cry out; some curse or exclamation as she was dragged down the bank after the retriever. She was giving the dog a good telling off now, but he couldn't have cared less, his big bushy tail wagging with joy as he bounded off again, dragging her with him. They scrambled back up the bank, the woman exhausted already. She bent down to remove the lead and, sensing real freedom at last, he tore away, haring along the bank and swooping back down to the water. He ran along its edge, sniffing and pawing, springing backwards sometimes from some new discovery, as if he'd been bitten. At any moment, the dreaming Rosie expected him to plunge in, that she'd see his golden head bobbing on the brown water, and it seemed the woman feared this too, because she was calling frantically from the top of the bank. For some reason, though, the young dog seemed to think better of it, trotting back up the tussocky bank to the woman. She probably had a bag of treats in her pocket.

Rosie stirred and opened her eyes, shivering and pulling the old gardening fleece more closely around her. A large cloud had drifted across the sun, blocking out the warmth and sending the temperature plummeting downwards. She remained where she was, reluctant to move despite the chill.

Why had she dreamed of Antonia again? And had it been merely a dream? She'd overheard Antonia talking to the secretary about walking the dog by the river, so this could just have been a dream based on that memory. But, no! It had been too clear for that; as vivid as a video clip. The whole feel of it had been something far more real than a dream. So, that meant she'd been visiting Antonia in her sleep and she didn't like the thought of that one bit.

Getting up, she made her way back through the trees towards the gap in the hedge and squeezed through, staggering as her foot caught on a long strand of ivy. She wasn't watching her feet carefully enough, too busy wondering whether Monica would listen if she told her about this dreaming business now. She was hardly the fanciful sort, dear old Monica, but there was no one else to turn to and she needed badly to talk.

The sky had clouded over completely now and the light in the garden had changed; moody, as if suddenly offended. She gathered up her basket, trowel and gloves and replaced them in the remains of the shed, its poor old door protesting loudly at being disturbed again.

Back in the house, she could hear no sound from next door, but she sent Monica a quick text. She took a shower and washed her hair, pulling all manner of fir needles and dried leaves from her garden-brushed mop. By the time she had dried herself, there was a reply. 'Pub later'.

The Red Lion was busy when they arrived at about eight, several groups of diners having arrived at once. All competing to deliver their own news or gossip, their voices were steadily growing louder as they passed menu cards and freshly filled glasses around. It was a good Saturday night atmosphere, typical of a popular pub; full of good humour and laughter, accompanied by a lot of glass clinking. Monica and Rosie skirted the jostling, noisy crowd by the bar, dodging between extended elbows and dripping glasses to find a small table by the window. While several drinkers hovered close to their table, still debating the contents of the menu, the girls made small talk.

They'd both decided to make an effort with their appearance and it felt good to be out. Monica's usual dark jeans and sweater were lightened by a bold brass necklace from New Look and Rosie had really gone to town with a new shirt, pencil skirt and the sort of shoes she shouldn't have walked so far in. While the group at the bar debated loudly whether to order whitebait or pâté, the girls looked out of the window and wished the lot of them would just go away.

Dusk was falling, amber street lights coming on over the river on South Brink, where traffic slowed on approach to the junction, red stop lights flaring briefly. Before long the last of the daylight would melt away, but in this brief interval between light and dark the colours of day were still discernible; faded and distorted, but still there. A swan idled gracefully by, his whiteness displayed in a brief glimmer of sunlight, a last ditch effort before the curtain of night finally fell.

The noisy group left the bar at last, their voices gradually diminishing as they filed into the dining room. A small gathering of elderly gents still occupied one end of the bar, hugging their pints to their chests, their heads shaking in despair over the woes of some goal keeper or other who'd apparently been letting in too many lately.

'So,' grinned Monica over her glass, 'Tell me all about it.'

Rosie paused, trying to find the right words to explain the inexplicable.

'You might not take this seriously,' she began, 'there isn't a logical explanation for this and I know you like to have one, but I really need to tell someone. It's been going on for years...'

'What has?'

'Dreaming; clear dreaming, but more than just that. Most of the time, like everybody else's I suppose, the dreams are the normal sort of nonsense. You know, hazy and mostly forgotten as soon as I awake...'

'Yes, I can relate to that.'

'...but sometimes, just sometimes, they are completely different.'

Monica took a sip of wine and leaned forwards, as if expecting to share a great secret.

'Sometimes I dream I'm in a particular place and everything, every detail about it is very clear. Sometimes I recognise the place I'm in, other times I don't. But, always during these experiences it's as if I'm truly there, watching real people getting on with their lives. Another thing; the time of day or night I see these things tends to match the time in the dream. For instance, if I fall asleep and dream in the daytime, the scenes in the dream are daylight ones. If it's night, I see night time or evening happenings.'

'All right, so they're clear dreams. That can't be very unusual, surely.'

'Perhaps not, but you see, just occasionally someone sees *me*.'

'You mean you dream that someone looks at you.'

'Well, yes. They stare, as if seeing a ghost. They actually look right at me. Monica, what I'm trying to say is, that I believe at these times I'm not just dreaming but am really there, in those other places, seeing real people doing real things. And this has happened often enough now for me to accept that these things are more than just dreams.'

Monica was looking doubtful, biting her lip. Rosie blundered on.

'And I've seen *him*, Monica, that's what I really needed to talk to you about. I've seen Henry. I've been there, in his garden and his house.'

'But of course you have! You're still obsessed with the pompous twerp and keep it all to yourself, refusing to talk about him. Keeping it all bottled up means your subconscious makes him materialise in dreams. It's logical, I'm afraid.'

'No, Monica, I really see him. I've seen her too, his partner, or whatever he calls her.'

'The other woman? Well, you're bound to see her, aren't you? You've created a picture of her in your mind and now she's made her way into your dreams. The mind works like that!'

'No! She's more than just a face I've dreamed up. I know it's really Antonia! I know because...'

Rosie clammed up suddenly. She was about to say she knew it was really Antonia because she'd seen her in the flesh. She'd seen her when she'd foolishly visited Henry's office. That had been *after* first seeing her in a dream and Antonia had been perfectly recognisable. It was absolute proof that these visions were more than mere dreams, but she felt unable to say so. She just couldn't bring herself to admit that she'd been to Henry's office. Monica would be horrified at such stupidity.

But Monica was still looking at her, waiting for her to finish her sentence. The pause had been too long already and in the end her little speech petered out uselessly, '...because I just know it, Monica. I just know it.'

Monica was looking nonplussed, sipping her wine and looking as if she needed another one.

'Sorry, Rosie. I can see you really believe it, but you've got to admit it's a bit hard to swallow. You need your holiday, need to get away for a bit and think about other things. I wish I could come with you, but I can't afford to, not with going to Australia at New Year. And anyway, dear old Berkant's emails from Turkey have come to an end... I suppose he's found himself more convenient lodgings for when he visits England. I don't really give a damn, but neither do I fancy running into him again. Honestly, of all the hotels in Turkey, why are you torturing yourself with going back to the Melek? Everything about it will be miserable. As it is, you're thinking of him far too much. Becoming obsessive, in fact. No wonder you dream about him! You even dream up a world for him to live in. The people you see with him aren't real. They're all figments of your imagination! I hate to say it, but you really do need to get out more.'

Rosie laughed, seeing things from Monica's angle. There was clearly no point in mentioning the research carried out on astral travel. Monica would just wave that away too, and without knowing that Rosie had her own proof in the shape of Antonia, how could she be expected to understand?

'You're right about the Melek,' she said at last, deciding to stay on the new subject, 'going back there will be tough, but I've decided to do more exploring this time. I'll avoid the Club Dancing and the pool games...'

'I don't believe you. You're a push-over!'

'True,' she laughed, 'another drink?'

Rosie went up to the bar and ordered the drinks, surprised at how much lighter she felt, just from being able to talk about things. She'd never really expected Monica to believe it, anyway. Taking the two glasses of wine back to the small table by the window, she gave her friend a confident smile.

'So, enough of my hogging the conversation,' she began, 'you didn't tell me about Berkant defecting...better still, let's talk about Australia!'

Chapter Sixteen

Rosie. Thursday 7th May

Rosie has overslept. She stirs, becoming aware of the strength of sunlight filtering through the closed curtains, and knows it is late. For a moment panic squirms in her stomach before she realises the alarm is switched off because today she's on leave. Today she is packing for her holiday. Today it will not harm her to sleep.

It is not long before she is sleeping again. Her suitcase is lying open on the floor next to the bed, piles of ironed clothing placed beside it on the carpet. Hanging from the top of the wardrobe and the door handles are dresses and skirts, ready to be packed. She is so well prepared for her holiday in fact, that she could have managed without this day off, but a day's leave was owing to her and now she is glad to have the leisure time.

She looks peaceful as she sleeps again. There is no indication of the images that are flashing through her mind and being projected with cinematic clarity before her eyes.

She dreams that Antonia is walking along the river bank again. She looks fresh faced and energetic and the dog's lead is swinging from one hand, while Arnold is bounding and leaping with his usual joy and abandonment some distance away. Antonia keeps her eye on him as he gallops up the bank and down again, barking at the water, then backing away from it, as if challenged by some unseen water creature.

'Arnold!' the woman booms powerfully, but the retriever takes no notice whatsoever, enjoying his freedom and the fresh May air. Antonia looks resigned and not altogether bothered by his disobedience. She walks down to the water's edge where the ground is boggy, back-stepping hastily as her immaculate trainers begin to take in water. Small clumps of wild flowers peep out from the sodden grass; blue speedwell and shiny yellow buttercups.

Antonia pauses and calls the dog again and this time, perhaps taking into account which side his bread is buttered on, he races back along the bank and slams his weight lovingly against his mistress' legs. She bends down to caress his golden head and smiles.

'Had a good run, boy? Let's go back to the car now and drive to the office to see Daddy...' Arnold seems to sense that his daily dose of freedom is nearing an end and has other ideas, so he leaps away again, streaking back down towards the water, practically somersaulting with joy.

'Having trouble, Antonia?'

The voice from behind startles her despite its calm tone and Antonia spins round to see Julia standing there. The secretary is smiling. In fact, she seems her normal, friendly self, but there is an edge to her voice and to her whole manner that Antonia can't quite work out. She nods curtly at her, mumbles something dismissive but fairly polite and looks as if she wishes Julia would walk away and leave her in peace.

'Thought I'd pop out for an early lunch,' Julia remarks in that conversational, sunny way of hers, 'There was nothing I needed to do in town, so I thought I'd come here, since you make it sound so attractive. I can see why you bring Arnold here. It's really peaceful, isn't it?'

'Arnold loves his walks and this is as good a place as any,' Antonia manages to say, though it is clearly said through gritted teeth, 'Must be getting back now, though...oh for heaven's sake, Arnie, get out of the bloody water!'

Arnold has padded down the bank to an area where recent high water has flooded the grass and left behind a shimmering pool. The water is hardly deep, a few stems of long grass and buttercup heads managing to peer bravely above the surface, but the dog is in nearly up to his knees, splashing about and having fun. His tail is swishing, spraying an arc of water around his backside.

'Looks like he's enjoying himself,' Julia laughs and the comment seems to grate further on Antonia's nerves. She strides away, down the bank to remonstrate with the dog, tugging on his collar and finally managing to attach his lead and pull him onto dryer land. Antonia's trainers and the lower part of her jeans are soaked and the rest of her clothing looks pretty damp too. The dog's tail, face and under belly are so wet that he looks smaller somehow, his golden hair darker. When he and his mistress return to the top of the bank Julia is still there, waiting. Antonia ignores her this time, struggling as she steers Arnold back to the car. Julia follows her.

'I thought you were going for a walk,' Antonia says, 'Your lunch hour will soon be over at this rate.' She opens the back of the Mercedes, trying to persuade the dog to enter. The woman's continued presence is really getting to her now and she is no longer able to hide her irritation. 'Arnie, will you bloody well get into the car! We have to be going, unlike some people who seem to be sticking around.'

Arnold, however, is clearly disinterested in his mistress' desire to be leaving, resisting with super-canine strength her attempts to get him into the car. Then, suddenly he pauses in his resistance and Antonia seems to brace herself, knowing what is coming. He shakes himself with an almighty spin-dry action that most washing machines would be proud of, his body a blur as water droplets are flung from his fur in every direction, soaking the remaining dry bits of Antonia and most of Julia.

Julia is laughing. Antonia is not.

'Why are you still here, Julia? Why aren't you in a pub, doing something useful, like boozing as usual?'

'Because it's far more fun here, seeing your dog get the better of you. Anyway, I don't need pubs. I have my supply right here, as I'm sure you know.'

She opens her shoulder bag and takes out an almost full 70cl bottle of gin, displaying it as if it's a lot in an auction.

'Of course I damned well know! Everyone knows about your seedy little habit. As I've said before, you are very lucky to keep your job!'

159

Julia does not reply, but she is no longer laughing or smiling. Her face looks white. Antonia has her back to her, trying to heave the unwilling dog into the back of the car. As she turns, she just has time to see that Julia's arm is raised, the bottle with it, then she crumples to the wet grass, Arnold looking curiously on.

Now there is confusion, a sharp feeling of panic, a hand still gripping the bottle neck. There's a filing cabinet with some sort of label on the front and the sound of ragged, tortured breathing as the bottle is dropped into a drawer. The breathing has turned to sobs. Helpless, terrified sobbing.

Rosie awakes, rolling on to her back with a groan. She stares at the ceiling for a while, the pictures from the dream replaying in her mind with increasing horror.

The clock shows her it is almost midday. How could she have slept so late? She staggers out of bed and wastes no more time in getting under the shower. She needs desperately to talk to someone. She needs to tell Monica.

Monica is at work by now, of course, but Rosie dresses hurriedly and skips breakfast, hurrying out of the house and part runs, part walks up the Brink towards town. She hasn't bothered Monica at work before and has only visited the Poet's House Museum once. She's forgotten how far away it is. She ought to have brought the car. She walks along Nene Quay, then along the old Lynn road out of town, eventually reaching the Georgian museum.

The Poet's House is displaying its neat welcome sign on the grass outside and a few visitors are strolling about. Monica has been creating a herb garden at the front and along the side of the house, reproducing as closely as possible the original Georgian layout of the garden. Rosie hardly gives it a glance; she'll look at it another time when she feels calmer.

She attempts a smile at a few of the visitors before entering through the reception door. Monica is there, in conversation with a young female assistant who is having trouble with the till. She looks up, surprised to see her friend. She opens a door behind the counter and beckons Rosie through.

She waits for her friend to speak, seeing that she needs to.

'Monica,' Rosie almost whispers, 'I think Antonia is dead!'

Chapter Seventeen

Rosie. Friday 8th May

Perhaps it wasn't entirely by chance that Rosie left home so early that Friday morning. She told herself that it was just a bit of luck that the packing, sorting out last minute jobs and locking the house had all gone so smoothly. Unusually, there had been no last minute phone calls, no awkward emails that couldn't be ignored, no frustration about lost items or things she'd forgotten to pack. It had all gone perfectly to plan and soon she was driving away, her bags in the boot of her small two-seater car and with far more time on her hands than the hour and a half needed to get to Stansted Airport.

It was sunny as she drove, a good omen for her holiday, and there was absolutely no need to hurry. All this was thanks to far more than just good luck; she knew deep down that she'd left early because she'd always meant to.

Try as she might, she could not dismiss the dream about Antonia's murder. Monica had been scornful of it, as she'd known she would be. She'd reminded her that some dreams were simply dreams, that Rosie had been over-tired and that her subconscious had created that horrible little scene as a result of thinking too much about the same people. She could well be right, but the dream remained in Rosie's thoughts and would not be shaken off. Last night, before she'd fallen asleep, she'd come up with the idea that if she could catch a glimpse of the man himself or even of Antonia, she would know there'd been no truth in the dream and would be able to forget all about it.

Deciding on which route to take to the airport was easy; no last minute wavering this time. She left Wisbech along the Outwell road instead of taking the road through March. Both routes would take her to Stansted, so where was the harm? The road was quiet, the late morning traffic light. Although the day was not all that warm, the effect of the sun intermittently lighting up the Mazda's black dashboard gave the illusion of heat and helped to boost her holiday mood and flagging confidence.

There was no harm in going there just once more, she told herself. There was nothing to lose in seeing the office again if it convinced her that all was well and that what she'd dreamed had been no more than a lively flash of imagination. Yet, still the thought of going anywhere near him felt like invading his territory, made her feel like a stalker. Her heart was thumping in uncomfortable protest already, and she hadn't even reached Downham Market.

As she entered the town, she had to wait at the crossing barriers while the train from London, its tail of carriages spreading back across the main road, waited at the tiny station. She was soon on her way again, making her way along Bridge Street towards the square and the grand Victorian clock tower. As before, she turned left along the one-way street and searched for a parking space. The only space available was closer than the one she'd used before, slightly past but almost opposite the office. It was far from ideal, but she pulled into it anyway. Its proximity to the shop front made her wish she'd brought a pair of dark glasses or a large newspaper, which was absolutely ridiculous of course.

This time she had no intention of going into the office. If she was ever to see Henry again it would have to be with more forethought than by strolling uninvited into his workplace. She wasn't at all sure what she could expect from this morning, but she sat and waited anyway. According to the dashboard clock, it had just gone twenty past eleven, not too far from the time of day when Antonia had taken the dog for a walk last time. With any luck, Rosie might see her and she'd have the proof she needed that all was well. There was plenty of time yet, no need to worry about her flight for now.

To keep her eye on the office door, she had to look back over her shoulder and peer around the head-rest, which was uncomfortable, but it gave her some measure of cover. Even so, she needed something to do, or appear to be doing. She opened the glove box and rifled through the untidy stack of contents before pulling out a map of Cambridgeshire and Norfolk. It was the awkward, folded kind, the sort she could never fold back up again and usually felt like chucking out of the window, but right now it was very handy. She laid it out flat and draped it over her knees, lifting it high to study an imagined route with great concentration. All the time, she kept half an eye on the office door, but there was no movement. No one entered the building and no one left. Now and then a passer-by would catch her eye and the surrounding shops seemed to be doing a steady trade, but at Mason and Blanchard there was no action at all.

She clicked on the car radio, but a pair of dull, monotonous voices discussing fly-tipping did nothing to hold her attention. On another station they were playing the sort of music that ought to have been put out of its misery years ago. She yawned. Nearly twenty-five to twelve. What did she think she was doing? Maybe she was waiting in vain. Perhaps the office was closed for the day...

A movement at the door caught her eye and she sank down in her seat. Anna Sobers, the City Life inspector, came out of the office carrying her neat black leather briefcase. She looked disgruntled, as if her meeting today hadn't gone too well. Perhaps, thought Rosie with uncalled-for bitchiness, Henry hadn't flirted as much as usual, or worse, perhaps he hadn't been there at all. Anna moved quickly away, passing Rosie's car without noticing her and crossed the road, disappearing from sight.

Rosie sighed. She couldn't hang around forever. More minutes ticked by and she thought about folding the map and driving away, but then at last the awaited moment arrived. The neat, green painted door opened for a second time.

Stepping out of it, into the faltering sunshine of a May morning, was the very man she had waited a year to see.

She stared, unable to believe that she really was looking at him again after all this time. Her neck was straining against the head-rest as she tried to take in as much as she could while he was still right before her eyes. He was even better to look at now, she decided. His charcoal pin-striped suit looked far better on him than his summer holiday clothes had done, far more in keeping with his conservative nature.

He walked over to the kerb and glanced down the road towards the on-coming traffic, as if expecting someone, and unconsciously providing Rosie with a prolonged opportunity to look. Luckily, the direction he was facing was away from where she sat and ogled, but even so she felt vulnerable, as if the intensity of her watching eyes would alert him.

Briefly, she glanced down at the map as it began to slide from her knees, but when she looked up again he was still there, looking slightly peeved and checking his watch. He shrugged and turned decisively on his expensive heels, apparently giving up on whoever he had been waiting for. Rather than going back into the office, though, he disappeared through the wide coaching entrance next to the building.

Rosie slumped in her seat, her thoughts confused, the rawness of her feelings taking her by surprise. Seeing him again was hurting far more than she'd anticipated. She tried to think logically. Had she achieved what she had come for? Perhaps. Peeved he may have been, but he certainly didn't look like a man whose partner in life had just been killed.

Less than two minutes later, a black Jaguar XF saloon nosed its rather important way through the coaching entrance and across the pavement. The car, with Henry at the wheel, paused for a moment at the kerb like a big cat preparing to pounce, waiting while a few humbler cars passed by. Then it swept into the road, joining the one-way system and passing the place where Rosie hid and spied as it gathered speed. She caught a glimpse of him as he passed. His expression was impassive, the look of someone just getting on with his day. The car looked like the perfect extension to Henry's character; conventional, safe, and fittingly expensive. She knew all over again, just by looking at his neat, ordered, immaculately painted office front and his gleamingly perfect motor car, that he could never have left this world for her, even if she'd asked him to.

The car, and Henry with it, had disappeared from sight in seconds, leaving her with an empty, sinking feeling. So that was that. Her wish had been granted and she'd seen him again. She'd seen that he looked nothing like a man who was bereaved, but really that proved nothing. If something bad really had happened to Antonia, he may simply not know it yet.

So, where did Rosie go from here? Could she ever hope to see him again? With irritation she brushed away a few stray, self-pitying tears with the back of her hand. It had been utterly stupid to come here and open old wounds and there could hardly have been a worse time than when she was on her way to "their" hotel without him. She had been feeling better lately and now she had erased that progress in one clumsy move.

She struggled to regain her composure, trying hard to recapture a shred of the self confidence she'd found once and could find again. She folded the map, badly as usual, cursing the paper that refused to behave and return to its nice, neat creases. She managed finally to get it roughly into shape and she stuffed it into the glove compartment, fastening her seat belt and getting ready to leave. Her fingers were on the key in the ignition, ready to turn it, when a further movement at the office door drew her attention.

Julia the secretary had appeared and was standing on the pavement with a tall, smartly dressed, silver haired man in his late fifties or early sixties. They were both laughing, the man confidently, the secretary politely. At first glance, Julia's face was amiable, but to the trained eye of a fellow people-pleaser such as Rosie, there was a distinct look of duty beneath the masking smile. It looked as if Julia was seeing a client of Henry's out and was having trouble terminating the conversation. She was clearly trying hard to remain polite and pleasant, while wishing he would just go away and leave her to her sandwiches, or whatever else she wanted. Rosie was oddly fascinated and couldn't help continuing to watch, her hand still gripping the ignition key, but not yet turning it. She empathised with the secretary, knowing what it was like to stay teeth-grittingly nice to certain clients who rewarded you with nothing but inconsideration and rudeness.

There was something else that Rosie remembered to note. Julia was not behaving as if she'd just killed anyone. Looks could be deceptive, though.

The secretary had almost escaped from the client. The man had begun to walk through the coaching entrance towards the car park at the back, calling out a vociferous farewell that even Rosie could hear from her car. Julia began her retreat towards the office door, but just as she reached it he hailed her again, his head reappearing around the corner. Julia's smile was thin, but she went obediently, standing with him for a further few minutes while he plunged into an earnest, frowning monologue. He must have thought of another query he wished to air and, sadly for Julia, it didn't look like a brief one. She looked cold. They were standing in the shade and the morning air, untouched by the thin sunshine, was fresh. She was pulling her cardigan around her, but if the man noticed her discomfort at all, he was unbothered by it. Rosie watched as Julia nodded then shook her head without managing to get a word in, and then the pair of them disappeared around the corner towards the car park.

Rosie had no idea what made her follow them, but she found herself unfastening the seat belt and slipping out of the car. She dashed across the road, narrowly avoiding collision with a boy on a speeding bicycle who was sporting a mean looking helmet and a poisonous glance.

She sped to the pavement and slowed down as she approached the wide entrance, peering into it in as casual a way as she could manage. No one there. She ventured into the short, brick passageway, assuming the air of someone who had innocently lost their way. As she reached the end of the passageway she slowed her steps, peeping cautiously around the corner to look into the small car park. It was only large enough to serve Henry's office, providing just enough space for three or four cars. With Henry's gone, there remained only a small red Peugeot and the client's silver saloon, which was parked in the very end space.

The man had opened the boot and was showing Julia some papers. Poor Julia looked colder than ever, her arms wrapped around her under-dressed body while she tried to look interested. She must have been desperate to get back to the office. Neither she nor the client noticed Rosie's quick glance at them around the corner before she pulled back swiftly and walked back towards the street.

She smiled ruefully to herself. How had she allowed her obsession with Henry to become so bad that she'd begun to spy on his secretary? This had to stop right now. She glanced at her wrist watch.

Time to go.

Chapter Eighteen

Rosie. Friday 8th to Friday 15th May

The taxi driver was a man of few words. Having taken Rosie's instructions with a silent, moody nod of the head he seemed totally engrossed in his own world and his own haphazard style of driving. Normally, she wouldn't have paid much attention to the absence of seat belts in the back, but as the car accelerated out of Fethiye and hit the dusty Ölü Deniz road, she began to find the thought of them very attractive.

But so far, so good. She'd been here for three days now and was trying to do as she'd promised herself; she was getting out and about more and spending the minimum of time lounging around the pool, immersed in memories. Today she had been to Fethiye, taking the dolmuş as before, but had decided to vary things a bit and hail a taxi for the return journey. Now she was beginning to question the wisdom of such a whim. She closed her eyes tightly as the driver accelerated to overtake a lorry loaded with swaying steel milk churns. Spitting loose gravel from beneath its tyres and spraying an arc of grit along the roadside, the taxi swerved back into its own lane, only just avoiding collision with a dusty blue Renault. Rosie let out a squeak of fear from the back seat and the driver grunted.

After a few more hair-raising miles they overtook the plodding dolmuş, Rosie eyeing it longingly. She thought of how stuffy, noisy and overcrowded it would be, could almost catch the heady whiff and close proximity of too many over-heated armpits. Right at that moment though, even with all its disadvantages taken into account, the dolmuş seemed like bliss compared to this taxi and its fun-fair ride. In record time, the car reached the top of the valley. Below them, spreading like a Turkish carpet displayed for their admiration, was the coastal village of Ölü Deniz. She could see the hotel from here and could never look at it like this without thinking of her departure a year ago, when she'd left Henry behind. After a rapid, swerving descent, the taxi crunched to a stop in front of the Melek Hotel, showering dust and grit over a bikini-clad group, who dived spluttering into the reception hall. Rosie clambered out, feeling dizzy and grateful to be alive, placing the amount of lira the driver demanded into his impatient palm.

Walking through the lofty coolness of reception, she exchanged a wave with Selma, who was trying to explain to two German guests about the sun beds.

'No,' she was enunciating in English, her patience clearly wearing thin, 'the brochure only says the beds around the *pool* are free…'

'No, no, quite clearly have I read right here that also the beds are free on the beach.'

'I'm sorry, but the beach doesn't belong to the hotel, so we couldn't offer you free sun beds there. You see, it says,' Selma turned the brochure to face her and quoted from it, ' "Sun beds around the pool are free. There are also sun beds available on the nearby beach." You see, it doesn't mean beds are free on the *beach*.'

'Well, in fact I would like to see the manager.'

'Well, in fact I *am* the manager, Herr Werner…'

Rosie threw Selma a sympathetic glance, glad to be so many miles away from the problems of her own job. It was good to have a break from the everyday pettiness of work, even if this hadn't been the wisest of destinations. Even now, walking down the path towards her room, there were so many snap shots from the past that appeared unbidden before her eyes; Henry walking, Henry speaking, Henry smiling, and many other memories besides. Thankfully, the room she had this year was nowhere near to either his or her own from last year, but everything else was there to remind her.

There were so many familiar faces. Many members of staff remained from the previous season; Selma in charge of reception, Mustafa the Head Waiter, even several of the seasonal staff, such as animators and waiters. They all seemed to remember her, which made her feel welcome and did something to stave off the loneliness.

The evenings were the worst times to be without him. Sitting alone at the bar was no fun at all, even though many of the staff made the effort to stop and chat when they weren't too busy. The other guests seemed mostly to be families. She'd realised too late that this week was half-term for most of England, and for much of the day the pool was full of children, squealing and dive-bombing their little hearts out. Even in the evenings, with the little loves tucked safely into their beds, their parents seemed interested only in chatting to other couples, usually about their kids. Rosie missed Monica almost as much as she did Henry. Every evening she was reminded of the mistake she'd made in coming here again and after the first awful night she gave up as soon as the show in the amphitheatre was over and went to bed early.

Back in her room after the taxi ride, Rosie changed out of her dress and put on shorts and a T-shirt, only to realise with a glance out of the window that the weather had changed for the worse. She pulled on a pair of cotton trousers and a long sleeved top, bundling up the rejected clean clothing and pushing it into a drawer. The day had clouded over and a strong sea breeze had begun to blow across the garden, moving the tall oleander bushes like crowds doing a Mexican Wave. The Turkish weather in early May was very changeable, sunshine fading easily into cloudy indifference.

She locked her room and left the key with the overworked Selma, then took the quiet path that led through the gardens towards to sea. On quieter days such as this, when the weather had driven most of the families indoors, birdsong became the prominent sound. The music from the bar was turned down and hardly noticeable, carried out to sea on the breeze. There was a nest of martins tucked behind a light fitting on one of the arches, reaching out with their tiny beaks in unison, whenever a feeding parent flew home to them. Slim sparrows were everywhere, feeding off crumbs left over from breakfast, and the jays were there again too, swooping from one low perch to the next, flashing blue, then gone again.

She had reached a fork in the path, one way leading to the pool, the other to the beach, when a manic cry rent the air. A whirling dervish of a creature came hurtling towards her, arms waving and a pink frilly hat flying from his head. He almost knocked her over in the effort of enfolding her in his arms, arms that were dressed for winter in a thick woolly jumper. Zeynel! She laughed and managed to fit in a hello between his deafening cries.

'You coming to see de show tonight?'

'Of course. I always come to see the show.'

Then he had gone and she hadn't a clue whether or not he'd heard or even needed a reply. She suspected that he had even less English than on first impression, and that the bit he'd mastered had been picked up as set phrases from guests. Although he managed to deliver the question or phrase fairly fluently, she had the feeling that he hardly ever understood the reply.

She carried on along the path, turning towards to sea and taking off her flip-flops to walk on the sand. The sea had turned to grey, flecked here and there with foam. The innocent wavelets, which had lapped so peacefully on to the beach earlier in the day, had become steely waves that rolled, broke and fizzed on the sand. She felt better out here by the sea, far from people. Long ago, the sea had claimed her parents and because of that she'd never been able to swim in it, but simply watching the water like this, with its ever-changing mood and colour, brought her no fear, just a sense of peace. She took a deep breath of fresh sea air and felt calmer, willing away the host of unwelcome thoughts that were forever threatening to overwhelm her.

She kept to the water's edge, the cool wind soothing her face and the wind tearing at her hair. She headed towards the lagoon at the far end of the resort, having to leave the sand after a while and follow the path behind drifts of pine woods that reached down to the water. The locals called the lagoon the Dead Sea, or Ölü Deniz, because its water was well known for remaining calm, even during the wildest of storms. Protected by a sand bank, there was very little movement on its calm surface to disturb the clouds of mosquitoes that buzzed and hummed above it. The area was strictly protected as a nature reserve and an air of calm surrounded it, completely different from the lively atmosphere at the other end of the beach, where the Melek stood. As Rosie paused, drinking in the peace and looking out across the water, a small tortoise dawdled across the path and disappeared into the bushes.

By the time dinner was over and the show began, the temperature had fallen further and the audience was noticeably smaller than usual. The faithful few who bothered to attend were huddled in several layers of inadequate summer knitwear and perched on thin cushions to ward off the rising chill from the stone amphitheatre steps. The cushions were being handed out by a solemn boy with a perfectly chiselled Ottoman face. Rosie remembered seeing noble features like his in art books and museums. He reminded her of the well known painting of one of the sultans; Süleyman the Magnificent.

Someone trotted down the steps behind her and interrupted her reverie, perching briefly by her side. She gave the newcomer a polite smile, thinking it was another hotel guest finding a seat, before realising that it was Berkant, dressed once more in his clown costume. The costume looked even more faded and damaged than ever, a few of the buttons hanging by a single thread. Berkant had been absent from the animation team so far this season, visiting his family in Marmaris and, despite everything, she was glad to see him back. Another familiar face.

'Monica says hello,' she added after they'd exchanged the customary hugs and fond greetings. Actually, Monica had said no such thing; the message she'd given her friend to deliver had been far ruder, but Rosie decided to edit it a bit. He looked confused for a moment, obviously thrown by the name, and Rosie began to wish she'd edited nothing out. Then he collected himself and smiled ruefully.

'Her emails stopped,' he muttered with a straight face.

'That's funny. That's what she said about yours.'

'Oh. Maybe...my address. My computer…problems...' He trailed off sheepishly.

'That's what they all say,' she stated. No hard feelings. Monica had been philosophical about it and he'd hardly been the love of her life. He waved as he descended the rest of the steps and reached the stage.

The days passed uneventfully. The animators and other staff were her main companions and after the first few days she gave up travelling around and settled down to do what she'd meant to avoid; she stayed close to the hotel and joined in with as many activities as possible. Contrary to her expectations, she was finding that a full programme of activities gave her less time to brood, whereas all those bus and taxi journeys with their hours of gazing out of windows, gave her far too much.

Even so, each of the day's many small rituals and each turning in the winding garden paths brought reminders of Henry. She had her regrets too. She knew she'd made things worse with her anger and her rejection of him at the end. Whatever he was guilty of, she'd helped to turn a blissful holiday into something sullied. Now, she couldn't even bring herself to walk past the part of the grounds where his room had been because her own spiteful words still seemed to hang in the air there. She was spending so much time regretting her own actions, in fact, that she'd almost forgotten his deception. She only knew that she missed him. She missed him terribly.

The weather warmed up again by the fourth day and she made the most of it, sunbathing by the pool. It didn't last long, unfortunately, the sun only staying around for two days before retreating once more behind a heavy bank of white cloud. It wasn't cold, despite appearances. To most winter-blighted Brits, the balmy air felt pleasantly like bathing in warm milk.

Rosie went for a few walks along the sea front, but by the sixth day of her holiday, she found that reading on her favourite sun bed by the pool had become more appealing. The cloud cover didn't really matter. Lying on the sun bed beside a gnarled olive tree, a baggy T-shirt covering her bikini and a book on her knee, she was content to day-dream. There was far less noise from the pool that day. Some of the families were still around but the children seemed to be in a quieter mood. Perhaps subdued by the cloudy weather, they swam lethargically or propelled themselves through the water on inflatables as big and bright as giant wine gums.

The animators had suspended all pool activities for the day, as was usual as soon as the weather clouded over. With their long working hours and very little time off during the season, which stretched from early May to late October, Rosie suspected they welcomed poor weather because it gave them a rest. She didn't blame them.

There was a storm brewing. Everyone could feel it. The sky was growing heavier by the minute, the great mass of cloud looming ever closer and turning from white to grey. Like smoke escaping from massive chimneys, banks of dark cloud gathered over Mount Babadağ, then drifted closer on the thick, tepid air. The children were being called out of the pool, the giant wine gums stacked inside the pool house, while parents dried the children on large multi-coloured towels and ushered them down the path towards their rooms. Only a few adults stayed behind, a few people like Rosie, who weren't troubled by the coming storm. The animators made occasional appearances, wandering forlornly around the pool to fetch coffee or bottles of water from the bar before returning to their office. Sometimes they made an effort to stay a while, sitting huddled together at the bar like wood pigeons perched on a branch, feathers fluffed up against the cold. They were dressed from scalp to toe in woolly hats, sweaters and trousers, while staring in puzzlement at the German and British guests who remained doggedly on their sun beds, dressed in next to nothing.

By three o'clock the occasional low rumblings of thunder had become an almost continuous background noise. The storm was hovering ever closer.

Perhaps she had fallen asleep for a moment, because with an uncomfortable jerk of the head Rosie came to suddenly. Her book had tumbled face-down on the ground and Zeynel was crouching to pick it up. His Marlboro gripped firmly between his chilled lips, he was trying to smooth the crumpled pages. She thanked him with a smile as he handed the book to her and he squatted down on the spreading roots of the olive tree by her side.

'Cold,' he mumbled through the Marlboro, before removing it from his mouth with one frozen hand. 'You OK? You sleeping?'

'I'm OK, thanks. You really feel the cold, don't you?' she laughed, looking at his pinched face. He only seemed to understand one word and nodded.

'Summer coming soon.' He looked down at his trainers, taking little thoughtful puffs on the cigarette. 'Where is he?' he added after a pause. The words, though spoken in an unusually quiet and hesitant way for Zeynel, seemed to boom powerfully into the silence. He raised his eyes slowly to meet hers and his glance stayed there, holding hers for what seemed an age, and during that time she went on looking back at him without knowing what to say.

'England, I suppose,' she said at last, quite uselessly.

He frowned to himself, grunting something under his breath and grinding the cigarette butt into the sandy earth between the olive roots.

'Don't like him,' he said simply. In all their conversations, however limited, she'd noticed that he always went out of his way to avoid saying anything negative about anyone, and so from him that short statement spoke volumes. Suddenly, as if embarrassed

176

he'd said too much, he stood up, removing his blue woolly hat and popping it playfully onto her head so that it fell over her eyes. He removed it again and then he'd gone, hat and all, the crushed cigarette butt by the tree roots the only clue that he'd ever been there.

It surprised her that Zeynel even remembered Henry, let alone disliked him. In a single season the staff must talk to thousands of guests. If some of them returned for a second holiday, it was only natural that they'd recognise them, but in recognising Rosie he'd remembered Henry too. He'd remembered that he didn't like him.

The sky, leaden black now, grumbled more violently, as if the tension from holding back the storm was getting too much. Sometimes the grumbling seemed to emerge from the mountains themselves, one crouching giant trading threats with another. It was easy to see how the legends of Greek Gods had come to be. The valley seemed to cower before the might of the angry sky and growling mountains. As snakes of lightning flashed and darted, it wasn't difficult to imagine them as spears hurled by displeased and vengeful gods.

The wind was joining the battle of the gods now, its fist tearing at the olive branches above Rosie's head and flinging tiny unripe fruit across the terrace. A parasol, a mere toy in the hands of the gods, flew past her and was hurled into the pool, as with a sudden cry of alarm the barmen began to dash about, stacking parasols and chairs under the wide overhanging roof of the bar.

'Rosie!' cried Süleyman the Magnificent as the rain began to descend in fat, soaking drops, 'you must come in now; it's dangerous!'

As if to illustrate his point, a mighty body of wind tore across the terrace, scraping white plastic chairs and tables along with it and tossing glass ashtrays on to the paving. A discarded newspaper released itself from a fold in one of the sun beds, separating into sheets and sailing through the air like a flock of startled gulls. A page of it came straight for Rosie as she ran for cover and she caught at it with one hand, preventing it from wrapping itself around her face.

She joined the others seeking refuge from the storm under the wide thatched roof of the bar. She flung down her bags and rubbed at her limbs with a damp towel, dressing in a hurry. She had to admit she was cold now.

'Coffee?' Süleyman was anticipating her response, already pouring the hot liquid into one of the thickly potted, white cups. She accepted it gratefully. It was cheerful around the bar, bonhomie developing easily in the small group of escapees from the storm. There was a lot of laughter, the German and British holiday makers determined to make the most of it. Among them sat Berkant and Zeynel who, despite their pinched faces and shivering bodies, were trying to laugh it off. Only Süleyman the Magnificent remained solemn as he calmly and efficiently worked his way around the bar, serving hot drinks.

The building, having no front wall, offered only the minimum of protection against the weather. Its overhanging thatch did its best to keep the storm out, but couldn't stop the sudden gusts of wind that carried bursts of rain into the shelter like the breaking of mighty waves, spraying everyone in the process. Outside, the surface of the pool had become a frothing, wild sea, water rocking and spilling over the sides as another chair skidded into it, carrying abandoned towels and sun cream bottles as it went.

Berkant had ducked down behind the bar and was doing something with the music system. Abruptly, the background medley of 1990s hits that had been drowned out by the storm was replaced by the insistent, familiar opening bars of the Club Dance music. There was a chorus of groaning around the bar, a few laughs and a few curses, but then, quite unbelievably, a few people began to dance in the confined space between the crisps stand and the ice cream cabinet. Berkant was leading five Brits and a German in the dance, their jerky, restricted movements

178

silhouetted against the background curtain of falling rain. Rosie was laughing out loud, loving the silliness of it.

The storm continued to rage, rain lashing down and the wind tossing leaves, olives and small branches under the cover of the bar. Much of the wooden bar top was wet now, the ground soaked and covered in debris. The remnant of newspaper she'd caught earlier was still lying on the bar top, completely water logged and stuck to the wooden surface. Idly, Rosie peeled at its edges and picked it up, some of the soaked paper tearing off as she moved it. It was an English paper, but it was impossible to tell any more which one. Süleyman offered her another coffee and she accepted with a smile while making some remark to Berkant. They were laughing at Zeynel who was going through the motions of the dance, listless and chilly. He had found a straw sombrero, probably something that had blown in, and had tied it over his woolly hat, the strings secured tightly under his chin. Rosie still held the soaked newspaper between her fingers and had begun to make a ball of it to toss into the bin, but as the ink blurred and the photographs merged in the screwed up mass, something caught her eye. Hastily, she tried to unravel some of the paper. A woman's face filled the lower left hand quarter of the page. It wasn't a good picture, but it was good enough.

Her heart gave a slow, twisting lurch as she stared at the remains of the picture, fixated on the woman's face. Antonia's face. This was it then. It had come; confirmation.

Had she still been expecting it? She didn't know, couldn't think, her brain jamming like a crashing hard drive. Her eyes were still scanning what was left of the crumpled mess of paper in her hands. She could hardly make out the tiny section of print beneath the photo, but she read enough to learn that a Norfolk woman, Antonia Grey had been found dead by the river. Rosie felt the blood leave her face as she allowed the sodden ball of paper to fall to the ground.

The date had been missing from the paper, torn away at some point during its destruction, but the English newspapers on sale here were always at least a day old. Added to that, it had probably been hanging around for days, passed around from person to person, so it was impossible to tell when all this had happened.

She was staring blindly ahead, trying to take in what the paper had told her. Antonia was dead. Antonia had been killed. Someone had killed Antonia. Around her the storm raged with unabated violence. The music had stopped and she became gradually aware of someone calling her name. It came again, then again, but still she could not respond.

'Rosie!' Zeynel was sitting next to her on one of the high bar stools, still looking miserably cold. She hadn't even noticed him pulling up the stool. Rain, great volumes of it, were sweeping under the shelter and had drenched one side of the oval shaped bar. The previously spread out group had gathered into a tighter huddle under the one remaining dry section of the shelter, the area where she'd been sitting the whole time. She looked around her to see everyone packed tightly together, looking far less amused now. The laughter had died away, leaving only the sounds of rain on the thatch and the smashing of stray bottles and glasses by the poolside. The downpour was still so intense that they could hardly see the far side of the pool.

'Rosie, are you OK?' Zeynel tried again.

'Yes,' she smiled unconvincingly, making an effort to speak, but he continued to look at her with curiosity. There was no way she could explain to him what she'd just read, so she attempted another smile and took a sip of the coffee that Süleyman had placed in front of her on the wet bar top.

She could never have explained to Zeynel that the man he did not like had just re-entered her life. A year after losing him, and in the very same place, she had the strange feeling that Henry Blanchard might just have walked back into her life. It would have been hard to explain why; she just felt that it was true.

Henry had blown back into her life in an Anatolian tempest via a page from an out of date newspaper.

Chapter Nineteen

Rosie. Saturday 16th May

'Oh, come on! You can't pull out now!' Monica was standing crossly on the doorstep, arms folded. It was already three o'clock and the concert was due to start at half past. She'd wanted to get there early and find a good place in the garden for their fold-up chairs, but that was hardly going to happen now. She'd been looking forward to this for ages, apparently.

'Really not in the mood,' Rosie was muttering, 'Didn't get back until gone midnight and I can't stop thinking about...you know.'

'Come on, it'll cheer you up. Anyway, there's nothing you can do to help matters. Best thing you can do right now is to stop worrying and think of something else. Have you got a jacket? You'll need an umbrella too. Weather looks threatening. I've got the picnic; you can pay me back later for your share...'

'But I feel involved, Monica. After all, I dreamed it, didn't I? It can't be a coincidence. The local paper says it happened by the river, just where I dreamed it did.'

'Please get your jacket, Rosie. We'll be late. I've got your bag. Where's the house key? You are not involved. You had a dream. That's all. You need to stop thinking about it. You've become obsessed.'

'Suppose I have...'

'Please, Rosie. The key?'

'It's here. All right, I'm coming.'

By the time they had walked along the Brink to the National Trust house, the Blues Brothers tribute band had already started proceedings and was well into the second number. The lady standing at the front gate of Peckover House looked weary. She was holding a list in her hand, her eyes scanning down it to see how many more ticket holders had not yet arrived. She was down to the last few stragglers and looked like she needed to sit down. Seeing the girls, she greeted them with a cheery smile.

'Looks like rain,' she observed philosophically as she checked their tickets, 'Good thing you've got your umbrellas.'

'Will the concert end early if it does?' asked Rosie, not sure whether she wanted it to or not.

'No,' smiled the National Trust lady, 'In all the years we've been holding these outdoor events it's rained more often than not, and everything just carries on. The band's under cover, at least!'

The girls walked through a side gate, through the courtyard and on to the back lawn where a marquee had been set up. Two men in black with bowler hats were dancing and singing beneath its shelter, in front of an audience of happy, smiling people who sat on an assortment of blankets and fold-up chairs. Some of them had even brought tables, setting out wine glasses and cutlery and really getting into the spirit of the thing. Most people were already raiding their picnic baskets, wine glugging merrily into glasses or paper cups. Finding a space near the back, under the arching stems of white lilac, Monica and Rosie set up their chairs and opened their own basket of goodies. Monica had been to Morrisons earlier, making up a fine picnic of king prawns, crab claws and filled rolls, and she presented it proudly, popping the prosecco cork and pouring the effervescent liquid into two plastic stemmed glasses. Rosie had to crawl under the seat in front to rescue the cork, which she dropped into the basket.

'Cheers! Here's to forgetting things you can't do anything about!'

'Cheers!' replied Rosie, but didn't comment on the other bit.

The air was damp and chilly, the sky an ominous shade of grey. It was a stark contrast to the climate Rosie had just left behind. Even before the storm, the air in Turkey had been warm; here it was distinctly cool and everyone was bundled up in jackets and trousers.

Strangely, though, and quite unexpectedly, Rosie began to enjoy herself. The music was cheerful and loud without spoiling the atmosphere of the garden. There was a heady scent of lilac filling the air and in the flower beds that bordered the lawn shrubs were swelling towards their summertime fullness, flowers bursting through once tight buds. Despite her preoccupations with the Blanchard household, Rosie found herself lulled into a sense of harmony and restfulness. The old, beautiful and scented garden felt as if it had always been there, its magic lulling her into peace. Perhaps it was just the prosecco talking, maybe more, but whatever it was, Monica had been right. This really was the best way to take her mind off things.

It wasn't long before people were on their feet and dancing, filling the area of lawn just in front of the marquee with movement and laughter. Monica turned the bottle upside-down to confirm that it really was empty and then leapt up to join the dancing. Rosie smiled as she watched. Some of the change she'd witnessed in Monica while they'd both been in Turkey that first time had been long lasting and it was good. Monica was waving at her to join the dancing throng of adults and children, young and old. Abandoning her half eaten salmon roll, she happily obliged.

They were still dancing when the rain started; large, cold drops that landed on Rosie's scalp and ran down through the roots of her hair on to her forehead. There was a general groan of disappointment, but the dancing went on at first, children continuing to skip around the lawn in their candy coloured summer clothes. Then the rain intensified, showing that it meant business, falling fast and soaking everyone on the lawn. The dancers ran back to their seats, seeking the cover of flimsy umbrellas which they clutched valiantly, covering their rickety chairs and damp picnic baskets. Sheltered by their marquee, the band continued without a pause and the music and laughter went on, groups huddling together under umbrellas and sharing the last of the food.

Huddled into her waterproof jacket, drops of rain escaping the umbrella and dribbling down her neck, Rosie was enjoying the eccentricity of it all. It was so very British, this carrying on despite the weather. Inevitably, it reminded her of the Turkish storm, which of course led her thoughts back to Antonia and Henry, and her mood faltered again.

The rain was still falling as they walked home, the concert having ended promptly at six o'clock. Rosie was tired, still recovering from the long journey home the day before, and she turned down Monica's suggestion of going out again later. Piles of unwashed laundry still littered the floor of the spare bedroom where she'd unpacked her case earlier, and something had to be done about it.

Alone in the house, she scooped up the washing from the carpet, carrying it downstairs to feed into the washing machine. She squeezed laundry gel out of the almost empty bottle, pressing buttons to set the machine gushing into life, and all the time the gloom that had hovered nearby all day was closing in, staking its claim on her.

It was impossible not to think of Henry and all that he must be going through. His life with Antonia may not have been perfect, but the shock of what had happened to her must still be enormous. In the few days since Rosie had read the wet newspaper in Turkey, she'd been thinking of him even more than ever. She'd been hoping that her dreams might grant her a glimpse of him, that they might even take her to him.

But it hadn't happened. Just when she needed to travel in her sleep, she couldn't. Nothing had come to her but sleeplessness and the old enemy; the nightmare of being pulled down in the water, seaweed dragging at her ankles and refusing to let go.

She found her Mickey Mouse mug and made some instant coffee, going to sit on her favourite window seat. She looked out at the wet garden, watching as rain drops formed and swelled on the tips of yew branches, quivering in the breeze before finally letting go and falling to blend with the glistening soil below. She was glad to see the garden again after a week away, glad to be home in many ways, but a stray thought that had come to her while making the coffee kept returning, disturbing her peaceful view from the window. As she'd been pouring boiling water over the coffee grains in her mug, she'd recalled something from long ago and now she couldn't stop thinking about it.

As a seventeen year old who was beginning to search for information on the Out of Body Experiences she was having, she had come across an interesting book in the public library. The book explained that it was possible to induce an Out of Body Experience while conscious. Apparently, she could leave her body while awake and control where she went and what she did during this time. She'd borrowed the book, reading it over and over again. After a while, she'd felt confident enough to try some of the exercises in the book for herself. She'd mentioned this to no one. Her parents had long since departed and her grandmother would have been horrified by such foolishness. Eventually, one afternoon while her grandmother was out of the house, Rosie had begun to practise the techniques explained in the book.

At first, nothing had happened, but she'd refused to give up, trying every afternoon when she had the opportunity. It had taken months of practice, but very gradually, aided by the natural psychic ability shared by many adolescents, she had begun to see small signs of success.

One rainy afternoon during her usual practice session, she'd felt that she'd succeeded in freeing her arms from her body. With delight and astonishment she'd watched her spirit arms as they moved quite independently of her other, earth-bound arms, which still rested by her side. It had lasted no more than a few seconds, her sudden success startling her and bringing her arms right back to where they'd started. She'd collected herself and tried again, gradually achieving more and more. Then at last, several weeks later, she'd managed to free her whole body. For a few moments she'd seemed able to float above herself, before panic pulled her back.

She'd begun to understand at that stage that panic, coupled with the mind's instinctive fear of allowing the spirit to leave the body, was the most difficult obstacle to overcome. (There was no such problem while a person slept, of course, since the controlling conscious mind was resting and the spirit was freer to move around.) After that, she'd disciplined herself and learned to master her nerves, struggling and willing herself on. Several weeks of practice later, she'd found that she could move around the room at will while her motionless body remained stretched out on the bed. When she'd wanted to, returning was easy. She'd only have to think of it and she was back, safe in her body again.

Now, at the age of thirty-one and not having practised for years, would she still be able to do it? She finished her coffee and thought of all the reasons for not trying. What if she couldn't get back? What if...

She quickly ran out of reasons for not trying, acknowledging that the worst thing that could happen would be that nothing happened at all. She desperately wished to try. In fact, she wanted to go one step further than in the past. She wanted to see if she could visit Henry. She knew she couldn't expect too much after so many years without practice and her desperation to succeed might be the very thing to prevent it. It was a bit like wanting to dream a particular dream and wishing too hard for it before you went to sleep. For some reason, wanting a thing to happen too much could block it altogether.

She swilled out her coffee mug in the sink and unplugged the telephone socket, switching off her mobile. She just had to hope that no one rang the doorbell. She settled herself on the sofa, trying to empty her mind of all her worries. She took deep, slow breaths, feeling her body relax and slump on the cushions of the sofa. She watched the shadows on the wall opposite, observing the play of light as the breeze moved damp fronds of buddleia outside, projecting a puppet show on to the wall. Her eyes closed, the shadows continuing to play in her mind as she hovered on the brink of sleep. It was tempting to let go altogether and catch up on her sleep, but she resisted it, urging her spirit body to separate, to fly. Her body felt heavy as her thoughts concentrated themselves, willing with all her might for her spirit to break free.

But nothing happened. For endless minutes nothing happened at all. She stood up, walked around the room for a while and told herself to be patient, to try again.

She settled once more on the sofa, watching the patterns on the wall, then closed her eyes, still resisting sleep. This time, the procedure seemed less difficult and she was determined not to give up. She concentrated hard, keeping her thoughts focussed. And then, refusing to give in to surprise or nerves, she became aware that one foot, then the other, had freed themselves from her body. She could feel them in their new positions as gradually she lifted the whole of one leg, aware as it, too, became free. Willing herself on, she felt the rest of her spirit body pulling away, emerging from the physical body that did not want to let go.

And then the wind tunnel hit her. The sudden roaring of noise that engulfed her, buffeting her with its sheer volume, was totally unexpected. It came at the very moment of separation from her body, immersing her in deafening, howling wind, as if in a tunnel. Like a storm that she could hear but not feel, it was overwhelming and relentless, and an alarm sounded in her mind, panic setting in. And then she was back right where she'd started, lying on the sofa.

She sighed in frustration. She had forgotten about the wind tunnel, as she used to call it, that almighty sound of roaring wind that had always bombarded her at the moment of separation. She should have been prepared for it. She fidgeted a little to make herself comfortable on the sofa and yet again went through the preliminaries.

Once more she relaxed, guiding herself through the various stages until she reached the point where separation was imminent. With her mind she urged and pushed, willing herself on with new determination. Then it came again, that sudden loud whooshing, like countless giant fans blowing all at once in a tunnel. It enveloped her, almost overwhelmed her, but this time she remained calm, allowing the separation from her body to complete.

And then, quite suddenly, she was free. Below her, her resting body lay peacefully on the sofa. She could see her face as if sleeping, turned slightly to the side. She felt no fear at all, only peace and an increasing sense of euphoria. The ceiling was right above her, but it was no real obstacle. She told herself where she wanted to be and the ceiling was no longer there. She was flying. She was free and happy and far away from the room where her body waited.

The place she found herself in was silent, full of shadows. The curtains were drawn and the atmosphere in the house was pervaded by a strong sense of misery.

She was upstairs on the landing, where the walls were painted pale lemon and decorated with family photos in neat frames. She reached out towards the banister rails but could feel nothing. She moved tentatively forward, heading for one of the doors that led from the landing. Through the half opened door she could see little of the room that lay beyond; just a darkened, curtained place with a wardrobe door left ajar and a dirty plate abandoned on the carpet. Avoiding the plate, she moved into the room.

A man lay on the bed, fully clothed. He looked haggard, a scrappy beard of more than one day's growth darkening the lines of his face. His eyes were closed. A glass of brown liquid was still clutched in his hand, though it looked forgotten, and she wanted to reach forward and put it on the side table for him. A huge feeling of compassion filled her, yet she could not reach him. She moved further into the room and tried to speak, but the words would not carry; she could only stand and look at him.

There was a flicker beneath his eyelids and then slowly his eyes opened, unfocussed at first. Gradually, his gaze was lifted, moving towards the space before the curtains where she stood. She followed his eyes with her own, reminding herself that he wouldn't be able to see her, but then he was frowning, as if he were struggling to make something out. He blinked and suddenly he was looking right at her.

For a moment, just for a heartbeat, his eyes looked into hers. Awareness, understanding and recognition were all there and in that moment he seemed to collect himself and become again the man she remembered.

It was just a look. It was just one moment of eyes meeting, but the connection felt so strong, like a wire holding them together. And then it was over, Rosie being pulled abruptly back.

As if by an elastic band stretched beyond its normal tolerance, she was yanked back into her waiting body, looking at the ceiling above her own sofa.

Chapter Twenty

Bruce. Monday 18th May.

The ten days that had passed since Antonia's body had been found by the riverside had felt more like a month. Bruce had hardly been home at all, his seventeen year old son pretty much running their household by himself. Bruce's waking hours had been taken up with keeping an eye on Henry and working late to catch up lost time. Fortunately, his new boss was the understanding sort, otherwise the job would have hit the buffers right from the start.

It had taken days for the shock to sink in. Antonia, for all her faults, had been so full of life, with so much living yet to do. They had first found out what had happened when the police turned up at Henry's house that Friday night. Some unfortunate dog walker had found Antonia, alerted by Arnold, who was running around on his own, trailing his lead and in a right state. The police had been all kindness and consideration, apparently. After they'd left, Henry had called Bruce. Bruce had never seen a man so bewildered, so shaken. Just to see him, anyone would have believed that he'd cared for the old girl after all. Arnold, home at last from his ordeal, had apparently suffered no loss of appetite and was chomping his way through meaty chunks from his favourite bowl. Henry had been sitting in the old Windsor chair in the kitchen, caressing the dog's back. His eyes were glazed and Bruce had scarcely been able to get a coherent word out of him.

During that first weekend nothing much could be done except talk about the same thing, over and over again. The cronies had flocked round to help, of course, all of them meaning well, but it had been Bruce who had taken charge, handing out little jobs to them like the scraps of meat he found to placate the mournful Arnold. They'd all tried to cheer Henry up, offering him meals at the pub in a hearty, 'got to eat old boy, keep your strength up, you know,' sort of way, but Henry had politely refused. It was all Bruce could do to get him to eat anything at all. In his ham-fisted, well intentioned way, he'd made up all sorts of man-snacks in the kitchen, most of them accompanied by the smell of burning and loads of tomato sauce. Henry appreciated all of this, Bruce knew, but could eat hardly any of it.

On the Monday the police had visited again. Bruce had had to go to work, but as far as he could understand, rather than offering condolences this time, they were asking quite a lot of questions. Obviously, they had to find out who'd done this to Antonia, but Henry had been surprised by the depth of some of their questions. Apparently, they'd also been asking for any witnesses to come forward, who might have been on or near the riverside that Friday, but as yet no one was providing any clues. Henry had last seen Antonia that Friday morning before he'd left for work. He'd half expected her to call in just before lunch, as she sometimes did, but she hadn't shown up. The assumed time of death was a bit vague, thought to be between late morning and mid-afternoon.

During the week, the police investigation had seemed to gather speed. Julia had phoned Bruce in panic on the Wednesday, his mobile going off while he was working under a 1980's John Deere tractor, his hands black with grease and dirt. He'd ignored the phone at first, but when it kept on ringing he'd cursed roundly and wriggled out on his back, managing to bang his head on the engine sump in the process and adding another layer of grease to his already thickened hair. By the time he'd staggered to his feet, the mobile had stopped ringing of course. He'd phoned her back in some irritation; unusual for him, but his mood had soon softened when he'd heard her anxious voice. The police were there at the office, she'd told him, having a good look round. Without warning, they had apparently blundered their way in, asking a load of questions and were snooping around Henry's room.

After that, it had become clear that their chief suspect was Henry. They'd visited him again at home and continued to bother Julia at work. He'd remained at home all that first week, but had decided by the next Monday to return to the office and try to return to something like normality. Normality, of course, was out of the question, but there was nothing useful he could do at home. He couldn't start the funeral arrangements until Antonia's body was released for burial and that didn't look like being any time soon.

On that first Monday of Henry's return to work, ten days after Antonia's death, Bruce went into work early. He put in a few hours to finish a job, before managing to slip out and call into Henry's office. Julia, he thought, might need some support, this being Henry's first day back and all that. From outside, the neatly swept pavement and sparkling windows gave the impression that all within was normal. It was only when Bruce entered reception and the leaden atmosphere that filled it, that the change became obvious.

Julia, grey faced and exhausted, sat behind the long desk as usual, but her customary welcoming smile was missing. She offered him a watery, toned-down greeting, lifting her glance slightly from the file she was attempting to work on.

'He's in his office, Bruce. He went in at nine and I haven't seen him since. He refuses coffee and there's no way he's going to be able to see any of his clients. I've just phoned everyone in the diary for the second week running to postpone their appointments.'

He gave her an encouraging smile, pushing back his hair from his eyes. His hand came away loaded with grease from that morning's work on a Massey Ferguson. His face was probably mucky too; he ought to have checked.

'How about the locum? Did you get hold of him?' Someone had to start looking after the firm's clients while Henry was unable to do so, which was why Bruce had been encouraging Julia to call in the locum. He was a neighbouring financial advisor who had been on their books for years; emergency cover for times like this.

'At last, yes. He'll take any new business that comes from seeing our clients, of course. It worries me. Once they do business with the locum, will they ever come back?' she appealed.

'Of course they will, love! They'll understand. After all he's done for them, all these years, I should damn well hope so!'

She didn't reply, but he reached across the desk to touch her shoulder with his cleaner hand and went through the door to Henry's office without bothering to knock.

Henry looked up with neither surprise nor greeting, peering at his visitor through sleepless eyes.

'Thank God it's you,' Henry muttered, 'Thought it was that thug, Wayne Crisp again.'

'Has he been here today already?' asked Bruce in amazement. Henry just nodded drearily. Detective Inspector Wayne Crisp and Detective Sergeant Penny Lunberry were becoming uncomfortably regular visitors.

'What did they want this time?'

'They were quizzing poor Julia again.'

'For...' Bruce shook his head, 'She was upset enough about what they were asking her last week...but never mind them for a minute...Julia says she's been trying to bring you coffee all morning, so why don't you just let her? It'll do you a bit of good at least. Don't suppose you had any breakfast, either? Thought not...'

He opened the door and beckoned to Julia, who within a minute had presented her boss with a large cup of fairly fresh coffee and a plate of biscuits. Bruce had a cup too and drank his thirstily while Henry played with the spoon on his saucer.

'I know she could be a bit much,' Henry was muttering, 'but who would do that to her? She had so many friends. She was hard going, yet I never heard of anyone who disliked her as such, at least not enough to kill the poor...'

194

'I know, mate. I'm so sorry. I can't offer anything in the way of explanation, but I do know there's no point in you sitting around like this. You need to eat. Come on, let me take you down to the pub and get you an All Day Breakfast.'

'After that burger and chips you turned to cinders last night, how could I possibly still be hungry?' Henry grinned in a brief attempt to lighten the gloom and Bruce nodded philosophically.

Henry began to rise from his chair, relieved to have some distraction. His coffee was still only partially drunk, the biscuits left untouched. Bruce walked to the door and opened it cheerfully.

'Julia!' he called, 'We're going out for...'

But the person who filled the doorway was definitely not Julia. The stranger was enormous; big boned and fleshy, with an ill-humoured face that sprouted something between a weedy beard and neglected stubble. His dark hair was greasy and his suit looked two sizes too small. Behind him trotted a small woman with straw-like hair that was cut into such a severe bob that her round face looked like it was wearing a helmet.

'You're back,' observed Henry pointlessly.

'That's correct, Mr Blanchard. Can we speak alone?' The words, delivered with a strong Norfolk accent that might have been attractive in anyone else, clattered out at high speed.

Henry grimaced, pulling himself together.

'I'd like Mr Ryan to stay, Detective Inspector. This is Bruce Ryan, an old friend and client of mine, and these officers, Bruce, are Detective Inspector Crisp and Detective Sergeant Lunberry.' Despite the grim circumstances, Bruce had to admire the way Henry was dealing with the situation, refusing to let this man take total control. The man nodded his curt consent. He's right, Bruce thought. This bloke *is* a thug.

'Mr Blanchard, we were just passing and thought you'd like to be kept up to date with our investigation.'

'That's very efficient of you. Second time this morning.'

'True, but things are moving along nicely and I'm sure you're as keen as we are for Miss Grey's murderer to be caught. By the way, I couldn't help noticing earlier that there's still no picture of Miss Grey on your desk. Still shoved in the drawer, is it?'

'What?' uttered Henry, obviously perplexed, 'Ah, you mean...' He opened the desk drawer, fumbling amongst papers, old diaries and bits of stationery until his fingers closed around the heavy silver frame of Antonia's photograph. He retrieved it with an irritated look and put it back in its old position, next to the picture of his dad. 'I can't remember when it went in the drawer. Honestly, does it matter?'

Bruce noticed that Henry was looking flustered, the veneer of professional cool wearing thin.

'Of course it doesn't matter, Mr Blanchard,' DI Crisp replied with a barely disguised smirk, 'It just seems curious to me that the picture of your dearly departed partner in life has been so casually discarded. But, that aside for a moment, we wanted to bring you up to date. Unfortunately, we've still had no response from the public to our appeal for any witnesses to the murder, but there's plenty of time yet. Regarding the cars, Miss Grey's vehicle has been looked at by our forensic team and you should be aware that tests are now being carried out on your own car. We should have the results very shortly now...'

He paused, looking meaningfully at Henry, as if he expected him to speak. He didn't.

'What?' voiced Bruce instead, 'Why do you need...Henry, why didn't you say? How did you get here? I could have...'

'Hire car,' Henry replied, ignoring DI Crisp, 'Didn't see the point in mentioning it. I'm sure my Jaguar will be back very soon.'

'But what has your car got to do with it? It was only Antonia who went to the river bank, wasn't it?' Bruce was sounding worried.

'Yes,' Henry assured him, 'she liked the place for some reason.'

'So,' said the inspector, stating the obvious, 'when we have the results we'll be back.' He nodded at the sergeant as they left the room.

Henry and Bruce watched the retreating bulk of the inspector, followed by the diminutive figure of the silent sergeant without wishing them farewell.

'So what was all that about?' asked Bruce, flabbergasted. 'That visit achieved nothing whatsoever!'

'Apart from getting under my skin. So you see where their investigation is heading,' observed Henry, 'They think I did it and they're trying to unnerve me. They've poked around the house and the office and now they're running tests on the cars and some other bits they think they've found. What next, do you think?'

Bruce just shook his head in exasperation.

'Come on, let's go and get some breakfast.'

Julia watched them leave, looking on with a deepening sense of melancholy. She'd missed nothing of the conversation with the police, having listened at the door. She followed the two men with her eyes, watching them through the window as they drove away in Bruce's car. Then she went on filing; file after file, until it was done.

The Dog and Duck was the best choice within easy distance for an All Day Breakfast. Fortunately, its landlady Jeanette Radley was absent that morning, so the men could eat in peace without Jeanette's well meaning but exhausting sympathy and chatter.

Bruce had been uncomfortably aware that the police investigation had been homing in on Henry, but the thought of two visits from them in one morning really alarmed him. He wanted to stay off that subject for a while, though. He was keen to see whether a plate of sausages, greasy bacon, mushrooms and huge fried eggs would do anything to tempt his old mate back into eating. Amazingly, there was only a moment's hesitation before Henry's knife attacked one of the sausages and soon he was really getting the hang of it, hoovering the lot up in record time.

'Blimey mate. And there was me thinking you were off your grub! Or was it just my cinder-burgers?' Henry didn't answer, apparently deep in thought.

'I need to talk to Julia,' Henry said at last as he polished off the last of the mushrooms, 'She was very upset on Friday. She phoned me at home and I can't have been much help to her. She thought she was being disloyal, but I tried to tell her it wasn't true. She'd only told the police the truth and the worst they can do is waste their own time, trying to make something of it.'

'So...what did they ask her? What was she so worried about?'

'Apparently, they wanted to know what sort of life insurance policy I had on Antonia. In their view, if I stand to gain anything on her death it gives me a motive. They put poor old Julia on the spot and demanded that she showed them our file; Antonia's and mine. Of course, she didn't really need to look at it. She'd only finished the work on it a few months ago.'

'So...she had no choice, then? She told them?'

'Of course. Straight forward policies...we each took out £750,000 on each other.'

'Blimey, mate! Does sound a lot.'

'Nothing unusual about it. It was designed to pay off the mortgage and provide whoever survived the other with a bit extra...more important if she'd survived me, of course, because she didn't work. As it happens, it's going to be pretty useful for me, however callous that sounds, because the business is going to need some injection after I've let it slide like this...'

'Yeah, I suppose...'

'But, apparently the questions became worse after that. Julia hadn't even had chance to put the file away before
198

they started asking her about my relationship with Antonia, whether we got on well together, that sort of rubbish.'

Bruce shook his head and took a gulp of beer, pushing aside his empty plate.

'Julia would never tell them anything...'

'True...and the poor girl did her best. Apparently, she just stuck to the point that I kept my work and home life separate and that she wasn't privy to how good or bad my relationship with Antonia was.'

'Good girl.'

'I agree. They'd have made something of that, wouldn't they? There I was, arguing day and night with Antonia, lured by the temptation of £750,000 in cash. All I had to do was bash her over the head.'

'Blimey, mate. You can see where they're coming from...'

'Thanks, Bruce, thanks a million. Even a Neanderthal like Wayne Crisp needs better "evidence" than that.' He emphasised "evidence" with a twiddle of his two fore-fingers, moving them like tiny windmills, 'Oh, and I nearly forgot. They also found Antonia's old golf clubs in the office cupboard. They were still in there ready for the charity shop. I hadn't got round to taking them and DS Lunberry seemed to think one of them could be the murder weapon, for goodness sake. They've taken them away for testing.'

Bruce shook his head.

'Good luck to them. They've got nothing and are trying to put the wind up you. I mean, all that about Antonia's photo being in the drawer! They're piling on the pressure, hoping they'll panic you into giving yourself away. When they realise there's no more to find, they'll give up. In the mean time, I think you're doing a good job with them, mate...right, must go! I'll drop you back at the office and get back to work while I still have a job. I'll drop round and see you later at home, OK?'

'Don't worry about me, Bruce. I really appreciate all you're doing, but your lad Jimmy might like some company for a change. Oh, and I meant to say earlier, either you've grown a quick moustache or there's a great slick of engine grease under your nose.'

'Thanks mate. You might have mentioned it earlier,' grunted Bruce, taking a blackened handkerchief from his pocket and wiping it roughly over his face, 'and just remember, all they've got is a set of old golf clubs and a life insurance policy.'

'And my car. Don't forget my car. And meanwhile, whoever killed Antonia is getting away with it. Absolutely bloody marvellous!'

By the time Bruce reached home, there was a note from Jimmy on the kitchen worktop. He'd done his homework, apparently, and had gone round to his mate's. Normal for a seventeen year old, Bruce supposed, but he knew it was high time he spoke to the lad, made sure things were OK. After a quick plateful of tinned spaghetti on toast, he dropped in to see Henry again because, despite Henry's protestations, he felt he ought to.

When he arrived, his friend was in a far more relaxed state. Certainly, the amount of whisky he was getting down him was helping, but it was more to do with the fact that he'd had no further visits from the police that afternoon. The cat was snoozing peacefully on Henry's lap, her small paws kneading his rounded stomach as occasionally she broke into a purring expression of contentment. Arnold sat by his master's feet, his face a picture of mournfulness. The dog really had been Antonia's greatest fan, thought Bruce.

He was on his way out when he noticed Antonia's glasses case on the living room window sill. He'd seen it there many times before, of course, during the ten long days since her death, but now it occurred to him that it might be easier for Henry if there were fewer reminders of her lying around. Not surprisingly, Antonia's things were all over the house, but especially in the kitchen. They were

200

just as she'd left them; a white jacket hanging on the back of a chair, her packet of sweeteners beside the teapot and a paperback book lying face down close to the sink, still opened at the page she'd reached. Henry had been too sunken in gloom all this time to take much notice of these things, but Bruce wondered whether the time had come to remove them. Things were hard enough for his old mate as it was.

He called out a farewell, glancing back into the sitting room. Henry, Polly the cat and Arnold the retriever were all dozing peacefully. Bruce smiled, quietly picking up the sweeteners, jacket, book and glasses case. He also removed a photo he'd spotted at the last moment, of Antonia with Arnold at Christmas, but on second thoughts put it back on the kitchen window sill where he'd found it. After that morning's scene with the police making so much fuss about the photo in Henry's desk drawer, he thought this picture had better be left alone. The other things could go, though. He opened the door of the stuffed hall cupboard and pushed them inside, out of Henry's way.

Chapter Twenty One

So it really had come to this. They had actually done it, brought him in, arrested him.

Staring at the opposite wall of his cell, he was having trouble getting his thoughts in order. The last few hours had gone by in a haze of confusion, anger, fear and indignation, yet still there were moments when he felt oddly detached, as if he were watching someone else in a bad TV sketch.

He had always been cautious by nature, always making sure he stayed well within the law. He was careful not to exceed speed limits too blatantly and to declare every last morsel of income on his tax returns. His only real transgressions in life had been his numerous affairs, which although they'd been sins against Antonia rather than the state, they'd still made him uneasy. Perhaps this had added to the thrill of cheating but it had still worried him deep down. And look where all that caution and law abiding had brought him!

To this hole. It may have been a newly built facility on the outskirts of King's Lynn, but no amount of disinfectant could ever get rid of the smell of the place; yesterday's fear and all it threw up. If he paced the cell from back to front he could manage four paces before reaching the white wall opposite. From side to side it was even shorter; just a couple of paces between the hard shelf of a bed with its thin blue mattress and the wall with the loo attached.

At one end of the cell was a heavily glazed window, its row of narrow panes letting in a pitifully dull glimmer of light. In one top corner of the cell was a curved light fitting, plain and inoffensive, but from the opposite corner the eye of a CCTV camera watched. Apparently, they could listen now too if they wanted, and if he needed attention, instead of yelling out or thumping on the door, as they did in all the old police dramas, he could speak to them through a new-fangled electronic thing. For added nosiness, there was also a good old fashioned window in the door. Just beneath it someone had started to write 'bastard' with God only knew what, but had only managed to reach the second 'a' before giving up. That half-formed word really irritated Henry, adding to the tension that was building up inside him as he whiled away the long hours. The word kept catching his eye, however hard he tried to reposition himself not to see it. If he could have found anything to carve with he would gladly have finished the word himself.

His arrival at the Police Investigation Centre in Saddlebow had been even more humiliating than being walked out of his office that lunch time in front of the terrified Julia. They'd brought him here in the back of one of their cars. Then he'd been photographed, his DNA recorded by taking a mouth swab, and his finger prints captured using some sort of modern gizmo. Even worse, they'd taken his personal possessions and locked them away in a box. His wallet, his watch, even his belt for heaven's sake, had gone, so now he couldn't tell what time it was or how long he'd been here. That was one of the worst things for him, not being able to tell how time was passing.

He was still struggling with the fact that they thought he had killed Antonia; that he'd murdered his own life partner, wife, call her what you will. To be suspected of doing such a thing, a thing he knew he was absolutely incapable of, was bad enough, but to be arrested in front of Julia and then locked up while they made up their minds how to interrogate him...how had he let it come to this?

He'd been asked if he wished to speak to a solicitor, but his mind had gone blank. Then he'd remembered Rob Searles, the larger-than-life lawyer who'd dealt with a few business matters for him a few years ago. He seemed to remember that Rob had a partner in the firm who dealt with defence and that sort of thing. The custody sergeant had known whom he meant and the phone call had been made. Then he'd been asked if he wished to inform someone of his arrest, but there was no one he could think of. Julia was already aware of the situation and would tell Bruce, whom he knew would see to things at home for him. In the end he'd phoned William, his brother in Dorset. It had been a peculiar conversation. The brothers rarely communicated these days and William had just sounded stunned. Hardly surprising, really.

While the arrival of Kevin Green of Green, Searles and Pick was awaited, Henry had been left in his cell. Time had stretched on and on, feeling like hours, before finally he'd been taken to a small, bland room where he'd encountered Mr Green for the first time. His heart had sunk at the sight of him. With pale eyes that darted behind smeared spectacle lenses, putty coloured skin, a tiny grey beard and a limp handshake, Kevin's presence had done nothing to lessen Henry's fears.

Like the cell, the room they'd sat in for their short discussion was simple, painted white and furnished with just a table and four chairs. Introductions over, Kevin had paused for a painfully long time while Henry waited with mounting frustration. At any moment, he'd been thinking, they could be summoned into the interview room and this chance to speak alone would be over, wasted. His frustration had surged tsunami-like with each silent moment, and still Kevin had waited, as if collecting very slow thoughts.

Unable to stand it any longer, Henry had begun to speak, filling the silence and blurting out the facts as he saw them. The solicitor, looking faintly startled, had listened for a few minutes, jotting down the odd note and nodding. Then, at long last, he'd sat up straight in his chair and looked ready for action, tapping his pencil on the edge of his notepad as he began to take charge of the interview.

Briefly, he'd gone through police procedures and time limits for holding Henry at the centre.

'One thing you may not be aware of, Mr Blanchard,' he'd pointed out, 'is that a different team of investigators will be speaking to you here.'

'What? No DI Crisp?' It had felt like the first half-decent news of the day, but then of course, the new people could turn out to be even worse.

'No. There's a specialist team here, working on the evidence collected so far against you.' He quickly summed up the evidence the police had, which sounded quite thin, even to the pessimistic and worried Henry.

Apparently, they could hold him for twenty-four hours initially, after which they could charge him, bail him, release him or apply to hold him for another twelve hours. To keep him in, they'd have to have a good reason, though. Then, if after that first thirty-six hours they still had a good enough case to continue to hold him for questioning, they'd need permission to do so from a magistrate. But, Kevin had assured him as he removed his glasses to wipe some of the smears on to his polka-dot tie, it was unlikely to come to that. The evidence they had, or at least had told him about, was flimsy, all of it circumstantial.

Henry had listened to Kevin's dull monotone, trying to glean inspiration from his words, but he wondered whether, if all that stood between him and a life sentence was this pale faced, nervous little man, it might be better to give up hope now. Where was the forthright Rob Searles when he needed him? He wanted someone who oozed confidence, who would storm in here, tell them what for and get him out of this nightmare.

The only person to storm in, however, had been a constable who came to move them into the interview room. They'd paced along a white corridor to another room with a central table and four grey chairs. Here though, as Henry had soon discovered, the chairs were screwed to the floor. He'd slid himself on to one of them, his heart pounding and his fears climbing.

Despite Kevin's assurances about the flimsy nature of the evidence they had, the two strangers who had entered the room to interview him looked pretty confident. The older man, who'd introduced himself as civilian investigator Mike Newton, seemed reasonable enough, but then you could never really tell. He had a roundish face and a greying full head of hair that kept flopping over his eyes. He wore a tweed jacket, a pink shirt and a striped tie and he folded his tall form on to his chair with the sort of agility that Wayne Crisp would have envied. The other officer was young, probably mid twenties, with a pale, narrow face and blond hair cut severely short. He'd been introduced as Detective Constable Sykes. There'd been a pause while the constable clicked and fiddled with the black video recording machine next to him, informing it that the time was 14.56 and getting them all to tell it their names. Then the senior officer had begun a few preliminaries, such as why Henry was there, etcetera, before assuming a chattier mode.

He'd talked a bit about Downham Market and Henry's business, as if he'd just read the case notes for the first time and was feeling his way. Henry, who had learned much from his dealings with DI Crisp, was not fooled into lowering his guard, but Mr Newton had phrased his preliminary questions in such a perfectly amiable manner that Henry could only answer in the same way. After that of course, the questions and the chat had lost their veneer of pleasantness and Henry had braced himself, aware of Kevin sniffing nervously at his side.

The constable had leaned back in his chair, his face serious and conscientious, as Mr Newton changed tack.

'How would you describe your relationship with Miss Grey?' he'd asked, one hand subconsciously pushing back his errant fringe. Oh, here we go, thought Henry.

'Like many marriages and civil partnerships of several years' standing, I suppose,' he'd ventured reasonably. There was no reaction from his solicitor, so he continued, 'the usual ups and downs.'

'So…more ups than downs? Or more downs than ups?'

'More ups,' he'd said hesitantly, 'We were fine. We got on together most of the time.'

'Well, that's certainly a different point of view, Mr Blanchard. The ladies at Miss Grey's golf club don't seem to agree with you, though.'

'What? You asked *them*?'

'Our colleagues did. The ladies, Miss Grey's personal friends, certainly do not share your view of your relationship. In fact, I'd say the general opinion was quite the opposite. One lady,' the investigator consulted his notes briefly, 'Mrs Dorothy Brownlow, mentioned your constant quarrelling. She said she was surprised Miss Grey stayed with you and endured your constant affairs with other women, but that Miss Grey stayed because she loved you. Your partner sounds like she was pretty loyal, Mr Blanchard, but all that loyalty must have been a mixed blessing…'

'What the hell do you mean?' Henry had snapped, taking the bait. Kevin had given him a warning glance. 'Dottie Brownlow *would* say that! She and her golfing buddies are the very least likely people to give a fair assessment of our home life!'

'Well, the sergeant carrying out the investigation at the time did wonder if that were true,' nodded Mr Newton, his face a picture of reasonableness, 'so she asked your secretary, Miss Turner, the same question, thinking that she'd give you a fairer assessment. Sadly, though, Miss Turner appeared to find the subject difficult. The sergeant reports that Miss Turner was clearly being evasive. The poor woman hardly knew what to say, apparently. And then there was the photo of Miss Grey that you'd pushed into your desk drawer; hardly a sign of a harmonious relationship, was it? So, I'm back to the same point, that your relationship with Miss Grey was far from easy and that her loyalty must have been a mixed blessing. On the one hand, her staying with you meant you could continue in the security to which you'd become accustomed. You

208

could remain in your rather nice house, which I understand Miss Grey's father contributed generously towards, and continue your high standard of living. If you'd gone your separate ways you would have lost your fine house and much of your comfortable lifestyle. On the other hand, it must have been inconvenient to be saddled with her when you so obviously longed for freedom. Did she find out about your latest affair, Mr Blanchard?'

'No! Absolutely not! And anyway…'

'Because you *had* begun another affair, hadn't you?'

'What? No, I...'

'It was getting more and more frustrating to be tied down, wasn't it? Especially when it was to a woman you could barely tolerate. Especially when you could have been with Miss Turner…'

'What?' Henry had cried, bristling with indignation, 'What the hell do you mean? I'm not having an affair!'

'Oh, that's interesting. Miss Grey's friends seem to be of quite another opinion. Several of her friends individually described how Miss Grey treated you at your parties, ridiculing you in front of your guests. Several of them also mentioned, er... your closeness to one of your guests in particular; your secretary, Miss Turner.'

Noticing another of Kevin's warning glances, Henry had paused this time before speaking, giving his anger time to die down. When he'd started to speak, it was with a return to his usual measured tone.

'Understand this. I am not having an affair with anyone. Neither with Julia Turner nor with anyone else. If my relationship with Antonia had its low points it was not because of that.'

'What was it because of then, Mr Blanchard?'

'I don't know! I'm not a marriage counsellor!'

Henry had gripped the smeary-edged table at that point, pulling his fingers away with a sudden repulsed jerk when he realised that, despite its newness, the under surface of the table was encrusted with something disgusting. His sudden movement had elbowed Kevin in the side and he'd muttered an apology. There'd been a brief exchange of looks between the two police officers and Mr Newton had nodded to the constable who'd wetted his lips before addressing Henry. His narrow, slightly nervous face had cracked into something resembling a smile.

'Come on, Mr Blanchard, we've all been there. The worn out relationship, the times when you can't stand the sight of the little lady you live with. I know I have!' he'd laughed thinly and Henry wondered how he managed to be so experienced and cynical at such a young age. 'Then along comes some gorgeous woman who'll do anything for you and it's OK at first...quick, sneaky meetings when no one's looking. Actually, though, it was easy for you, wasn't it? All those hours at the office, all those lunch times...no wonder your poor old missus started to call in on her way to walk the dog! That must have really got to you. There she was, dominating not only your home life, but starting to interfere with your working life too. It would have got to me, don't mind telling you. I'm not surprised you snapped. I really feel for you there. And I should think the lovely Miss Turner was objecting too, wasn't she? She must have wanted you all to herself. And there's a limit to how long a woman like her will put up with sharing you. Did she give you an ultimatum? Was that it? Her or me sort of thing?'

Henry had listened with increasing incredulity, his hands still wiping themselves automatically on his trousers. If this stupid boy in his woolly polo necked sweater thought he was winding him up, trying to make him snap, he was sadly mistaken.

'No,' he'd said calmly, 'Nothing like that happened at all. As I said, we were not having an affair.'

The detective constable had given a little sigh, shaking his head and exchanging another look with the older man. Mr Newton had risen from his chair then and had begun a slow walk around the room.

'Mr Blanchard, we know how you value your home, your cars, your very pleasant lifestyle and all the trappings

210

of respectability. In fact, no one we've spoken to could imagine you without these things. Splitting up with Miss Grey would have meant dividing your valuable assets, especially since much of the house's deposit money was provided by her family. However, it doesn't take a genius to work out that if, instead of just going your separate ways, Miss Grey happened to pass away, you would do very well out of it indeed. In fact, you'd be able to claim on a very healthy life insurance policy to the tune of £750,000, enough to pay off Miss Grey's family and leave you plenty of change. You could keep your house and your pride and win your freedom at the same time, keeping your respectability intact. And just who set up that insurance policy? It was you, Mr Blanchard, wasn't it?'

'Yes, of course it was,' he'd agreed unmoved, 'it's my job. There's nothing unusual about two spouses or partners setting up policies on each other. In the event of the death of one partner, the policy on his or her life should be enough to clear all debts and leave some spare to help the surviving partner through the inevitably tough time that comes with bereavement. Antonia had an identical policy on my life.'

The investigator had just stared at him, sitting down again.

'On that Friday you knew exactly where Miss Grey would be because it had become a habit of hers, walking the dog by the river in the late morning. Even your faithful secretary will confirm that much. So, you left your office, taking care to place something suitably heavy in the car. One of Miss Grey's old golf clubs, wasn't it? You drove down there, found her car easily and joined her, and all the time you were waiting for the right moment when she was distracted with something. Perhaps, for instance while she attended to the dog. And then you used that club as a weapon on her.'

'You don't have to answer that,' Kevin Green had put in.

'Oh, but I do,' Henry had retorted, his voice surprisingly calm, 'I didn't go anywhere near the river that day. I waited for Antonia for a while, just to see if she'd show up. Sometimes she dropped into the office, sometimes she didn't. I'd finished my meeting in the office with a client...it was Bob Southwood, actually. I'm sure he wouldn't mind you checking that...'

'Already have,' the constable's voice had sounded bored.

'...Oh, and then Anna called in. I'd forgotten that...'

'Anna?'

'Yes, Anna Sobers from City Life. She often calls in on a Friday. When she'd gone, I decided to drive to King's Lynn for a change. I looked in a few shops, bought a sandwich and a newspaper and then came back to the office.'

'Which shops, Mr Blanchard?'

'W H Smiths, Boots and Waterstones, since you ask, but apart from the sandwich and paper, I just had a quick look round. Didn't buy anything else.'

'So you drove all the way to Lynn, just for your packed lunch and something to read, when you could have strolled round the corner and bought them in Downham? That seems strange to me. A waste of petrol, as well as time. And do you happen to have kept your parking ticket to prove all this? Or a receipt for your paper or sandwich?' Mr Newton had paused, hoping for an answer. Henry noticed that the man's reasonable manner had a very hard edge to it now. 'You see, our colleagues asked in those three shops and no one who was working on that day remembered seeing you.'

'Well they wouldn't, would they? The shops were busy and no one's going to remember one quick sale of a newspaper. And as for receipts, I threw them away. Why would I keep things like that? Damn it, I *always* throw them away! The parking sticker would have gone into the bin on Tuesday Market Place, where I left the car, and the others...well, I don't think I even took them from the cashiers.'

'Not exactly convincing is it? So, you'll see, Mr Blanchard, why DC Sykes and I are having trouble in believing you. We'd like to believe you drove all the way to Lynn just for a little look round, but unfortunately without any receipts or anyone who can help you prove you were there, it's difficult for us. The CCTV footage we've looked at doesn't show you or your car being in the vicinity of the market place at the time either. I'm afraid it all means that you have no alibi for the time the murder took place.'

'What? But that can't be! I think you need to look at the CCTV records again. I was there that lunch time, parked in Tuesday Market Place!'

'Very well, but I'm afraid the bad news doesn't end there. As you'll remember, tests were carried out on your car. Mud found on the tyres turned out to be an exact match with the mud in the lay-by that Miss Grey parked in. Tyre tracks left in the mud there also matched your car. Since you've made it quite clear that you never went to the lay-by or the river, how would you explain this?'

'I don't know!' Henry had spluttered in exasperation and alarm. He'd thought hard for a few seconds as a headache began to throb over one eye. 'Oh, of course!' he'd offered as light dawned, 'Three or four days before all this happened, Antonia's car was in for servicing and she borrowed mine. That explains the tracks and the mud on the tyres.'

The detective had made no immediate reply but his raised eyebrow showed that he didn't believe a word. It was all far too convenient.

'We can check the Mercedes' service history. You realise that, don't you?'

'Of course I do! Just go ahead and check. Walker's Garage. I haven't been near the river bank for months. And anyway, even if I'd been there, your theory wouldn't make any sense. How was I supposed to hide a golf club from Antonia before belting the poor woman with it?'

The investigator had shrugged his shoulders and the constable had taken over again.

'You tell us, Mr Blanchard. You tell us. We will soon have the results on the golf clubs that were removed from your office and we're confident that they'll prove what we already know. You may as well just tell us everything now and save us all time.'

There'd been a long silence, punctuated only by the solicitor's nervous pencil tapping and the constable's impatient sighing.

'Then you must wait for your tests,' Henry had said finally, 'Antonia used those old clubs for several years before I bought her a new set for her birthday, so presumably they'll be covered in her finger prints. I doubt you'll find anything more dramatic than that. Why don't you just stop mucking about and look for her killer?'

'Oh, we're not mucking about, Mr Blanchard, you can be sure of that,' the constable had said, sounding exasperated. The senior investigator had grunted something and the constable had leaned forward, speaking into the black machine again, ending the interview and the video recording and giving the time as 15.51.

Despite the older man's assured manner, Henry had detected uncertainty in his voice that hadn't been there earlier. Perhaps, after all, his solicitor had been right. They really did have nothing to hold him on and he was hardly going to help them out with a quick confession.

After another lacklustre discussion with Mr Green, Henry had been taken back to his cell and given something to eat that was mostly boiled potato with a hint of hake. He was suddenly very hungry, though, and tucked into the food as if it had been an All Day Breakfast, complete with sausages and the greasiest of bacon.

Because something, perhaps the tiniest flicker of optimism, was lighting the darkness he found himself in. Unaccustomed as he was to allowing optimism to rule his thinking, he gave permission for the flicker to take hold and glow.

Chapter Twenty Two

Julia. Tuesday 19th May, 4.30 pm

Julia's day hadn't been much better.

If only the phone would stop ringing, just for a few minutes. If only it would stay silent long enough for her to clear her head and do something useful; anything but answer the same questions over and over again.

When news had first broken of Antonia's death, the phone messages had been full of sympathy. Cards and well meaning emails had flooded in with offers of help for the bereaved man. Clients whose queries were not urgent had agreed to phone again another time, when things returned to normal. The clients whose needs were more pressing she'd referred to the locum. She still hated doing this. She worried that Henry's client bank would gradually be lost to the new man while he helped out, but what else could she do? Of course, Henry would have hated the thought of throwing away business, but during the last ten days or so he'd hardly noticed what was happening in the office.

But today the tone of the phone calls and emails had changed. It was still less than five hours since Henry had been arrested, yet somehow everyone knew already. Suddenly, people who only last week had been promising support and assuring her of their understanding, had turned frosty, demanding immediate answers to their queries and information about Henry. However much he had done for them in the past, often without a fee, and however improved their financial situation was as a result of his advice, he and his work had suddenly become tarnished for them. After some of the comments Julia had heard that afternoon she wondered how she would ever be able to speak to certain individuals again. Their pompous voices were edged with self righteousness and her desperate explanations, that Henry was merely helping the police, had gone unheard. But that was all he was doing. He was helping them. Yet, so far as many of the callers were concerned, there was no smoke without fire.

At least if they took their business elsewhere Julia would never have to speak to them again, but still she wanted to hold on to them, to keep the business alive for when Henry returned. She refused to consider the possibility of him being charged. He could never have done such a thing; she just knew he couldn't.

When the police had taken Henry away, Julia was left in a state of shock. She could hardly move, could hardly take her eyes from the window, from where she'd watched the police car move away. When at last she'd recovered the ability to stir herself, she'd phoned Bruce. His horrified silence at the other end had said it all. He obviously hadn't believed they'd go so far as to arrest Henry, that they'd be so short sighted. When he'd recovered himself, he'd told her he couldn't leave work that afternoon, but that he'd go to Henry's on his way home to feed the cat and dog. He'd had a spare key to the house for the last ten days, he explained. She took some comfort from his practical attitude.

As soon as he'd hung up, the other calls had continued. When it wasn't some sanctimonious client or an over-curious life assurance company inspector, it was the local press. The press were pleasant enough, of course, but she didn't know what to tell them, torn through her loyalty to Henry between not saying too much and assuring them that she knew he was innocent.

So, it was almost a relief when the office door burst open to reveal the grim faced Sergeant Lunberry. After all the stinging remarks from once loyal and polite clients, the sergeant seemed refreshingly honest. At least she was only doing her job.

Julia offered her coffee, which was declined with an impatient shaking of the head.

'What did you do, Miss Turner?' she began without niceties or the smallest clue as to what she meant, 'Did you remove one of them, or simply clean the lot?'

'Pardon? And it's Julia. Just call me Julia.'

'Come on, Julia. Don't mess me about. The golf clubs. You cleaned them, didn't you?'

'Well, yes, actually. I did. Henry was going to take them to the charity shop and they were caked with mud. I thought they ought to be cleaned up a bit…'

'Yes, I bet you did. How much does he pay you for all that devotion, Julia? Or do you do it all out of affection?'

'What? I do my job, that's all, and I'm paid a salary. I don't call cleaning a bit of mud off a few golf clubs before sending them to a charity shop devotion, just ordinary consideration. Who wants clubs that are covered in dried mud? Anyway, I had a bit less to do that day. Henry was out with clients and...'

'And which club did you remove from the bag?'

'Which club? All of them, of course. I cleaned them and put them back.'

'You know very well what I mean, Julia. I mean that you removed one permanently. Lost it, didn't you? I can think of very good reasons for you wanting to do that. I'm sure you did your best with cleaning them but perhaps you weren't sure about how thoroughly you'd removed the evidence, so you threw the doubtful one away.'

'They were all returned to the bag.'

'Oh yes? Then why is there no three-wood?'

'Three-wood? How on earth should I know? I just cleaned the ones that were there. I scraped off the mud and used kitchen cleaner on all the metal bits…'

'…conveniently removing all the evidence in the process.'

'Evidence of what? The only evidence I saw was of a hell of a lot of golf played in wet conditions.'

The sergeant was looking impatient and certainly not ready to give up.

'Then how do you explain the fact that in an otherwise full and expensive set of golf clubs the three-wood is missing?'

'I can't. I assumed it *was* a full set. Henry seemed to think so. I know absolutely nothing about golf and Henry doesn't seem to know much either. Perhaps Antonia broke a club and threw it away. Or it could be in Henry's house. Perhaps in the hall cupboard. That's where we took them from on the night of Antonia's party. They were swapped for new ones, you see. It was her surprise birthday present.'

'It was that, all right. When were you going to tell her, Julia?'

'Sorry?'

'About your relationship with Henry. Or was Henry still waiting for the right moment? Were you putting pressure on him to tell her, Julia? Is that why he snapped?'

'Snapped? I really don't know what you're talking about, Sergeant Lunberry.'

'Oh, I think you do, Julia, but we'll leave that for now.'

Without troubling herself with any form of farewell, the sergeant clumped noisily to the door and banged it shut after her. Left alone, Julia's eyes widened in surprise. The woman was clearly desperate, making up theories and hoping they were right, yet she was way off track. That had to mean that the police were having problems. By tomorrow lunch time, according to Bruce, if they couldn't show good enough reason to hold Henry for a further period, they'd have to let him go.

For the first time in what seemed an eternity, Julia felt tiny stirrings of hope.

Bruce. Same day, 6.45 pm

Bruce watched through the sitting room window as the car made its way up Henry's drive. He'd been at the house for half an hour already, having had trouble locating the cat, but he'd finally found her dozing in a sunny patch between two rhododendrons. She was now tucking into a dish of tiny biscuits from a box he'd found in the cupboard. As for Arnold, he hadn't been at all hard to find, flinging himself at the door as soon as Bruce's key was turning in it, the warmth of his greeting only slightly muted when he realised that Bruce was not Henry. Bruce had found the dog food in the same cupboard as the cat biscuits. Not having pets of his own, he was thankful for the big photos of dogs and cats on the various packets and tins that helped him to identify what was what. Without them, Arnold would probably be chomping on baked beans by now.

Bruce had done the bit of washing-up that was left in the sink. He'd thought he might as well, while he was there. If it hadn't been for the circumstances, it would almost have been peaceful; swilling the mugs and dishes to the messy vocal accompaniment of Arnold chewing his meaty chunks and slurping from his water bowl. Beside him, Polly had been munching intently on her cat biscuits and he bent down to stroke her dark, silky back. Her tail shot up, comforted by his presence. After all, Bruce was such a regular caller that Polly considered him family.

But now, that wretched woman had turned up again. He'd returned to the kitchen for a tea cloth to dry his hands on before opening the door. Antonia would never have approved. There was a hand towel hanging by the oven, she'd said quite often. Leave the tea cloth alone, Bruce.

'Evening, sergeant.'

Try as he might, his normal cheery tone seemed to have deserted him. Cheerfulness would have been wasted on her anyway. She grunted some sort of acknowledgement of his presence and strode through the door into the hallway, heading straight for the hall cupboard. As she tugged open the door, Bruce moved to stand behind her, peering over her shoulder into the gloomy depths of piled up and abandoned household items. She tugged on the hanging light cord, illuminating the small space with a dull, washed-out glow. Her hand brushed against a mop head, sending it rattling to the floor and upsetting half a dozen miscellaneous items as it went. She tutted irritably.

'I thought you'd already looked in there,' observed Bruce.

'This won't take long,' she offered by way of reply, casting him a disapproving glance, as if the state of the cupboard were his fault. She moved a few things aside, trying to manoeuvre herself around the new bag of golf clubs parked at the front of the cupboard and knocking a box of tea lights from a shelf with her elbow as she did so. The box smacked on to an old food mixer, releasing two dozen little candles which spun and wheeled themselves around the cupboard as if battery powered, their clattering and spinning going on for what seemed ages before coming to rest by the sergeant's mud encrusted boots. In the past, Bruce had often been guilty of entering Antonia's well kept domain wearing inappropriate footwear and now he could almost hear her voice, objecting loudly to this rude intrusion. Antonia's death had changed Bruce's attitude somewhat, enhancing the things he'd admired about her and making her once unendurable faults almost endearing. Now he knew what people meant about rose-tinted glasses.

Arnold appeared suddenly, charging into them and head-butting Bruce's legs before diving past the sergeant into the disaster zone that was the cupboard. The woman squealed and jumped aside as the golf bag was knocked over, its heavy contents clattering out of the front of the cupboard and all over the hall parquet.

'Get that dog out of here!' she yelled and Bruce grinned, reaching for the dog's collar without any real urgency. She bent down and began to replace the clubs in the bag, peering at the impressed numbers on each club head as she did so. She looked frustrated and irritated, obviously not finding what she was looking for, and she pushed the heavy bag aside. Bruce busied himself with Arnold, determined not to help her.

When he returned from shutting the dog in the kitchen, the sergeant had pulled on a pair of rubber gloves and was feeling her way along the loaded shelves at the back and sides of the cupboard.

'Are there any more golf clubs in here?' she asked conversationally.

'I doubt it. All Antonia's new ones are in the bag you just knocked over. Henry took her old ones away. I think they were going to the charity shop.'

She grunted. More items tumbled to the floor and she kicked them aside. Tins of polish, spare vacuum cleaner tools and dusters went flying into the corners as she worked. She had spotted a few boxes of bric-a-brac and bags of discarded items that were stacked towards the back of the cupboard and she moved gingerly towards them. Her hand knocked against a plastic bag of Airfix soldiers and she muttered something under her breath as thirty tiny Germans in combat gear dropped on to her feet. She kicked them away and moved on.

'Hey, careful with them,' protested Bruce, 'they're worth a bit on EBay.'

'What's this?' she demanded. She bent down, so that all he could see was her backside. Remarkably broad for someone so small.

'Don't know,' he replied in total honesty, 'I can't see past your bum.'

'This!' she insisted, standing up and clutching a framed photograph. It was a photo Bruce hadn't seen before. A much younger and happier Antonia and Henry beamed out from the frame, their faces close together, eyes aglow with something that looked curiously like love. Judging from their clothes, the picture probably dated from the nineties, when they'd first met.

'It's just an old photo of Antonia and Henry. What's the problem?'

'I'm wondering why Mr Blanchard appears to be in the habit of removing pictures of his partner from view.'

'I'm sure he's in no such habit. I've never seen that photo displayed, so it must have been stored away ages ago.'

'Oh yes? And this?' She was holding up a crumpled white mess that had once been one of Antonia's best jackets.

'Oh, that was me. When Henry first heard about what had happened to Antonia, her things were all over the house, just as she'd left them, of course. The other night I decided to clear up a bit. Perhaps I shouldn't have moved things, but he was in a bad enough state as it was, without having salt rubbed in his wounds, so I collected up a few things and put them in here. That jacket was on the back of one of the kitchen chairs. She'd left it there before she…I thought it wasn't good that he had to see it every time he went into the kitchen.' Good thing, he added to himself, that he'd left that photo of Antonia and Arnold where he'd found it.

'You sound amazingly considerate to me, Mr Ryan.' It didn't sound like a compliment.

'Well…'

'And this?' Now she was holding up Antonia's glasses case. She snapped it open to reveal the spectacles, prodding at them with her gloved finger.

'Now look!' Bruce could hardly keep his voice civil now, 'Yes, I put that in there too. So what? What would you have done if your friend was in such a state that he was practically swallowing whole bottles of whisky at a time and the house he returned to from hearing about his partner's death was littered with her personal things?'

'I doubt if I'd have risen to your level of consideration,' she said scathingly.

'Perhaps you wouldn't, but I can tell you you'll find nothing in there to help you to solve this thing.'

'Really? So what's all this?'

She was bending over a damaged cardboard box towards the back of the cupboard and had pulled a few items out of it. There was an old brass candle stick, a small steel case and a dented metal vase. She backed out of the confined space, carrying the objects she'd selected over to the window. The early summer evening light was still

222

good and she peered at the items briefly before laying them down gently on the window sill. She examined them one by one, turning them over in her gloved hands. After a few seconds she grunted and placed the candle stick on the floor, picking up the steel case. Bruce walked over to have a better look. It had been finished in brushed steel and was about fifteen centimetres by twelve in size, with a slim carrying handle that unfolded from underneath.

'Ah, I see what it is now!' he said, realisation dawning, 'It's Henry's sat nav. He never used it and it ended up in the cupboard, like everything else that nobody wanted.'

She clicked open the case and, as predicted, the pristine and unused gadget was there.

'Very expensive, top of the range satellite navigation system, a bit out-dated now, though,' she murmured, 'Shouldn't this be in Mr Blanchard's car?'

Bruce shook his head.

'No, Henry tried to get on with it, but he couldn't stand the thing. Said he preferred a good map and didn't need some irritating woman inside a machine telling him which way to go. Antonia bought it for him a while back, but I could never understand why. She knew how much he hates gadgets. In fact, Henry hates anything invented after about 1975!'

The sergeant didn't reply, but her whole attitude seemed to have changed. Unlike the candlestick, the sat nav was not placed on the floor, but slipped inside a plastic bag. The woman's small mouth seemed to have relaxed into a grim smile. She had turned to the third object now; the vase. It was so old, tarnished and dented that it was hard to tell what metal it was made of, but it was probably brass. Turning it over, the sergeant let out a muffled exclamation. She took another plastic bag from her pocket and slipped the vase inside.

'Why are you so interested in these things?' Bruce couldn't help asking.

'There are traces of blood on both items. Any idea how they got there?'

She looked smug. Bruce stared at the bagged items in bewilderment and saw that she was right. Smeared across the rounded body of the vase was the unmistakable dark brown stain of blood. Just a smear, though, hardly anything to get worked up about, but blood all the same. The sat nav case looked as if it had even less; just a faint stain by one of its hinges.

'I don't understand. I don't know how that would have got there.'

'You don't have to, Mr Ryan. Thank you for your time!'

She hadn't even left the house before she was shrieking triumphantly into her mobile and Bruce closed the door behind her, not understanding a thing.

There was a movement by his feet, the brush of something soft on his calf, as Polly wove her way around his legs, seeking reassurance. He bent down to caress her back, his eyes hardly moving from the front door.

'What the hell's going on, Henry?' he muttered, 'What the hell's going on?'

Chapter Twenty Three

Rosie. Wednesday 20th May, late morning.

There had been no local paper delivered for several days, no news since a sensational front page report of the murder a week ago. The on-line edition was more up to date, though, and Rosie scrolled down through the headlines on the screen of her office computer, the cursor sticking and refusing to budge every time she thought she'd found something.

Then she saw it; another photo of Antonia, looking glamorous, as if going out for the evening, and the headline, 'Arrest Made in Search for Antonia's Killer'. Her heart in her mouth, Rosie scanned through the two short paragraphs beneath the picture, but learned nothing more. Absolutely no clue as to who had been arrested.

Her heart kept up its harsh pounding for a long interval, all her instincts telling her it was Henry who was 'helping the police with their enquiries'. After all, didn't they always suspect the husband? She was desperate to know what was going on and wouldn't be able to rest until she found out. But how was she going to do that?

The morning in the office dragged by and she went out early for lunch. She wandered gloomily around town before sitting beside the turbulent, brown river to eat her sandwich. The water was higher than usual, swollen by the recent heavy rain, and she watched as a twig was carried along by the current, caught in an eddy for a brief spiral dance, before being released to seek its fortune out at sea.

After half an hour, she made her way back to the office building, her thoughts as turbulent as the river. She was still churning over the same fears in her mind as she closed the street door behind her, entering the gloomy hall and beginning to climb the stairs. She was so deep in thought that at first she hardly registered the voices that drifted down the stair well towards her. Automatically, she stood to one side to allow the man and woman to descend. They passed her without a glance, their chatter going at full speed.

And then, in a second, her dreary, worry-clogged mind woke up. Her thinking sparked into life as she looked at the two visitors who were leaving the building; the new smart-suited inspector from Emerald Investments and Anna Sobers from City Life.

'Anna!' she called out, walking back down the stairs to greet the inspector in the dark entrance hall.

'Hello Rosie!' the inspector responded with a big smile, 'Thought we'd missed you. Can I help with anything? This is Geoff Walker, by the way, from Emerald Investments.'

Rosie shook hands with the smiling Geoff. He'd just had a meeting with the advisors, he was telling her, his body language alive with enthusiasm and positivity. She was nodding, making all the right noises while her mind was working away. She let the pair leave and waited until the door was closed firmly behind them, before opening it once more and leaning out. She called Anna's name again and obligingly the dark haired girl returned, all smiles still. These things were always easier on a one-to-one basis.

'Anna, I wonder if I could ask you something?' Rosie began in a suitably hesitant way, 'I had a telephone call this morning from an old client. It was an appeal case I've been working on for a lady we later lost to Mason and Blanchard in Downham…'

Anna's attention sharpened visibly. Was Rosie imagining it, or did she look worried? She'd stopped smiling, anyway.

'Ah yes, the lovely Henry,' she said quietly.

'It's just that, well, this lady seemed rather upset on the phone and was telling me that something dreadful had happened to Henry Blanchard,' Rosie lied, 'I realise it sounds terribly nosey, but I know you go to see him in Downham and I wondered…'

'Yes, I'm afraid it's true,' Anna muttered, her face lowered. 'I visited his office yesterday and his secretary was almost in tears. Apparently, Henry's been arrested! It was his poor wife, you see. It's been in the papers, but I hadn't realised before that she was his….the names were different, you see…'

Rosie froze, unable at first to respond, and Anna stared back at her, looking equally stricken. Rosie managed to say something in the end, though she hadn't a clue whether it made any sense, and then Anna had gone.

Back upstairs in her own office, she sat at her desk and tried to work, which was impossible, of course.

So it was true. Henry was the one the newspaper was talking about, the one helping the police right now.

She wanted so badly to help him, but what could she do? What if they never found another suspect? What if he ended up doing time for something he'd not done? Because surely, Henry would be incapable of doing such a thing.

And there was nothing she could do, was there?

She looked up from the regulator's website on the screen in front of her as Raymond entered the room and walked over to the window.

'Due to rain later,' he informed her, peering skywards through the grimy glass. She pulled herself together with a supreme effort, closing down the website and leaning forward to make some attempt at conversation.

'What, again?' she heard herself say, 'The garden's almost water-logged as it is.' He nodded.

'Have we heard any more on that complaint from last week? The Matthews case?'

'I reviewed it and couldn't find any grounds. I wrote to Mr Matthews, so as far as I'm concerned, it's finished.'

She thought she was making sense and Raymond was nodding again, apparently satisfied with her reply, but the words sounded unreal, as if they had nothing to do with her. All she could think about was the mess Henry was in.

After a little more dithering, Raymond had gone and she was left staring at the computer's home screen and a pile of files that Alice had deposited there earlier.

Perhaps, just perhaps, there was something she could do to help Henry. She could tell the police about her astral travel, her Out of Body Experiences. She could explain what her vivid dreaming or travel had shown her, that Antonia had not been killed by Henry. But how likely were they to listen to woolly information like that? It was all she had, though, and surely it was worth a try?

There was, however, another thing that worried her. If they found out that she and Henry had known each other in the past, she could be stuck there for hours, answering lots of irrelevant questions, and that would help no one. She would try to help him, do what she could, but it would have to be done as a stranger who had dreams. She had to remain at a distance.

She glanced at her watch. It had only just gone one o'clock. She closed down the computer and picked up her bag and car keys, moving quickly before she changed her mind.

'I have to go out for a bit,' she called out to Alice and Jenny as she passed their desks, 'Won't be long!'

DS Lunberry had had a decent morning. She had a good feeling about the evidence she'd sent to the lab and at last she felt she had something worthwhile to report. DI Crisp had been in late and when at last she'd located him he was nursing a bad head and was in a worse mood than usual.

'I think we might have cracked it, sir,' she'd enthused, 'I think we've got him. The vase is the right shape, size, weight, everything. He hadn't even bothered to clean it up. The lab says they'll try to hurry up the results for us.'

'They'd better. We're cutting it a bit fine and we'll have to extend his custody. I'm going to have to ask very nicely.'

There was a movement behind them, followed by an apologetic cough.

'What is it?' he barked.

'A woman's here to see you, sir,' a constable informed him, 'A Mrs Rosalyn Stone.'

'Who the hell…can't she wait?'

'Not really, sir. Says it's in connection with the Antonia Grey murder.'

With the evidence against Henry Blanchard looking hopeful at last, the inspector had lost some of his hunger for fresh information. He'd been hoping for a few hours to catch up with some of the other work on his desk and this interruption was one more nuisance he didn't need. He cursed under his breath as he went through to where she waited.

A youngish, nervous looking woman was sitting awkwardly on one of the metal chairs in the interview room. She pulled her shoulders back and sat up straight as he approached and he managed a gruff, barely polite greeting.

'You might find what I have to say a bit unusual,' she began and he sighed inwardly.

Just what he needed. A total nutter.

Bruce. Same day, 1.15pm

More bad news.

Bruce put the phone back in his shirt pocket and stared at the dark pool of oil that had formed on the workshop floor beneath the Massey Ferguson. It was lunch time anyway, but news like this was going to need longer than an hour. Mac peered at him from his office, over the top of The Sun, and grunted.

'Go on, then. Make it up next week.'

Bruce nodded gratefully, uttering an apology and wondering whether this job could survive Henry's problems.

Picking up Arnold on the way, he drove to Downham. With the dog lolloping all over the car, driving was no easy task. Considering that this high octane canine behaviour was Arnold in mourning, Bruce hated to think how uncontrollable he'd been before. With no dog guard fitted in the car to contain him, Arnold was a nightmare of a back seat driver. One moment he was running up and down in the back and then he was jumping through the gap to sit at the front. Bored with that, he ran around a bit more before settling on the floor next to the driver's seat. He amused himself for a very short time with watching the traffic, barking at anything that took his fancy. His sudden bass baritone woofing, close to Bruce's ear, was enough to jar the wits out of the driver, who hollered a warning more than once. Arnold took no notice, just sat there, panting and drooling, while waiting for the next thing to bark at.

By the time they arrived in High Street, Bruce was exhausted. He managed to attach the lead to Arnold's collar and get him to walk in an almost orderly fashion to the office. While Bruce greeted a gratifyingly welcoming Julia, Arnold was eyeing up the potted plants in the corner. Julia eyed the dog warily and Bruce pulled him away.

'Come on,' he decided, 'we're closing the office and you're having a break. You need fresh air and so does the dog.' He could see from her ghostly white face and slow

230

reactions that she was in no state to receive more bad news. He would have to tell her, though, and it would be easier away from the office.

As he spoke, the phone rang. He snatched it up and muttered a quick greeting, listening for a few seconds before replying with tried patience.

'No, I'm afraid Mr Blanchard is still helping the police...it's kind of you to show concern...' He frowned, listening a bit more, then added a few more words and replaced the receiver.

'All the calls are similar,' commented Julia wearily, 'they're either feigning sympathy or they're downright cruel.'

'Come on, Julia. Let's leave this place for a couple of hours. And anyway, I need someone to sit in the back and control the dog.' She smiled faintly at the thought of trying to control Arnold, the great destroyer of her office.

The phone blared again as they locked the door, but they ignored it. They let Arnold on to the back seat of the old Vauxhall and Julia climbed in beside him, keeping his lead attached. As they drove out of Downham towards King's Lynn, she found it comforting to hold on to the dog. He seemed to like her company too, surprisingly content to sit still as he watched the passing landscape with big, sad, brown eyes. They by-passed Lynn, heading towards the coast, and for much of the journey Julia was quiet. Occasionally, Bruce heard her talking gently to Arnold, but other than that the journey passed in peaceful and companionable silence. At last, as the car bumped along the pot-holed entrance to an almost deserted cliff top car park in Old Hunstanton, Julia found her voice.

'What if he comes back to the office and I'm not there?' she asked. Bruce didn't reply at first, leaping out of the car instead to help her and the dog out. They followed the sandy, twisting pathway out of the car park, down the cliff side and through the dunes to the wide expanse of the beach. The air was cool and fresh, with little sign yet of summer, but the threatened rain had held off and the weather was pleasant enough to lift some of the gloom. Julia unclipped the lead from Arnold's collar and let him run. He made the most of it, tearing away towards the distant grey waves.

'I'm afraid, love, Henry won't be coming home just yet. They've extended his custody. They can keep him another twelve hours, apparently, so we have to hope he's out by midnight.'

'What?' her voice was little more than a squeak, 'How can they? I mean, they've no idea! That sergeant was going on about Antonia's old golf clubs being evidence. It was utter rubbish!'

'But then the sergeant found more so-called evidence in Henry's hall cupboard. I was there when she found a couple of bits she thought were important. I saw the look on her face. She was so damned pleased with herself.'

'But it can't mean a thing. Henry didn't do it!' She was panicking, her voice climbing higher up the scale. She seemed aware of it suddenly, taking a breath and adding in a more measured tone, 'they just have to let him go.'

'I know, love, and they will. Anyway, what's an old vase and a sat nav got to do with it? The detective sergeant said there was blood on both, but how can that make sense?'

They were striding across the damp sand, following the line of the sea and watching Arnold play at the water's edge. He was darting in and out of the waves, playing tag with the foaming water and picking up pebbles in his mouth before tossing them back into the sea. He seemed to have shaken off his pensive mood and Bruce noticed that even Julia's face was beginning to show touches of colour. It had been the right thing to do, coming to the coast today. He'd have loved to have made an afternoon of it. He could have bought them fish and chips and they could have sat on the dunes, just watching the sea, but he had to get back to work. He ought at least to put in a short appearance before the day ended.

Julia was frowning, trying to remember something.

'Did you say vase and sat nav? I remember the golfers going on about a few old things like that in a box. It was at Antonia's party. I think she'd cut herself somehow. That could explain the blood. Oh, for heaven's sake!' She laughed in sudden relief, 'They really are barking up the wrong tree!'

'Are you sure?'

She was frowning again, trying to recall events that she'd considered unimportant at the time.

'Pretty sure, yes. I'd had a bit to drink, so it's a bit hazy, but I remember a vase and Henry's unwanted sat nav, because the others seemed to find them funny. If they've found blood, I bet it's from nothing more than Antonia's cut finger!'

They laughed and she broke into a run, throwing up her arms and dashing along the beach towards the sea. He smiled as he watched her greet the wet dog, hugging him as if he were her own pet and not the wrecker of her office. She didn't seem to care that her clothes would be soaked, absorbing all that moisture from his fur. Her relief was obvious, even from this distance.

They were walking back towards him now, Julia's hand firm on the dog's collar. All three of them wanted Henry out of custody and Julia seemed so optimistic suddenly. But if, as she'd said, the police were barking up the wrong tree, which was the right tree?

Chapter Twenty Four

Rosie. Same day, Wednesday 20th May, 3.30 pm

Her interview with DI Crisp had been a total waste of time.

He'd laughed at her. Fair enough, someone walking in to regale you with tales of astral travel when you probably couldn't see your desk for work, must be pretty irritating, but the man hadn't even pretended to listen. She'd tried to tell him about her dream of the murder, but he hadn't let her finish. She had been prepared to explain the basics of how an Out of Body Experience happened, so that he would understand, but he hadn't given her chance. Anyway, she would have been wasting her breath. His thoughts had obviously been elsewhere; probably had a bag of chips going cold somewhere.

She'd never intended to mention seeing the secretary in the dream. Her only aim had been to make them see that Henry was innocent and to release him. She'd planned to be suitably vague about the perpetrator, mentioning that it had been a woman, nothing else. It was up to them to go looking for other suspects. But in the event he'd cut her off long before she'd reached the part involving Julia. To him, Rosie was just a fantasist. He'd even warned her about the consequences of wasting police time. The upshot was that she had failed to help Henry.

And the clock was still ticking, bringing no help for him. His twenty four hours were due to end any time now, and from what she'd picked up from DI Crisp, the time would probably be extended. The inspector had had that smug look about him, the look of someone with a trick up their sleeve.

So, Rosie had left the police station in Downham Market under a cloud of frustration and disappointment. She had driven back to the office, hardly aware of what she did or where she was. That had been an hour ago and still she hadn't managed to do anything useful. She was still sitting at her desk, staring at the computer screen and pretending to work, clicking on menus every so often to prevent the screen saver from kicking in and displaying its photo of a laughing chimpanzee. However endearing the monkey, the sight of him would soon have given the game away that she wasn't doing a lot of work. Behind her, Alice and Jenny were discussing nails; not the ironmongery sort, she guessed, but the ones you were meant to have done before going out anywhere. Jenny often had gel put on to hers, complete with a little picture on each finger end, then paid someone to take it all off again when it chipped. It sounded like far too much bother to Rosie, who was a file-em-down-and-hope-for-the-best sort of girl when it came to manicures.

Her worries about Henry continued to whirl around in her head and she was desperate to know whether they had, in fact, extended his custody. She thought of simply ringing the police and asking, but they'd probably still be eating chips and laughing after their last encounter with her.

Then she thought of Henry's office. She could ring, giving a made-up name and say she was an old client of Henry's. They were hardly likely to check. If she said she'd just invested in an ISA a few years back they wouldn't expect to recognise her name. She would sound like one of their many small clients whose details occupied a slim, never opened file in their alphabetical filing system. There was nothing to stop her calling to wish him well and asking whether he was back at work.

Checking that Alice and Jenny were still safely immersed in their manicure discussion, she dialed the number. She was surprised when it was picked up almost immediately. It was a man's voice; one she didn't recognise, and she plunged into her rehearsed lines, sounding almost convincing. The man didn't bother to check who she was, most likely tired of repeating the same words over and over again. He was polite enough, though, telling her what she'd hoped she wouldn't hear, that Henry was still in custody.

Did the police really think they had enough evidence to charge him, or were they just holding out and hoping for a confession? She let out a long sigh. Would they really charge him? Could she just sit there and let him go through all that without trying once more? She had one more card left to play, one she'd hoped she wouldn't have to use. Even after playing it, it was possible that they'd still not believe her, but she had to try.

As a compliance officer, she didn't really have the sort of job where she could just breeze out of the office whenever she felt like it, but lately she had been doing just that. Luck was on her side again this afternoon, with Raymond being out and the girls having moved on from their nail discussion to one about their favourite soap, "Emmerdale". She picked up her bag, closed down the computer, and made for the exit.

'Having to pop out again,' she sang cheerfully as she passed their desks. Jenny smiled at her vaguely and returned to Emmerdale.

4.30pm

There was an unpleasant silence; cynicism hanging in the air like wet curtains on a line.

'I rather hoped, Mrs Stone, that when you returned to say you'd witnessed something in connection with Antonia Grey's murder, you really had something worthwhile to tell us.'

Detective Sergeant Lunberry looked grey faced and jaded. The inspector had refused to see this nutter, as he called her, for a second time that day. He had sent the sergeant instead, to the room with the uncomfortable metal chairs and the chipped table, and already she could see why he wanted nothing more to do with this woman.

Despite this, DS Lunberry was reluctant to let go of any chance of getting to the truth. You just never knew. The evidence so far against Blanchard was merely circumstantial. The only thing they could pin any real hope on was a positive result from the vase and sat nav. Even with that, she had the feeling that they were still missing some vital piece of information, and however flimsy this story turned out to be, she had to sit through it.

'It's not conventional, I know, but in a way I did witness something.'

'No, Mrs Stone, you're telling me you had a dream. I have a lot dreams too, many of which I wouldn't care to share with anyone, and I certainly wouldn't use any of them to solve cases. Why do you believe your information is of any use to the police?'

'I've tried to explain, both to you and the inspector earlier. What I'm talking about isn't true dreaming at all. These events have happened all my life and I know from long experience that the things I see during them are real. There's been a lot of research done on them now and they are known as Out of Body Experiences or astral travel…'

'I know what *I'd* call them…'

Rosie ignored the interruption and continued.

'Astral travel is a better way of describing them in my opinion because during the "dream", if you want to call it that, the soul really does travel. In fact, everyone leaves their body at times while sleeping. It is perfectly natural and normal. What is less usual is for the dreamer to remember anything about where they've been. Even if they do, they usually put it down to a very clear dream. Far less usual is for the dreamer to be fully aware during the experience, and rarer still than *that*, is when someone you see in the dream sees you too, when they actually look back at you. That's happened to me several times and because of it I've learned that these events are not dreams, but astral travel.'

'Are you deliberately trying to wind me up?'

'No, it's just sad that I'm managing to.'

The sergeant sighed heavily and paced the room, well aware of how little of Henry Blanchard's extended custody time remained. The DI had been right. This woman really was a waste of time. What was it with these attention seekers? They heard about a local murder and they couldn't resist getting involved, bringing in any old trick to make themselves feel important.

'OK, Mrs Stone. Thanks for coming in. We'll get in touch if we need to follow any of this up.'

'But, I hadn't got to the important bit, the bit that involves the murder.'

'I believe you told DI Crisp about it this morning, in great detail.'

'No, he stopped listening. I really think I should say this, even if you choose to ignore it. It's not just that I saw what happened, I also saw the murder weapon. I even saw where it was put afterwards.'

DS Lunberry had been on her way out, facing a wall that was decorated with a faded Constable print in a scuffed gilt frame. She'd never liked the picture; it was the one with the big cart stuck in a puddle, and now she grimaced at it, turning reluctantly to face the woman again.

'You saw the weapon used to murder Antonia Grey?'

'I'm afraid so, yes.'

'OK...but make this quick.'

'Very briefly then; the weapon you should be looking for, according to what I saw, is a bottle. I saw that bottle being placed in an office drawer, a sliding sort of drawer used for hanging files...you know...'

The sergeant found herself nodding.

'A bottle?'

'Yes, a gin bottle, it looked like. Green glass and heavy, by the look of it, and it was filed away in an office drawer. I even saw something of the label on the drawer. Not much; something like H to H something...Hs? Hz?'

'That's it?'

'That's it. That's all I can tell you. I just thought you should have the information, even if you ignore it.'

'Yes...thanks again, then...thanks for...'

She never finished her sentence, leaving Rosie sitting alone on her uncomfortable chair by the rickety table. She got up slowly, feeling unsure about what she'd said. Perhaps she'd overdone it, but she'd had to give them that much to make them take notice. It had been the card she'd been reluctant to play. She just hoped it had been worthwhile.

Somehow she doubted it would be enough to help Henry.

DS Lunberry had hardly recovered from her bizarre interview with Rosie Stone when she came face to face with the looming presence of DI Crisp in the office doorway. He looked even less pleasant than usual and something was obviously wrong.

'Sir?' she prompted

'Forensics are back,' he grunted, 'The sat nav and vase both tested positive for Antonia Grey's blood and both items are covered with a mass of finger prints belonging to the victim, Blanchard and a whole load of others.'

'But…'

'So you know there's a but, do you, sergeant? Yeah, there is. There's no trace of body tissue or hair on either object. No way either of them is the weapon we're looking for. Being hit on the head like that would leave more than just a smear of blood…'

'Could they have been cleaned up?' she asked in vain hope.

'What? Cleaned up leaving them covered in prints?'

She groaned, joined by a colourful chorus of expletives from the two male constables behind her.

'So where does that leave us?'

'We keep this to ourselves for now and keep working on him, but without the murder weapon we're left with getting a confession out of him…'

'If it *was* him,' murmured one of the constables.

'Just one thing, sir. Rosalyn Stone…'

'Do I want to hear this?'

'Probably not, but she reckons she saw the weapon in one of the dreams she keeps going on about. Says it was a gin bottle and she saw where it was put and…I dunno, sir, but she mentioned a filing cabinet. Wouldn't it be worth just checking the drawers in Blanchard's office?'

'We've already searched his office.'

'Yes, his own room, but not the outer office where there are a lot of filing cabinets. Surely it's worth a try, sir? We'll never get another extension as things stand.'

'The woman's a fraud. We both know that.'

'Let me check it out. What is there to lose?'

DI Wayne Crisp shrugged his huge shoulders and gave his consent with a nod. She was right. The bloke was never going to confess and they had nothing. If they didn't come up with some better evidence, they'd have to let Blanchard go.

It was about an hour before he heard from the sergeant again.

'She was right, sir. Bottle was there, where she said.'

'She planted it,' he sighed, 'Too damned perfect. Things are never that perfect.'

'That's what I thought, and the bottle was full too. I thought…if someone needed to keep a bottle handy by their desk and it had been there since the murder twelve days ago, the bottle would hardly still be full, would it? I reckoned it was probably a new one, so we searched the bins round the back. Man in the office next door says the blue recycling bins aren't emptied again until Friday morning, and that they're done fortnightly, meaning that they were last emptied on the day of the murder. If the bottle was finished after that, chances are that it would still be in the bin…'

'You're a bit sharp today, sergeant,' the inspector observed drily, though he was sensing from her unusually animated tone that they might just be getting somewhere at last, 'so what did you find?'

'Three empties, sir! All the same size and shape as the full one. Gordon's Gin, 70cl bottles. I also checked the

240

ordinary trash bin, but it seems the faithful secretary is also a good recycler and all the glass was in the blue bin.'

'Bring the three empties in. Better include the full one too. We'll have them tested and no way is Blanchard going anywhere now. I'll get the request in to the magistrate. Oh, and sergeant, I still don't buy this dream crap. Get everybody's prints checked, including the secretary and the Stone woman. And everyone who uses that office. We can't afford to muck this one up.'

'Yes, sir, I thought of that too. On our way to see Mrs Stone now.'

DI Wayne Crisp put his phone back into his shirt pocket. He was almost smiling.

Chapter Twenty Five

Henry. Mid July

Lying down, Henry was staring at the wall opposite his bed. He'd become used to doing that lately. He found he could lose himself after a while, lose all track of time too, which had been useful when all means of telling the time had been taken away.

Even now, he hardly knew how he'd come through that second night in the cell. When they'd informed him that his custody had been extended for yet another period he'd feared he would lose his mind. His solicitor had explained that the police had found further evidence, but it meant nothing to him. He couldn't understand at all why they were interested in Julia's drinking habits or her bottles.

That night had gone on forever, the long, unmeasured, wakeful hours an eternity to him. He'd thought morning would never come, that the thin strips of glass in the window would never lighten. At long last, though, the usual bustling, morning noises had taken over from the night time ones. The poor old bloke along the corridor, who kept calling out piteously, had shut up for a bit when breakfast came and the woman in the cell next door, who kept up a constant and varied flow of obscenities, had changed her subject matter to complaints about the food.

The morning had worn on. He'd kept expecting to be called into the interview room again to talk about whatever they'd found, but nothing had happened and the hours had dragged past without news, without variation.

He'd just been catching the whiff of boiled vegetable and thinking that lunch was on its way, when the truly unexpected had happened. A sergeant had come in and left the door open. It had taken a ridiculously long time for the man's words to sink in, as if Henry's brain had seized up altogether. The sergeant had repeated himself, holding open the door.

Kevin Green, the solicitor, had taken him home and seemed quite cheerful, but Henry had remained frozen, as if he'd lost the ability to feel anything at all. Kevin had been explaining things, telling him that, at his insistence as Henry's solicitor, the CCTV footage had been rechecked. Apparently, on further inspection, Henry's Jaguar had been spotted on the footage; blurry and at the very edge of the image, but there all right. That image of his car, parked at the right time in the busy market place, had provided him at last with an alibi. So, Kevin had redeemed himself after all and Henry was suitably grateful. Apart from that though, nothing much that the solicitor told him had really sunk in. Henry's strangely frozen senses were just unable to process any more information.

Later, Bruce had arrived. Good old Bruce; whatever would he have done without him?

Henry blinked, still staring at the bedroom wall. He had to get up. There were things he had to sort out, things he had to apply his mind to. Bruce had been the one to get through to him about poor Julia. He'd repeated what the solicitor had tried to convey, that they'd found the evidence they needed on one of Julia's empty bottles. With her finger prints all over it, and traces of Antonia's blood, tissue and hair somewhere on the base of it, Julia was the obvious new target for them. Bruce was devastated, his relief at Henry's release ruined only moments later by this new nightmare.

Henry thought about Julia now, who was possibly in the same cell as he'd occupied, staring at that unfinished word on the wall. It would get to her as much as it had him. She would be going through hell.

Over the next two weeks there was much to occupy Henry. There was the funeral to arrange and Antonia's family to cope with. There was a small party of them that he felt obliged to offer a bed for the night, since they had to travel up from Dorset. Antonia's mother was silent and constantly tearful and he pitied her, but as it had always been, Antonia's father remained unexpressive and uncommunicative and it was impossible to reach him. The whole, long episode had been a nightmare for them all, but even in good times long past, there had never been any warmth between them and Henry. Though he was no longer under suspicion, it was clear that they still didn't know how to treat him. Mostly, they ignored him. He had never been one of them and they weren't about to change that now.

At last, the cloud of the funeral and all that went with it passed and gradually Henry found himself able to think of other things. He felt as if he were recovering from a long illness, spending long days in sleeping or doing very little.

The cronies had started to reappear as soon as he'd come home; Pamela with her well-meaning cakes and casseroles, Sylvia with her honeyed, reassuring words. Even Eugenie, Ronnie and Malcolm had shown up; Eugenie with something out of her freezer, the twins with a bottle each. He was grateful to them all, but he was still unready for much of their company. Antonia's golfing friends had all attended the funeral, of course, but he hadn't heard from them since and he doubted whether he ever would again.

Bruce continued to call in often, but now he was the one who needed consoling. Julia had been charged with the murder because, according to the police, there was more than enough evidence against her. Henry, who for the life of him couldn't imagine that she was guilty, had found her a much livelier solicitor than the conscientious but uninspiring Mr Green. He'd found the new lawyer in Norwich and was paying the bill, though try as he might, the man didn't seem to be getting anywhere.

Things, therefore, were still far from happy. Without Julia, and with Henry still trying to get himself back to normal, the Mason and Blanchard office in Downham Market was temporarily closed. The locum was still helping out from his own premises and, as Julia had feared, was gradually taking over the firm's clients. Very soon, Henry knew, he'd have to return and start to rebuild his business. The life insurance policy had finally paid out and was doing exactly what he and Antonia had meant it to do; it was funding this crisis time. It would be very useful for paying off Antonia's family and the remainder of the mortgage, as well as providing a back-up for income until the business was up and running again. There was so much to do and yet still he felt incapable of starting.

His sleepy recuperation continued for several more days. The doctor told him not to rush things, that he had to give himself time. He'd been through too much to expect an instant return to action. It felt at times as if he'd been drugged, the way he seemed to float pointlessly around the house and unkempt garden. Sometimes he went shopping for food or walked the dog, but he was glad when he made it home again without meeting anyone he knew.

Then at last, one fine morning in early July, something seemed to change.

He'd left his bedroom window slightly open and the first sounds to stir him that morning were of birdsong. He frowned, wondering briefly why he'd never been properly aware of it before. It was joyous.

As he lay there, the frown disappeared from his brow and a new emotion stirred within him, something that felt curiously like happiness. He wondered whether he'd ever heard birdsong as sweet as this. He sprang out of bed and heaved on the heavy sash window, hearing its surprised squealing as it opened as far as he could push it. Warmth and sounds drifted up from the summer garden, storming his long-deadened senses with overwhelming brightness. He was smiling as he leaned out, feeling the soft touch of the breeze on his face.

Beyond the patio stretched the long grass and smothered flower beds of the wilderness that had once been his garden. Gazing at it with the benefit of his newly discovered optimism, the garden was still beautiful to him. It was vibrant; full of life and joy, simply hidden beneath a layer of neglect that could soon be swept away. As if to confirm this idea, Polly the cat crept out from under a mass of dead lupin spikes and looked up at him, her little mouth forming a silent miaow. It was a request. It was a request for him to return to life, to go down and join her. She must have been hungry too.

He picked up his dressing gown from the floor where it had fallen in a heap the night before and ran down the stairs. He threw open the back windows and doors, running out with bare feet on to the warm stone. The little cat, tail high, came to greet him and Arnold came rushing out from his bed in the kitchen.

Today Henry would get into the garden and work. It was a good place to start; first the garden, then the rest of his life.

Before making himself breakfast, he picked up the telephone and spoke to Mrs Saunders, the eternally cheerful lady who had managed the housework for Antonia. Mrs Saunders had never had a first name, according to Antonia's telephone book and Henry's memory. She was simply Mrs Saunders, a smiling and efficient presence in an immaculate yellow apron who worked wonders in the house. She seemed happy to hear from him, glad to resume work, and they agreed that she should start the next day. As he rang off, his eyes rested on the telephone book that Antonia had kept for years, amending it with every change of number and address. He flicked through the pages, looking at her handwriting, the large looped, confident letters recording all the names that had made up her world.

'You poor old girl,' he whispered, 'So sorry it had to end like that.'

He shut the book with a decisive snap. He must try not to be maudlin today. There had been so much grief, so much anger and gloom already, and knowing that Julia was in custody, had been charged, and must therefore be going through far worse than he had, was enough to darken any day. It was hard to remain cheerful when Julia was still suffering, hard to forget her predicament even for a few minutes at a time. He felt guilty about the way he had taken her for granted, trampling over her feelings, and for the way Antonia had treated her. Had she been tried to snapping point? Could she really have done it? He found it very hard to believe.

His old, faithful friend Bruce was suffering too. He had become close to Julia during Henry's problems and on his release, news of the growing closeness between Julia and Bruce had been very welcome. It had seemed inevitable that any day soon they'd get together properly. And then the law had pounced on her, cutting off normal life with one brutal swipe. Henry was pinning his hopes on the solicitor he had hired for her. The bugger was certainly expensive enough.

But the sun was pouring in through the windows and the open door to the patio. The light lay like a golden pathway across the carpet, holding a host of tiny dancing motes of dust within its rays. It was drawing him back towards the garden and his heart could not help but be lifted, a heart that had been so compressed and dark for so long.

He stepped outside and breathed in the scents of hidden flowers. He walked across the patio and inspected the flower bed by the wall. A golden cloud of marigolds billowed around the hydrangeas where small green buds were beginning to show. Elsewhere, though, the beds were a mess of long grass and dock leaves that threatened to smother the lavender and brave old roses that peered through. The area beyond the lawn was the most neglected. The old shrubbery had become a thicket surrounding an island of long grass and neglected aluminium garden furniture. He had to admit it was a bit of a jungle.

He was mulling things over, making plans as he walked. He had to get back into the office and hire a temp to take care of the administration until Julia came back, or heaven forbid, to replace the poor girl if she never did. Then he had to get out there, see his clients and try to win some of them back. It was going to take time and it would be anything but easy, but he was ready for it now. Almost, anyway. Today there was the garden and there was this new life and the sunshine. Today he would be happy.

After breakfast, he set to work. He found an old pair of wellies in the back of the garage under the long abandoned work bench. At least three generations of spiders seemed to be living in them, weaving mini webs inside and around them, so that he had to wipe them out with an old rag before he could wiggle his feet into them. They flapped strangely against his calves as he walked down to the ancient garden shed. He couldn't remember the last time he'd worn the boots and he had the feeling that they weren't even his, that they'd been left by the bloke Antonia once employed to do the garden. He couldn't even remember the man's name, but recalled that the episode hadn't been a success. There'd been some argument about him chucking fag ends in the water butt or something. Henry couldn't quite remember.

The shed door creaked open to reveal more cobwebs, this time strewn across an array of rusty rakes, forks and spades, as well as his trusty mower. The hairy state of the grass reminded him how long it had been since the lawn had had a cut; well before the awful events of the last few weeks. He made a mental note to pick up petrol next time he was out and get the old machine going again.

The garden had never been well tended. It had been his job to cut the grass and he'd never been very good at it. Antonia had made half-hearted attempts to weed the flower beds on the occasional sunny day without social commitments. Pulling on a smart pair of leather gloves and tottering outside with her weeding basket, she would snip and tug away at unwanted plants, but it had never been enough. Henry knew it was time to hire a regular gardener to help him tame this wilderness and he made another mental note to sort that out. In the meantime, though, the peace of manual work on this glorious day suited his mood. He picked up some long handled shears and prised a rusted fork from the stack, sending a long legged spindly creature scuttling across the board floor. He located the old wheelbarrow behind the shed and, dropping the tools into it, wheeled his equipment away to start work.

He began with the flower bed nearest the house, removing dead stems of foxglove and aquilegia, together with masses of long grass, and tossed them into the barrow. He worked steadily, cutting back long tendrils of honeysuckle and digging out briar roots to make space for the struggling magnolias. Slowly but surely, he was getting somewhere. He was happy.

In the quiet of late afternoon, with the sun sloping in through windows on the side of the house facing west, a weary but contented Henry settled into his favourite chair with a gin and tonic. Tomorrow, he decided, he would get into the office and make an early start. He was almost looking forward to the challenge, encouraged by how much difference he'd made in the garden in a single day. That would be tomorrow. But today, before he had any more to drink, there was one more thing he had to do.

His solicitor had told him how the evidence that had shifted suspicion from him to Julia had been received, about the bizarre nature of it all. It had taken a while for these peculiar facts to sink in, that Rosie Stone, a woman he'd last seen fourteen months ago, had somehow come to his aid. While the police were still awaiting the forensic results from the bottle, Henry had remained their main suspect and his solicitor had had trouble persuading them to re-examine the CCTV records. When they'd finally agreed to it, it had been this rechecking that had eventually confirmed Henry's alibi, but the real breakthrough had come through the discovery of Julia's finger prints on the bottle. And all that had apparently resulted from some loopy story Rosie had told the police. Whatever or however or why ever she'd done this for him, he owed her thanks. He could not simply ignore it.

He walked over to the bookcase where his leather bound classics had sat for years, undisturbed by Antonia and only rarely picked up by him. He lifted one of his old favourites from the shelf and opened it respectfully. "A Christmas Carol" by Dickens. Whatever the season, he loved the book, loved its simple, inspiring message. He leafed through it and pulled out from between the pages a tiny folded sheet. On it, jotted diagonally across the paper in hurriedly formed digits, was a telephone number. It seemed so long ago now that he'd made a note of it, ready to use if he ever had the nerve. At last, that time had come.

For better or for worse, he had a debt to repay.

Chapter Twenty Six

Rosie. Mid July

It had been Jenny who had put the call through, her tone so casual, as if announcing someone from a life company. Then suddenly there it was; his voice on the line.

His voice. How many times had she heard it in her mind, remembered it from those happy, long ago days of last summer? Ever since his release she had wondered, hardly daring to, whether he would get in touch, but the days, then the weeks, had gone by with no word at all. Now at last she was truly hearing his voice again, the rich, reassuring tones of it. She'd had to pull herself together to concentrate on what he was saying.

He wondered whether she'd like to meet up briefly, he'd said, perhaps go for a walk somewhere, have lunch? He just wanted to thank her, apparently.

So here she was, walking towards town on an overcast Saturday morning. She hadn't been able to think straight when he'd asked her to suggest somewhere nearby they could go to. She'd uttered the first place name that had come to mind; Peckover House with its garden and the estate which stretched behind it. She had no idea whether this was quite what he had in mind but, especially when out in the wide open fields, they'd be able to talk uninterrupted.

She'd agreed to meet him in the car park and she made her way there on foot, turning into Chapel Road from North Brink, slowing her steps as she drew nearer. She was more than ten minutes early, so she took a detour around the rugby field next to the car park, keeping close to the trees and taking her time.

The car park was full. The place was teeming with Saturday shoppers, visitors to Peckover House and people filling their car boots with produce and second hand treasures from the auction hall nearby. It ought to have been difficult to spot his car amongst so many others. He'd omitted to tell her on the phone what the car looked like, but of course she'd seen it once outside his office. Even so, it could be hard sometimes to locate your own vehicle in a full car park.

How strange then, that she saw his Jaguar straight away. The sun was doing its best to break through the heavy bank of white cloud and for a moment it glimmered on the roof of a dark car entering the car park. From where she stood, all she could see was its dark top making its languorous way between parked vehicles in search of a space, but she just knew it was his. Then it turned and was heading in her direction; his black Jaguar. It nosed its refined way into a space that was overhung by a canopy of horse chestnut, facing the rugby field.

His face was thinner than she remembered it, and more lined. He was well dressed, as usual, in immaculate, expensive looking chinos and a green polo shirt. She watched him lock the car as she walked to meet him, smiling a little cautiously, the whole situation feeling unreal to her. His smile looked uncertain too. So much time had passed since their last meeting and this encounter might be anything but easy. Their brief relationship, ended so long ago, in a place so far away, seemed strangely irrelevant now. It felt like having a pocketful of Turkish Lira and trying to spend it in Tesco. It just had no place here.

His eyes followed her as she approached, his smile broadening. He stood by his car, one foot lifted and poised behind the other, the toe tapping the ground gently. It was a stance she remembered and the familiarity was comforting. Then at last she was standing in front of him. For an awkward moment she thought he was going to shake her hand and she had a faint recollection of thinking this once before. Then he seemed to realise what he was doing and corrected himself mid-gesture, his face breaking into a renewed toothy, natural smile as their eyes met.

'Good to see you, Rosie,' he said, a bit too formally but warmly, the light in his eyes as they met hers alleviating the awkwardness.

'You too,' she replied, sounding even starchier than he did. It was better when they began to walk, setting off across the rugby field towards one of the tree lined drainage ditches that divided the estate into different areas.

'Can we get across the brook?' he asked, seeing no obvious bridge.

'Brook?' she laughed, 'We're in the Fens, remember. This is a drainage ditch, which happens to look pretty because of all the trees. Water's low at the moment, so we can walk across. No problem.'

'Ah, yes, the dear old Fens,' he laughed drily.

The sun kept breaking through the clouds, the day gradually brightening as they crossed the ditch and walked on. Their conversation was beginning to flow more easily and already she was dropping the notion that their old relationship was somehow irrelevant. He felt so familiar to her, the months between their last troubled meeting and this nervous one falling away to nothing. She noticed that they were both still avoiding any mention of last summer and of the last few weeks, but there was no hurry. It could wait.

As they skirted the Wisbech Cricket Club's ground, several men dressed in whites were busy removing the big canvas covers from the pitch.

'Looks like they'll be playing soon,' Henry observed. We could stay and watch if you like,' he was smiling, teasing her a bit, knowing she was no sports fan.

'Monica would love to. You remember Monica?'

It was the first reference to the past, but a nice, safe one. He nodded thoughtfully as they approached another ditch.

'There's a lot we need to talk about, Rosie.'

The second ditch was as dry as the first but deeper, its sides of compacted earth smooth from long use as a crossing place between two fields. Children making dens and adults cutting across the National Trust estate had made a gap between the elders and hawthorn, so that the ditch was easily accessible from both sides. In wet weather it could fill quickly, becoming impassable, but the recent dry conditions made crossing easy.

He took her hand as she stepped down into the ditch. She tried to concentrate on her feet while her heart leaped. She wanted to carry on holding onto him when they were back on level ground, but he dropped her hand again, looking serious suddenly.

'There's a lot I need to say, Rosie, and much I have to thank you for. Your contacting the police like that. You didn't have to. None of this had anything to do with you, yet you walked right in and helped me. Before you spoke to the police things were looking bad for me. I'm very grateful to you, but have to say I don't understand why or quite how you intervened.'

She let a few seconds pass before replying.

'I did it because I knew you could never have done what they were accusing you of and I couldn't stand by, doing nothing. I didn't have much hope of them listening, but it was worth a try. In the end, although they made it quite clear what they thought of me, it seems they acted on the information I gave them. I suppose they were getting desperate by then.'

'But my solicitor said it was all about dreams, that you were some sort of psychic. He said that the police listen sometimes, even if reluctantly, to psychics.'

She shook her head.

'I'm not a psychic.'

'Bit of a witch, though, Rosie,' he was grinning, trying to alleviate a subject they both found awkward. She smiled too, allowing another pause before going on. She told him about the dreams she'd begun to have as a child and how she'd gradually come to understand what was happening to her. Then she went on to the research that had been carried out and which had given her some answers. The account she gave him was more personal and detailed than the clinical summary she'd given the police, but still it was no easy thing to explain. When she reached the words "astral travel" she caught the expression on his face and sighed.

'So you see? Can you imagine how the delightful Detective Inspector Wayne Crisp reacted to it?'

'Well, yes,' he agreed cautiously, 'and I'm afraid I'm not much better at understanding than he was…but go on…how did all this help me?'

'It's complicated, but very briefly, since you and I, well, parted in Turkey, I've had a few of these clear dreams that involved you and people I later realised were part of your world. During one of them I saw something that, if true, meant you did not hurt Antonia.'

He looked dubious, as well he might.

'The bottle. You saw the bottle, my solicitor said.'

'I did… but we've all afternoon to talk about it. Let's come back to it later,' she suggested brightly, feeling the need for a change of subject. He smiled as if relieved, reaching for her hand again. He hardly seemed to notice he'd done it.

They passed a line of ancient beech trees, then made their slow way back over the grassy fields to the car park. Crossing the road and cutting through to North Brink, they headed for Peckover House.

The small shop where they had to pick up their tickets was swarming with people. Before they reached it, however, a bright and breezy lady in a black National Trust shirt approached them in the dark hallway, waving an item at them that looked like an old fashioned calculator.

'Are you members?' she almost sang, 'I can scan your cards here and save you having to queue, if you are.'

Henry grunted amiably, putting the twenty pound note he'd proffered back in his pocket and beginning a frantic search through his wallet. Behind them, the queue was growing longer by the second, but finally, with a triumphant flourish, the membership card was produced.

Judging by how deeply it had been buried in his wallet, Rosie thought, it didn't get much use. She had her own card ready and both were promptly scanned by the cheerful lady who was no doubt keen to clear the queue.

They wandered from room to room in the house, even though Rosie had seen it many times before and Henry looked too distracted to take much in. He seemed to find the exhibition room upstairs the most interesting, reading about the Quaker Peckover family who had lived in the house for around a hundred and fifty years. Rosie, meanwhile, was studying a sketch map of the region in Saxon times. She felt him join her after a while, his feet making the old floor boards squeak in indignation. The room steward coughed behind them.

'The sea reached as far as Wisbech then,' said the man and they turned politely to face him. There were several other visitors in the exhibition room, but perhaps Rosie and Henry were the only ones showing any real interest.

'The sea...the Wash, do you mean?' asked Henry.

'That's right,' nodded the steward, his auburn hair catching the sunlight that stole through the half-closed shutters at the window, 'Between the water-logged Fenland, the river and the sea, this town was just a tiny island of wildfowlers and fishermen back then.'

Henry smiled, attracted by the thought of all that isolation.

'Sounds peaceful.'

The steward smiled back and continued his slow perambulation of the upstairs rooms, acknowledging Rosie's thanks with nod of his russet locks.

'I wonder if life was as uncomplicated then as it sounds,' mused Henry.

'I doubt it. Life's always complicated and it would have been a lot harsher than what we have to put up with now.'

He looked thoughtful, taking her hand again and leading her down the wide stairs and out through the back door into the garden. This was Henry's first glimpse of the garden, having visited the property only once before, for an inside evening event with a group of Antonia's friends. He gazed around in admiration as they strolled along the Wilderness Walk. It was a peaceful, shady path, bordering the lawn where Rosie and Monica had sat to listen to the tribute band a couple of months earlier. It seemed an age ago.

Henry was less interested in individual plants and flowers than he was in the overall structure and feel of the garden. He admired each fresh view as they turned a corner or ventured down a different path. He began to tell her about his own garden and his new interest in it, how he was enjoying working in it. It was good to come home to, he explained, after a long day in the office, even if he only spent a few minutes working and the rest just sitting in the evening sun by his old garden shed. He was animated and happy as he talked, even quite philosophical about his first few days back in the office and the inevitable problems that had greeted him.

'It'll take time,' he acknowledged, 'I know I'll get there in the end.'

Rosie let him talk, murmuring the odd reply, just feeling happy. She was enjoying every moment of this day with him, aware that it exceeded all her expectations and hopes. It felt utterly natural to be with him again and all her early nerves were long gone. He was admiring one of the fish ponds, laughing at something and she laughed too. The sun broke through the clouds with a determined effort, flooding the garden with an extra dimension of light and colour.

'You know, Rosie,' he said quietly as he watched the golden fish dart between clumps of water weed, the sun glinting on their backs, 'I'm so happy. Just being back in my own home…I never appreciated how precious that freedom was before. Every simple thing seems special. And now with today being so…I feel so guilty about being this happy. How can I be happy when poor Antonia has lost her life, when it ended so cruelly? How can I allow myself to be content when my secretary, a dear lady called Julia, is in custody? According to the police, there's no doubt she killed Antonia. The evidence seems stacked against her. Even the hot-shot solicitor I hired to represent her admits there's not much hope of avoiding a sentence. How, when she is going through all of that, do I have the right to be happy?'

Rosie was quiet for a moment, taking his hand from where it had dropped by his side.

'You have every right to be happy, Henry.'

They walked again and he released her hand gently, putting an arm around her and pulling her close to his side. He was very quiet and she was extremely aware of his closeness. They entered the Reed Barn courtyard, where several tables had been set out and a few families were sitting peacefully in the sun.

'Let's have lunch out here,' he suggested, 'It's warm enough, isn't it?'

'It would be a pity if we didn't,' she agreed happily.

The Reed Barn seemed dark, coming in from the brightness of the garden, its ancient brick walls looming high above them. They queued by the display of huge, cream laden sponge cakes and hefty slabs of fruitcake, choosing what they wanted from the chalked display boards on the walls. Henry insisted on paying and was given a little flag with a number on it, being told that their food would be brought out to them. He looked embarrassed.

'What's the matter?' she laughed as they seated themselves at a neat table with a checked cloth in a sunny corner of the courtyard.

'I'm sorry, Rosie. I meant to take you to lunch in a proper restaurant. I didn't mean you to have to queue up and order from a board!'

'It's perfect, just as it is. What could be better than eating outside on a lovely July afternoon in such beautiful surroundings?'

He was fidgeting on the iron garden chair, glancing around as he replaced his wallet in his inside jacket pocket. He noticed the flowers that decorated every table and the herbs in lovely old pots that nestled in groups against the warm brick of the courtyard walls.

'Yes, it *is* perfect, isn't it?' he reconsidered. Then he was laughing again, a big toothy grin making his face look boyish and completely happy, 'You're right. It's absolutely bloody perfect.'

He remained thoughtful for a while, his face growing sober. She knew the mood had to change. It couldn't be held back any longer.

'I'm utterly sorry that I wasn't honest with you when we met. I regretted it as soon as the deception began and there was never going to be a good time to confess.'

'I know,' she said, 'It's OK; all water under the bridge now.'

'And then…Antonia. The way she had to die, Rosie. It was terrible. She was difficult; most people knew that, but what happened to her was appalling. I feel so sorry that such a dreadful thing happened to her, but the truth is that as a couple we were miserable. I can't be a hypocrite. We were both unhappy, yet for some reason we never admitted that it had to end. And then the end came in the worst possible way.'

'Did she ever know about…what happened in Turkey?'

He shook his head.

'Not exactly, but she had a feeling. I suppose I was just so miserable when I got home that it was hard to hide. She was bound to pick up on it.'

'You were miserable? '

'Of course I was! I knew I'd brought it on myself, but the way you just walked away from me, after all that had happened between us.'

'I'm sorry. I really am. I was so arrogant, so self righteous. I should at least have listened to you. I really regretted it.'

He smiled faintly.

'Really?'

'Yes, really.' For some reason they were both laughing. Perhaps it was just a release of tension and it didn't feel out of place. He was holding her hand again.

'I never forgot you,' he said quietly.

'I couldn't forget you either, though I tried. I tried so hard and it didn't work at all.'

They were quiet as a cheerful waitress bustled to their table with tall glasses of orange juice and plates of food on a huge tray. His steak and kidney pie with chips seemed a bit unseasonable, but looked good. Rosie's Caesar salad looked appetising, but it was hard to think about food right then. They began to eat slowly.

'The principal reason for me phoning you, apart from the obvious need to see you again,' he began, pausing as he speared a chip, 'was to thank you for what you did to help me. You were explaining earlier about your dreams, the astral something or other...'

'Travel. Astral travel.'

'Yes, that's it. I can't pretend to understand, but I accept it's something you experience. You were saying earlier, I think, that in some of these...dreams...you saw me? Is that what you meant?'

She nodded, collecting her thoughts for a moment. Even now, it was a bit embarrassing to admit to being so obsessed with him that he dominated her dream world.

'On one occasion, I dreamed I was in a garden. There was a cat, some people standing on a terrace and I thought I saw you...of course, I couldn't be sure. It was all a bit indistinct.'

'But you did, Rosie! There were some friends with us on the patio at the back of the house and the cat had taken fright over something. We were all looking out into the garden and just for a moment I thought I saw someone, a shadow really, but it made me think of you.'

She smiled and continued.

'There was another time too, more recently. I saw you in your room. No mistaking the fact that it was you this time and I think you saw me too.'

He groaned.

'That was a very bad time. I was drinking far too much and felt dire. When I saw you standing at the foot of my bed I put it down to the drink!' He paused, thinking of Sylvia and her "ghost". 'I remember something else,' he continued, 'It was a while ago now, at a party. A friend of mine thought she saw a woman in the house, a guest we knew didn't exist. She was so convinced, yet we all gave her a hard time over it...'

'Yes,' she replied after a thoughtful pause, 'I think that was the first time I saw anything connected to you. There was no one I knew in the dream, but I just had a feeling you were involved somehow.'

'Well then, Rosie, it appears I've witnessed this astral travel of yours twice, so you could say I have evidence that it really happens. Being a cynical old bloke, though, I still find it hard to accept.'

'I understand. It takes a while to sink in.' She was grinning and he began to laugh.

'Got to say though, despite my doubts, next time I'm reading a private letter I'll be looking over my shoulder to check you've not materialised and aren't standing there, reading my secrets!'

She laughed, nearly choking on her orange juice.

'Don't worry, that's hardly likely. I'd never be able to see detail like that!'

They ate and drank in silence for a few seconds. He was obviously thinking things through, chewing pensively, forming questions in his mind. She waited, eating little bits of salad, unable to taste much of it.

'So, then, the dream you told the cops about...I suppose I need to know, though it's too nice a day to spoil, really, with such a gloomy subject...'

'You're right, it's far too happy a day, so I'll keep it brief and then we can move on to more cheerful things. In the dream I saw a tall, fair haired woman on a grassy river bank being assaulted by another woman with a bottle. A green glass bottle. I then saw the bottle being put into an office draw.'

She was holding back a little, but she couldn't bear to admit to him that she'd been to his office and had therefore recognised both Antonia and Julia when she saw them in her dream. She wouldn't tell him about that embarrassing little incident unless she really had to. The details of the dream could remain vague for now.

'That's what you told the police?'

'More or less, yes. The inspector wouldn't listen to much of it, but I told the sergeant more.'

'My solicitor said it was thanks to the precise detail you gave that the police decided in the end to search for the bottle.'

She paused.

'I wouldn't have called it precise, exactly, and neither of the officers seemed at all convinced...'

'Can I get you anything else?' the waitress was back, still smiling. Suddenly, Rosie wanted to break up this conversation and get away. She declined politely and the waitress began collecting the plates. Rosie scraped back the heavy chair on the cobbles and paused as Henry did the same. He didn't seem to notice her hurry, amiably reaching for her hand again as they took a different route back through the garden. He seemed as relieved as she was to change the subject and they began reminiscing about good times in Turkey, memories that seemed to come from another life. But she knew he'd whittle away until he knew everything. She knew he was just biding his time.

She walked back to the car park with him, refusing his offer of a lift home. She hoped there would be other times, but for now she needed to be alone and to think. They stepped through a gap in the fence and made their way along the edge of the tree-lined rugby pitch, rather than through the lines of parked cars. The branches of horse chestnut, laden with full summer leaf and small, spiky

262

green seed cases, arched low. Sunshine glinted through the splayed, hand-like leaves which moved gently in the breeze, as if patting the air. The sunlight touched his face as he pulled her towards him and she leant against him, forgetting everything for a moment as he kissed her. She never wanted it to end, that melting of grief and anger from the last long months. The past was dissolving into sweetness. The future was a thing to be resolved and they could have the world again if she just…

'When can I see you again?' he asked so quietly it was barely a breath.

'Soon.'

'Perhaps next time I could show you something of my world…the bits you haven't visited in your sleep,' he smiled, 'I'll show you the office and we could have lunch…'

'That would be perfect.'

'…because you've never seen the…' he paused and she struggled to turn her face to him, peering out from her safe nestling place against his shoulder. Very slightly, he was pulling away, a frown shadowing his face.

'Rosie, my solicitor said you gave the police detailed information about the drawer label, the one the bottle was in. I don't get it. You told me you don't see much clear detail in your dreams, so how could you have seen what a drawer label said? The writing on the labels is small. How could you possibly have made out detail like that?'

She sighed. She had to admit to being a love-lorn fool, then.

'Because I called at your office one day. I didn't want to tell you; it's just too damned embarrassing. But I wanted to see you again and I called in on my way home from a workshop. You were out, thankfully.'

'Aha!' he laughed suddenly, 'Oh Rosie, how wonderful that you came to find me! Do you know how often I've almost called you at work? I wish I'd been there that day, I really do. It could have changed everything. If I'd known you still cared, even still thought of me…oh, Rosie!' he

263

pulled her tight again, his face against hers. 'That explains how you were familiar with the office layout, how you were able to…'

Then the frown was back, comprehension dawning. He had pulled away, right away. She was standing alone suddenly. She felt cold. He was looking at her in bafflement with those eyes of his. There was no escape from them, nowhere to hide.

'It doesn't explain at all how you knew about the drawer label. No one would know what was written on it unless they opened the hatch and walked behind the counter. Yet, according to my solicitor, you told them what the label said. How could you have known? No one but Julia and I could have known how any of those labels read. And please don't tell me about dreams again. You've already told me it's not possible to read a letter when you're having one of your experiences.   Same thing applies to labels, Rosie.'

She looked at him, feeling small and afraid. She felt her way backwards, finding the tree trunk and leaning against it. His eyes were staring into hers, imploringly, begging her to tell him something easy, something he could understand.

'Rosie, darling, I think you should tell me what really happened.'

His eyes blinked, hurt, confused, still locked on to hers, looking at her in horrified silence. There was nowhere to run, nowhere to hide any more.

She told him.

Chapter Twenty Seven

Rewind

Those eyes of his. I just stood there, against that tree, and told him everything. What else could I do? There was no future at all with that great ugly lie stuck there between us.

I told him again about the dream, but this time I hid nothing. I told him how I'd seen Julia belting poor old Antonia over the head with a gin bottle before placing the bottle in the drawer beside her desk. The important thing about that dream, though, that no one noticed at the time because they weren't interested enough to listen properly, was that it was simply that; it was just a dream.

Just a dream.

All my true astral travel took place in real time. All the things I saw were truly happening at that very moment, such as the party in January and the spring evening when I visited Henry's garden, scaring his poor cat. Then there was the conscious out of body travel when I went to see him in his room during his darkest days. But when I saw Antonia's murder it was pure dreaming; a nasty nightmare best forgotten. How could it be anything else? I dreamed it more than twenty-four hours before Antonia met her end. If anyone had been listening to my repeated explanations, they'd have spotted that straight away.

I told him how, on that one visit to his office in the spring, I'd seen Antonia. I'd seen how arrogant she was, how badly she behaved towards Julia. I'd also learned a little about how Julia ran the office, and I'd caught sight of her drinking from a bottle kept in the drawer.

He never interrupted, just kept looking at me out of those wounded eyes and I had little choice but to plough on.

I reached the part about the drive to Stansted, still hesitating over how to phrase things, the rough bark of the horse chestnut tree digging into my shoulder blades as I leant against it for support. And still he listened, waiting.

I told him that I'd left early for the airport that morning because deep down, without admitting it even to myself, I had always meant to. I'd not been able to resist one more look at his office, one more chance of seeing him. And I'd been rewarded in a way. There'd been that one fleeting glimpse of him at the kerb side, then his departure in the car. The brief peepshow over, however, I'd been overwhelmed by a huge wave of disappointment and sadness. I'd found myself wishing that I'd travelled direct to Stansted and avoided more unnecessary pain.

But then Julia and a client had appeared at the office door and for some reason I'd stayed a little longer and watched. Perhaps I just couldn't tear myself away from that spy-hole into his world. I'd seen Julia and the man disappearing into the coaching entrance at the side of the building and without thinking I'd followed them. I still don't understand what made me do that, but before I'd doubled back I'd seen how engrossed they were in the papers the client was showing her.

I swear that I never planned it. How could anyone plan a thing like that, based as it was on pure chance? But the office door was unlocked, the secretary absent, and I knew where I was likely to find the bottle. Taking it was easy. I knew that putting it back, if I ever did, would be much harder.

I had slipped on a pair of leather gloves, left in my jacket pocket from colder days, and gripped the bottle by the lid. I'd seen plenty of films where the baddie did things like that.

I explained to his big, sad eyes that finding Antonia that morning hadn't been difficult. I'd known her car because I'd seen it before, on that spring day in Downham when she'd been so horrible to Julia. So, I'd spotted it straight away; its rear end just visible from the road. She'd parked it in the lay-by, close to the bridge.

She'd been making her way back to the car, as it happened, striding towards the grassy bank that separated the river from the road. Her crazy, beautiful dog was giving her trouble, as usual. She'd taken no notice of me as I strolled by, taking the air. The bottle was in my shoulder bag and I'd kept one gloved hand on it, ready. And I'd watched Antonia make her way up the bank.

I hadn't allowed thoughts to get in the way and she'd never seen me coming, being so wrapped up in her daily battle with the dog. Before I'd known it, the deed was done. It was a terrible thing to do. It took a lot more force than I'd anticipated, but then she was on the ground and very still and the poor dog was making a horrible noise.

I'd been terrified by then, appalled by what I'd done, but it was too late and I had to keep a cool head. I'd tried to drag her towards the water, but she was way too heavy, so I'd left her on the grass and driven away from there, the repulsive bottle back in my bag, and I knew I had to get rid of the thing. I'd been shaking as I reached High Street again, all that cold adrenalin that had allowed me to do what I'd done, long gone.

I'd had to steel myself to go back into the office. There'd been a line of people at the desk and Julia had looked under pressure. If anyone had come in behind me, I'd have left, dumped the bottle in a bin somewhere. Perhaps I should have done, but then there'd have been no evidence to call on, to take the heat off Henry.

Once I'd moved to the front of the queue, I told her I needed to make an appointment. I'd seen the diary wasn't on her desk and guessed she'd have to fetch it. I was right. Once she'd opened the hatch on her counter and disappeared through the back door, it was all too easy. She'd even left the hatch unbolted and I'd dropped the bottle into her drawer so quickly that I'd actually had to wait for her to amble back with the diary.

I could have fled, of course, but that would have made her suspicious straight away. So, instead I'd given her a false name and said I'd come in the following week for a financial review.

I wondered whether she'd missed the bottle in its short absence, but by the look of things she'd been too busy for that.

The strange thing was, that in the days that followed; in Turkey, then at home, as I'd watched the local news unfold, I could almost believe that I'd had nothing to do with Antonia's death. I'd found myself reacting to the news in as horrified a way as everyone else. Perhaps I'd become so efficient at blocking out memories that I truly forgot at times that I'd been involved.

It had only been when Henry became the chief suspect that I'd known I had to act. I'd decided to use that nightmare; that nasty little dream of Julia attacking Antonia. After all, it was that which had given me the idea in the first place. It wasn't difficult to make it sound like the astral travel I'd been experiencing all my life.

Unfortunately, though, the police had been even tougher to convince than I'd feared. I'd had to add that final piece of information about the drawer label.

It turned out to be the detail that freed Henry and betrayed me.

So, there it was, all done. My story was told and off my chest. For the record, I was nearly as sorry about Julia being arrested as I'd been about Henry, but at least now she would be freed and able to get on with her life. I was sorry about all of it, really, but that wouldn't make much difference now.

I had sung my song and his eyes, once so warm, then so wounded, were now so very cold.

But he let me walk away. For then, at least.

Step by step, I made my uncertain way across the grass, heading for home, and I don't even think he watched me go. There'd been no reaction from him, nothing at all, but already in my head I could hear sirens blaring, see blue lights flashing.

Afterword

Rosie. Two years later

It has been good to write, to put everything down on paper. Setting it all out like this, letting it flow from memory to pages of A4, doesn't make any of it go away, but it transfers it to somewhere I can cope with it better.

One day I shall be free again. They say that if I behave myself I shall be able to get out early. I intend to do just that; mostly I am good at behaving myself.

After serving a life sentence, even a shortened one, can life ever be good again? Do I deserve it to be?

I don't know, but as the clock ticks, as the pages on the calendar turn, as the leaves on the trees outside change colour with the season, the time grows nearer when I will know.

Monica visits often. She still doesn't understand what made me do what I did, but she is still there, my good friend. I really don't deserve her.

And Henry. Henry came to see me this week for the first time, sober-faced, polite, but at least he came. He didn't have to.

And one day, one day I shall be free.

Thank you…..

This book has been in my thoughts, half formed and dozing away, for years and finally the time has come to write it. I've discussed it over and over again with Tony, my dear and patient husband, and I thank him now for all of the listening and for his long hours of proof reading.

I am also very grateful to the following people who have helped me with certain aspects of the book:

Mariana Vidlak Brooker, for her patient explanations about astral travel.

Richard (Tom) Calton of RTC Plant Services Ltd, for his help on old tractors!

Tom Calton (tomcalton.co.uk) for the front cover photograph and the black and white image of the 'angel' statue in a niche.

Sergeant Andy Crown of Norfolk Police and Detective Superintendant Mike Howard of the Royal Hong Kong Police, for their information on police procedures. Any errors are mine alone.

Peckover House (National Trust).

Karen Scarr for her advice on a few technical matters…she'll know what I mean!

…and to my family and friends for their encouragement and to everyone who reads this book. What would I do without you?

Lightning Source UK Ltd.
Milton Keynes UK
UKOW03f1213310316

271231UK00002B/23/P